Blaze™

Dear Reader,

Well, I'm back at Harlequin Blaze. It's been a long time since my last superspicy novel for this hot line, and I have to say, I'd forgotten what fun it could be! Talk about steaming up the holiday season...I think any woman would like to unwrap Mark Santori on Christmas morning.

After the release of my novellas "There Goes the Groom" (in the *That's Amoré!* collection) and "Sheer Delights" (in the *Behind the Red Doors* collection) I heard from a lot of readers who wanted more of those Santori men of Chicago. They certainly interested me...five hot, hunky Italian brothers...hmm, what's not to find interesting?

Brother Mark is one of the twins, and is a hard-nosed detective for the city of Chicago. I wasn't sure where I wanted to start his story until I was trying on clothes in a department-store dressing room, and heard a very embarrassed-sounding guy helping his wife zip up in the next room. That immediately sparked a picture of a very sexy, hot, gorgeous man doing the same thing. Imagine the possibilities of being in the next room, listening to the couple next door and wondering all sorts of...interesting things.

That's the start of *Don't Open Till Christmas,* which was really a joy. I love the holidays and had a great time playing on the possibilities of a wacky town called Christmas. And, as you'll see, it was also fun going down memory lane in regards to toys, holiday movies, songs and traditions.

Hope you enjoy Mark and Noelle's story. And a very Merry Christmas to you and yours!

Best wishes,

Leslie Kelly

LESLIE KELLY
Don't Open Till Christmas

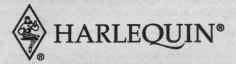

HARLEQUIN®

TORONTO • NEW YORK • LONDON
AMSTERDAM • PARIS • SYDNEY • HAMBURG
STOCKHOLM • ATHENS • TOKYO • MILAN • MADRID
PRAGUE • WARSAW • BUDAPEST • AUCKLAND

To the people who've made every Christmas of my life
utterly magical: Betty and Ray, Lynn, Donna, Karen,
Cheri, Lee, Toni, Chris, Paul, Holly, Jim and Lena.
And especially Bruce, Caitlin, Lauren and Megan.

And to Santa Claus: Thanks so much for the Barbie Country
Camper...the best Christmas present you ever gave me.

ISBN 0-373-79226-3

DON'T OPEN TILL CHRISTMAS

www.eHarlequin.com

Printed in U.S.A.

Prologue

TRYING ON a skimpy, beaded cocktail dress on Black Friday—the day after Thanksgiving—was bad enough. Hearing a couple having sex in the next dressing room? Well...that wasn't exactly what Noelle Bradenton would call priceless.

While slipping out of the sexy dress—which, to her consternation, highlighted some mashed potato-induced bulges on her thighs—she heard the conversation from next door. There were definitely two voices, one male and one female, coming from the other fitting room in the dress department of this upscale store. And there was no doubt what they were talking about.

"Would you please, just *do* it?" the woman asked in a loud whisper, sounding almost desperate. "Quit worrying—nobody saw you come in here with me."

"This is crazy," was the male response. The voice was deep, husky, holding both frustration and amusement. "Stop wiggling."

Unbelievable. Noelle could hardly fathom her rotten luck. Wasn't it bad enough that today was the official start of the season she detested more than anything except country music and underwire push-up bras? Did she *really* have to be reminded how utterly barren her sex life was by hearing a couple going at in a secret frenzy of dressing room passion?

"It's your fault, idiot," she whispered, not knowing what demon had made her venture into a downtown Chicago department store on the worst shopping day of the year. She *never* shopped on Black Friday, preferring to avoid the whole Christmas insanity altogether by doing her requisite gift buying online.

She cursed the day she'd won the Social Services department lottery for a ticket to the mayor's high-toned Christmas party, which was *so* out of her league. She'd probably spend the whole evening wondering how much money was being spent on champagne and mini quiches when it could have been used to help the women and kids in the shelter where she worked.

But she *had* to go, and there was no way she'd find a dress suitable for the party by shopping on the Internet. It was proving hard enough to do it in person. So here she was, stuck staring at a size eight dress taunting her about her size ten hips, frozen in a four-by-four space, about to hear a couple crying out in ecstasy as they did the deed on the other side of a paper-thin wall.

Oh, God, she hoped they didn't do it up against the wall adjoining *her* dressing room. It didn't look terribly sturdy, and might just come crashing down, leaving her to greet the bold lovers while wearing only a skimpy black bra and lacy panties.

She began to reach for her clothes, just in case, but froze again when she heard that sexy, oh-so-deep voice once more. "The sales counter is twenty feet away." The man sounded more amused than worried. "One of the employees could be heading over right now to find out why a man is in here with you."

"There are eight hundred and ninety-four women in line desperate to save an extra ten percent before the doorbuster sale ends," the woman replied impatiently. "Those clerks aren't going to look up from their cash registers until December 26."

Noelle grinned. The unknown woman sounded a lot like her, already disgruntled and cranky during the time of year when every other usually sane person turned into a carol-spouting, eggnog-drinking lunatic. She'd probably like to meet her under other circumstances—like, oh, say, when the woman wasn't naked and getting *done* in the next room. And if she didn't hate her for having such a daring sex life when Noelle's only recent orgasmic experience had been when she'd eaten a sliver of rich pecan pie after last night's turkey pig-out.

Pecan pie *and* mashed potatoes. No wonder the damn dress was laughing at her.

"Okay, there, yes. A little more…great, I think you've got it in," the woman was saying, sounding breathless.

She *thought* he had it in? Hmm. If the woman next door wasn't sure, maybe Mr. Sexy Voice wasn't such a stud after all.

Suddenly not feeling so bad—since, in her opinion, no sex was better than bad sex and I-*think*-you've-got-it-in was *way* worse than I-haven't-been-laid-in-a-year—Noelle giggled. If she ever worked up the nerve to have hot nooky in a public place, it would definitely be with someone whose equipment was big enough to leave no doubt in her mind that she was getting it.

"Okay, I did it. I'm done. Can you finish on your own and let me get out of here?"

Noelle rolled her eyes. *What a gentleman.* He'd gotten off…quickly…and was leaving his wife or girlfriend to take care of herself.

Yikes. Hearing a woman pleasuring herself in the next cubicle had an even higher yuck factor than hearing a couple of strangers going at it. Shocked out of her titillated lethargy, Noelle grabbed her jeans, determined to make a quick exit before the solitary moaning started. She heard quite enough of that in her own bedroom these days, thank you very much.

Bent over with one foot in the pants, Noelle hardly noticed the click of the door in the next booth. The words outside barely registered…just a man's voice saying, "Excuse me," before it rose in volume, almost shouting, "Watch out!"

Then came a loud bang, and in flew the door to the dressing room. *Her* dressing room.

"Hey, what are you doing?" she cried, immediately straightening as someone stumbled into the tiny space toward her. A someone whose forward momentum landed him right against Noelle, and propelled them back to the wall.

Noelle's heart flipped over about a dozen times as the stranger quickly braced both his hands on the mirror behind her head. That was the only thing that prevented them both from tumbling down onto the built-in bench seat.

It took a few seconds for her to grasp what had happened. During those seconds, with her pulse racing as she heaved in deep, surprised breaths, she took a look at the *someone* who was pressed against her from shoulder to knee.

"Oh, my God," she managed to whisper.

Because it was a male someone. A gorgeous male someone. An absolutely heart-poundingly sexy, to-die-for, somebody-quick-get-me-a-condom male someone.

His dark green eyes were widened in shock, and she could do nothing but stare into them for a long moment. With those eyes, she would have expected light hair, but his was jet black, cut short but still thick and lush. The kind of hair that made a woman want to tangle her fingers in it and tug him close to whatever body part he happened to be near.

She could think of a few. And a few more.

The stranger's lean face was slightly stubbled...another guy who hadn't shaved because of the holiday. The swarthy look only emphasized the squareness of his jaw, the hollows of his cheeks, and his incredible mouth. His sensually curved lips parted as he sucked in a deep breath of his own.

Noelle almost closed her eyes, in pure self-preservation, but curiosity demanded that she check out the rest of him. Pulling away a tiny bit, until the back of her head hit the mirror, she glanced down, noting the width of his shoulders clad in a black leather bomber jacket. The expanse of his chest beneath that jacket was impossibly broad and the tight shirt he wore emphasized a flat stomach and lean waist.

They were still pressed together from the hips down, but she didn't need to see anymore. She was *feeling* enough to know the man was perfect all the way to the floor. One of his feet was wedged between hers, and his firm leg, clad in soft jeans, scraped ever-so-deliciously against her thin panties.

Panties. She was clothed in nothing but the sinfully sexy black bra and panties she'd worn today for trying on little black dresses! Heat rushed through her body and she knew he must be able to see her blush.

"Hi," he said softly.

Noelle couldn't make her voice work.

"I was barreled into by a woman on a shopping mission."

And Noelle was barreled into by a man she wanted to lick like a six-foot-tall ice cream cone. She instead settled for licking her lips.

The man watched, his eyelids lowering a bit and his eyes growing darker. As if he'd just noticed her attire—or definite lack thereof—he looked down at her body.

Suddenly, Noelle didn't hate underwire, push-up bras so much. Because the stranger's jaw went tight and his breathing deepened as he noticed the curves of her average-sized breasts pushed to dizzying heights by the painful lingerie. Judging by the way he swallowed hard, and his whole body tensed in response, she'd say the bra was a very good thing indeed.

"Are you okay? I didn't hurt you, did I?" he asked, that sultry, deep voice rolling over her like a hot, heady breeze.

That voice. Oh, goodness, that voice. She recognized it immediately as the truth finally sunk into her lust-hazy brain. There was no denying it—the man pressed against her like a longtime lover was the stranger from the fitting room next door. The one who'd just been with another woman. *Ewww*.

She intended to put her hands on his chest and shove, repulsed at the very idea. Only one thing stopped her.

The stranger's physical reaction.

Oh, he was definitely reacting to their closeness, as she was. The air was thick and ripe, electric almost. Their faces were mere inches apart and they shared each breath. They also, without a doubt, shared a wild, uncontrollable excitement. For her part, Noelle knew it because of the sudden aching tightness of her panties and the rush of warm moisture between her legs.

As for him…well, his body's age-old response was rapid and completely unmistakable. Feeling him grow hard and huge against her hip, her legs went weak.

She wanted. She hungered. She needed. She craved.

He dropped a hand to her bare waist to steady her, the touch more sinful than helpful. "Did I hurt you?"

Shaking her head, she whimpered, unable to control the response to his obvious sexual arousal. Not to mention her own.

Suddenly, Noelle began to suspect she'd misread the situation she'd overheard in the next room, and not just because she *wanted* to be wrong. Thinking about it, she realized there had been no endearments or moans. In fact, she'd heard no unusual sounds at all. And the most important thing: the woman's suggestive words could not have meant what Noelle had assumed they'd meant. It was impossible. Because there was no mistaking the power and, er, *size* of the stranger pressed against her.

No way would any woman question his possession. Not with what Noelle now knew he had to offer. A lot. A whole, whole lot.

She whimpered again.

"This is like something out of a movie," he murmured, still making no effort to back off her.

She cleared her throat. "I guess it is."

"If it *were* a movie, you know what would happen, don't you?" His voice was low and thick with identifiable hunger.

She wasn't sure of what he meant. But she had a feeling….

"Sorry, sweetheart, but I'll regret it as long as I live if I don't go for it," he said, sounding apologetic.

Before she could even ask what he meant, he was dipping his head closer. Not giving her a chance to react, he caught her mouth in a kiss as hot and sensual as it was unexpected.

Noelle didn't think, didn't plan, didn't hesitate. She simply took the pleasure of the moment and ran with it.

Immediately turning her head, she parted her lips for him. Responding with a soft groan, he followed her lead and licked into her mouth. Noelle lifted her arms to his shoulders and tangled her fingers in his hair—as she'd wanted to the second she set eyes on him.

Their tongues met lightly, then drew apart, only to meet again in an instinctive rhythm that matched the crazy, sensual, erotic encounter they were sharing. She reveled in him, tasted him, let him taste her in return. The desire to sink down to the bench and pull him down on top of her was overwhelming.

But a noise outside intruded and reality began to sink back in. As if he'd realized the same thing—that he was in the arms of a nearly naked stranger—he ended the kiss and stepped back.

The sudden loss of his warmth and strength almost had her following him to demand more of the mind-numbing pleasure of his mouth. Before she could do it, though, a woman's voice intruded. "Excuse me, sir, this is a public place!"

The stranger whirled around. Even while doing so, he maneuvered his body to protectively block Noelle from view. The response was so automatic, so instinctive, she suddenly learned a lot about this sexy man.

Not enough, though. Not nearly enough.

She needed to know more. His name. His address. His marital status. The size of his…bed. Mostly, she needed to know if she was correct in thinking he had *not* just been in the arms of another woman right next door.

Fate, however, helped by a scandalized store clerk, decided she wasn't going to learn any of those things. Because as the unseen woman continued to whisper loud admonitions, the black-haired man in the leather jacket stepped out of the dressing room. The last glimpse Noelle had of him was the amazingly sexy view of his backside, clad in soft, faded jeans. And one flash of a smile—along with a quick wink—as he turned his head to look at her over his shoulder before closing the door behind him.

Three minutes later, once she was dressed and able to breathe normally again, Noelle stepped out of the dressing room. The fitting room beside hers where the mystery couple had been having their unusual conversation was completely empty.

And her dark-haired, green-eyed stranger was gone.

1

DETECTIVE MARK SANTORI had investigated a number of bizarre criminal cases in his six years as a Chicago cop, so not much surprised him. There'd been, for instance, the bank robber who'd hidden all his stolen money in his oven. He'd then gotten drunk, forgotten about the cash, burned it up and set his building on fire. One thing Mark had learned from that experience was that the red dye packs banks stuck into stolen money to mark it so crooks couldn't use it morphed into a number of interesting shades in intense heat. And, judging by the way the dye-spattered perp had been wailing when they'd taken him into custody, those suckers stung when they exploded in your face.

That had been a stand-out experience with the stupid criminals investigated by the anti crime division of the Chicago P.D., of which he was a member. But it certainly hadn't been his only one.

There'd been the purse-snatcher who'd had the crap beaten out of him by a couple of female impersonators leaving the Hidey Hole Club. The guy who'd tried to rob a liquor store using a plastic kiddie baseball bat and ended up getting his head split open by the owner's real one. The stupid bastard who'd nearly drowned in a barrel full of pickle juice—he'd hidden in it so he could rob a grocery store after hours. Not to mention the moron who'd broken into a home improvement warehouse and had tried to make his getaway on a stolen riding mower that went about two miles a day.

But this…well, this was pretty bad even for pathetic, scumsucking criminals. A ring of costumed Santas were stealing anything they could get their hands on during the so-called season of giving. Not that the holidays had ever given Mark much more than a whole lot of heartburn. Still, sticky-fingered Santas lifting the sugarplums right outta the stockings of homeless kids were pretty goddamn low, even to a Christmas-hating hard-ass like him.

"I had intended to send a uniform over to that women's shelter to keep them calm until you got there to take the statements," his lieutenant said as he prepared to leave the 10th district police station of Chicago, where he worked. "But this damn cold weather has caused some power outages and I needed extra traffic control."

"It's okay," Mark muttered, already wondering how to deal with a bunch of pissed-off social workers who'd been cooling their heels for a couple of hours. His notes showed the initial call from a women's shelter about the theft of some charity money by a costumed Santa Claus had come in before lunch.

"You have any leads yet?" Lieutenant Shaker asked.

"Not much. Harriet's gone back to Riley's to meet with some of the seasonal employees." Riley's was a department store that had been robbed a few days earlier and Mark's partner, Harriet Styles, was working that angle a little more.

If the robbery had occurred at Bloomingdale's, Mark might have done it. He'd have done just about anything to try to get a glimpse of the dark-haired seductress he'd kissed in the women's dressing room last Friday.

Mark hadn't been able to get the woman out of his mind in the week since they'd shared that hot, sexy encounter. He'd thought about her, wondered about her, dreamed about her.

Stumbling into her arms had—as he'd told her—felt like something out of a movie. Only, on the big screen, he would've at least found out the woman's name, if not her phone number, address and favorite sexual position.

But nuh-uh. He had nothing to go on when it came to the woman's identity. Zero. Zilch.

Much like the Santa crime spree.

"You really think this kids fund ripoff is connected to the others?" Shaker asked.

Mark nodded, his cop intuition still pinging, the way it had this morning when he'd first heard about the robbery at the shelter. "Yeah. This thing has escalated beyond pinching a few pennies from the bell-ringers on the street corners." Mark shook his head in disgust as he grabbed his jacket off the back of his chair. "I'll get over there now, I just had to take care of the Banner deposition this morning."

Shaker, a graying fifty year old, raised a questioning brow.

Mark knew what his boss was asking. "I nailed it. We're airtight on that case." He was set to testify in the trial of a slimy local businessman who'd been selling stolen goods rather than imported ones. Which was why he was late going out to the women and children's shelter to get statements about the theft of the shelter's holiday fund.

Disgusting. As if the holidays weren't bad enough, now even needy kids were being ripped off.

Frankly, as far as Mark was concerned, the holiday season was the absolute worst time of year to be on the job. Every December, crime went way up as desperate people with no money tried to do their gift shopping without visiting the cash register. Beat cops were exhausted from working second jobs as security guards for the high-end stores on Michigan Avenue. City officials were jumping up and down screaming about overtime pay even as they hosted pricy parties for the rich and spoiled. And lots of lonely people took swan dives off the balconies of their penthouses rather than toast in the New Year with only Pansy the poodle for company.

Christmas was second only to Valentine's Day in terms of holidays exploited by retailers to make more and more money. At least Valentine's Day turned people into sappy flower-buying Romeos for only a couple of days. The Christmas season now seemed to start in September right after the stores got rid of all the back-to-school junk. And it lasted until the final blue and orange polka-dotted tie had been returned in mid-January.

Yep, the holidays were always trouble, and this year, with the jelly-bellied burglars, things were a lot worse.

Heading to his unmarked car as he zipped his leather jacket against the bone-chilling December wind—a reminder that winter had come early this year—he consoled himself with the knowledge that criminals always eventually betrayed their stupidity. Hopefully this latest crime, which had targeted the most helpless of victims, would give him just the information he needed to nail the scumbags.

And hopefully the shelter workers weren't going to lynch him for taking three hours to show up at the crime scene.

GETTING RIPPED OFF by Santa Claus was one lousy way to start the month of December.

As an avowed Christmas hater, Noelle Bradenton had already begun to prepare herself for the general cheer, goodwill and onslaught of commercials for CDs containing a thousand of the most popular holiday songs ever recorded. She'd been happily ignoring the garland and decorations going up in the front office of the women and children's shelter where she worked.

Good-meaning invitations from friends had been ever so

politely rejected. Secret Santa plans had been ever so nicely refused. She had actually been walking around with a smile on her face, rather than her usual dismay that the most god-awful time of the year had rolled around again.

Up until this morning, when she'd realized the costumed Santa who'd come in to extend some holiday cheer to the scared kids in the shelter had robbed them, she'd really been looking forward to December 25. Because for the first time in her life, Noelle was going to spend the holiday season doing what *she* wanted to do.

While working her heart out to ensure a good holiday for the mothers and kids currently housed here—as well as some former tenants the shelter had helped get started in their new lives—she'd been secretly planning her own dream holiday, her own perfect Christmas. It had included no snow. No Santa. No frustrated shoppers elbowing their way down the crowded sidewalks on the miracle mile. No enraged husbands stalking their terrified wives and lonely children.

Just the sun. Sand. Rum laden drinks that contained neither egg nor nog. And if all went as planned, a hunky cabana boy or bleach-blonde surfer dude whose name she wouldn't even know, but whose body would become *very* familiar.

Oh, Lord, please *let there be a hunky cabana boy or sun-kissed surfer.* Because ever since last Friday, when she'd been in the arms of a gorgeous stranger in a Bloomingdale's dressing room, Noelle had been walking around in a constant state of arousal.

She'd been thinking about *him*—the man who'd kissed her, then disappeared without a word—during every waking hour since that day. And she'd dreamed about him—fantasized about him—every single night.

Noelle needed sex. Needed to touch and be touched, to take

and be taken. It had been almost a year since her engagement had fallen apart. A year since she'd had a man inside her. And, being honest about her ex, several years since she'd had really *good* sex, with a *great* man inside her. Or maybe that had just been in her dreams, too.

But now she was finished dreaming. She wanted physical pleasure and fulfillment. Wanted it badly.

So, fabulous, uncomplicated sex with a hot-as-sin man she'd never have to see again was what she'd decided to give herself for Christmas. The encounter with the stranger last Friday had sparked the idea. His kiss—and her response—had made her realize she didn't have to be celibate just because she wouldn't trust a man to shovel her sidewalk these days.

Erotic sex with a nameless, anonymous stranger had been the perfect solution. There'd be no repercussions. No heartbreak. No taking chances and leaving herself open for any soul-crushing betrayals. Short-term and uncommitted…that was about all her tattered heart would let her go for at this point in her life.

Her vacation had sounded like the ideal opportunity for blameless, unforgettable sex. She'd have been far away, in a steamy country that was probably full of men dying to make a lonely female traveler's fantasies come true. In a place as exotic and beautiful as St. Lucia—the Caribbean island she was supposed to fly off to on Christmas night—she'd felt certain she'd meet someone who could make her feel like a sexual, sensual woman again. Noelle hadn't even been sure that woman existed anymore. Until a stranger had proved she did a week ago in a small, public dressing room.

Maybe a black-haired surfer guy. Yes. Dark hair and green eyes. Sun, sand and beach. Heat. Passion. Desire.

Or…not.

"So long, St. Lucia," she murmured as reality sunk back in. *And so long, sexy stranger.*

Reality really sucked sometimes, because her vacation was suddenly looking more and more unlikely. Now that a fat pig in a red suit had absconded with all the Give A Kid A Christmas money the shelter had collected throughout the year, she didn't think any vacation was in her immediate future. Or food or rent money, for that matter. Because she was *not* going to let this robbery ruin one of the most important events this place offered, even if she had to pay for some of it herself.

The Give A Kid A Christmas program wasn't simply about buying some Barbie dolls and board games for needy kids. It was more about giving a true Christmas experience to children—and their moms—who might never have had one. It offered them a glimpse of the normal, happy family lives they could look forward to at the end of their long struggle for independence. Not fighting, abuse, addiction and rage, like many of them had experienced.

From the tree and decorations, to the toys, to the cookies to the pretty velvet Christmas dresses and the big turkey dinner, the program covered it all. And they didn't merely help the women and children currently living here, in the shelter, but also out in the community. A lot of them.

She couldn't let it be taken away from them. She *wouldn't* let it be.

"We'll replace as much as we can with a plea for donations from nearby businesses," she said to Casey Miller, who worked with her at the shelter, and who'd been with Noelle when she'd discovered they'd been robbed. Swallowing hard, she added, "As for the rest, well, I have some money I've been saving. I can pitch in."

"Oh, honey, tell me you're not giving up your dream vacation," Casey said, looking distraught. The skinny, red-haired caseworker knew how Noelle had been planning to spend her holiday season. "Isn't it all paid for already? Won't you lose your money?"

"I can pay a penalty and use the airline ticket another time." The thought cheered her up. The next one made her frown. "I will lose the hotel deposit, but thankfully they only required half up front. With what I'd saved to pay the rest, plus the meal and spending money I've been hoarding, I could make a dent in what we lost today." She didn't know who she was trying harder to convince—herself or Casey. Clearing her throat and nodding, she insisted, "I'd just be postponing my vacation. I'll go in the spring."

"In the spring, Chicago won't be full of singing elves whose mouths you long to tape shut, jingle bells you want to fling into the river and jolly Santas you'd like to run over with a lawnmower."

Casey was one of the few people who knew how Noelle really felt about Christmas. Nobody else at work was in on that secret, because the last thing she wanted was to make the holiday less special for the kids and their moms who already had so little happiness in their lives.

"A semi truck would be better for one certain Santa," Noelle said, still shaking her head in disgust at this morning's events. "How on earth did Alice let herself get suckered into letting that guy use the phone in the office—and leaving him *alone* to do it—when she knew the money was hidden there in the bottom of the desk drawer? And how did he find it so fast? It's almost like he knew we'd cashed out the account so we could go do the big shopping trip at that discount warehouse this weekend."

"He was a pro, and he fooled us all," Casey pointed out. "He was a pretty realistic looking Santa. The kids loved him."

"Well, the balls you hung on the tree in the lobby aren't

the only ones that are going to be bright red and broken into a million pieces if I ever get hold of him."

"I do hope you don't mean you're going to take the law into your own hands," a male voice said.

Noelle immediately whirled around, figuring one of Chicago's finest had *finally* shown up to take their complaint about the theft. She was about to lay into the officer for his late arrival. But her acidic comment about the three-hour response time died on her lips when she saw the man standing in the doorway to the office.

Because it was *him,* the dark-haired stranger. The one who'd kissed her one week ago in a Bloomingdale's dressing room. The one she'd made love to in every conceivable position every night since then. At least, in her head.

"My, oh my," he murmured, his eyes widening. So he obviously recognized her, too.

Noelle's first crazy thought was that the man had tracked her down to, uh, finish what he'd started. The idea was probably brought about by the fantasies she'd been having about the guy for the past week. Erotic fantasies, many of them including silk scarves and blindfolds. And chocolate sauce. Insane fantasies, really, because in a city the size of Chicago, she'd never expected to see him again. Yet here he was.

"I'm Detective Mark Santori," he murmured, holding up a wallet and displaying a badge.

A cop. Any thought that he'd tracked her down for personal reasons vanished. Since she'd known it was ridiculous, she really shouldn't have felt so disappointed. "It took you long enough to get here," she said, unable to keep the sharpness out of her voice.

"Hey, you never told me your name," he replied with a defensive shrug of his shoulders, his mind, obviously on last Friday's encounter as well.

Noelle frowned. "And you didn't wait around to ask for it."

"You two know each other?" Casey asked.

Glancing at her co-worker and seeing the avid curiosity on the other woman's face, Noelle felt heat rise in her cheeks. "I think I can take it from here, Case. Why don't you go see where Alice is?" she said. "I'm sure Detective...Santori is going to want to talk to her."

Casey nodded, but continued to look speculative as she walked to the exit, giving the cop a friendly smile. Once she'd gotten past him, to the doorway where he couldn't see her, she turned around and made a face of absolute hunger toward the dark-haired man's back. *To die for,* she mouthed to Noelle. Then she left the room.

"For your information," the detective said once they were alone in the office, "I went to smooth things over with the store clerk and give you a chance to, uh...get yourself together. I came back five minutes later. You were gone."

He'd come back. For *her.* Noelle couldn't keep her heart from lurching a little bit. Couldn't keep her panties from moistening a little bit, either. "Oh."

"So before someone comes barging in here saying we're in a public place, why don't you tell me your name?"

"It's Noelle Bradenton," she mumbled, wondering who that soft-voiced woman was. Certainly not a woman who would make out with a perfect stranger in a public place. No, she sounded every bit the small town girl who'd moved to the big city to become a social worker less than a year ago.

Darn...too bad she wasn't wearing her slutty underwear today. White cotton just didn't provide the self-confidence to act wanton.

It did, however, keep her grounded in reality instead of hot, sexy fantasy. Because one question popped into her head and demanded an immediate answer. "Are you sure you came back for me? Or was it for the woman you were with in the next dressing room?"

The guy visibly winced at having been busted. "You heard us, huh? I told her we were going to get caught."

Eww. She *had* been kissed by a man who'd just been going at it with another woman. How totally disgusting. "Maybe someone else should be investigating this theft," she said, her whole body snapping straight. "Instead of someone who gets his kicks by having sex in public places."

"Whoa, lady, back off," he said, his eyes narrowing and his lean jaw growing tight. He had no five-o'clock shadow today, and the man was even more attractive when smoothly shaven, darn him. He wore the same leather jacket, but beneath it was a black sweater. Instead of jeans, a pair of nicely fitted khakis slid over what she knew were a strong, muscular pair of legs. "It was just a kiss."

"*Just* a kiss?" She stepped closer as anger made her suck in a deep breath.

He took one step closer, too. "Yeah. A kiss. And I'd say you were every bit as involved as I was."

She inched even closer, wanting to smack the man for being so dense. Wanting to kiss his lips right off his face for being so hot. Wanting to cry because now, knowing his name and occupation, he *couldn't* be the seductive, nameless stranger she wanted to have wild, hungry sex with. "I wasn't talking about you and me. I was talking about the woman you were doing it with in the next dressing room."

The detective's eyes widened in shock and his mouth dropped open. He lurched back as if struck, an expression of utter dismay appearing on his face. "She was my sister!"

"Oh, my God, that's disgusting," Noelle said before she even thought about it.

"Jesus, lady, I was helping her button her damn dress. The

salesclerks were all busy and she harassed me until I came in to do it for her." Shaking his head, he added, "You're really twisted, you know that?" The handsome man was staring at her in genuine shock.

Hmm. She guessed he had a point. "Uh…sorry."

"You should be."

"How was I supposed to know?"

"Maybe because I kissed *you?* You really think I would have done that if I'd just been with some other woman in the next room?" She opened her mouth to answer, but he threw his hand in the air to stop her. "Wait. I don't want to know. Because if you *really* thought that, you must have some pretty bad opinions of men."

She couldn't deny it. After all, her most recent man—the man she'd dated since her senior year of college—had dumped her last year, two days before Christmas Eve. Two days before Noelle's birthday.

Two days before they were supposed to get married.

He wasn't the first man to have disappointed her, or the first one to break her heart. But he had been the most recent. So, no, she hadn't been feeling too kindly toward the hairier half of humanity. Which was why she absolutely was not going to get involved with one beyond getting naked and sweaty.

Emotions, commitments, promises and lies were right out of the picture. As were names. And she had the man standing in front of her to thank for her plan. It was just such a shame he'd gone and introduced himself, because now that she knew his name and occupation, that took him out of the running to be her sexual-healing stranger. Didn't it?

Clearing her throat and glancing down at the tip of her sneaker, Noelle mumbled, "I'm really sorry. I, uh…I guess I jumped to conclusions."

He didn't answer for a long, charged moment. Finally

working up the nerve to look him in the face, Noelle found him eyeing her speculatively. A slight smile played about those fine lips of his.

"What?" she asked, almost afraid to know what was causing that sparkle of amusement.

"You must have wanted me pretty badly," the man said. "If you thought I'd been doing…*that*…and you kissed me, anyway."

"Let's get this straight—you kissed me."

He stepped close again, this time close enough so she could feel the warmth of his big body, like she had last Friday. "You want to put it to the test?" he murmured. "Because I think it would be pretty easy to prove you were a willing participant."

Oh, yes. Yes, yes, yes, she wanted to put it to a test. Wanted to jump on him again and kiss him and take him the way she'd been dreaming of doing for the past seven nights.

Only, she couldn't. Because she was chicken. Because she was at work. Because she was wearing white cotton panties. Because he was no longer a nameless stranger. And because he was here to do a job…to help find the fat Santa who'd stolen the kids' toy money.

"Maybe we should just forget about it," she mumbled. "I assume you want to know about the robbery."

He didn't move away, continuing to watch her, those dark green eyes searching and assessing as he studied her face, her tense body, the way she had her hands clenched in front of her. Finally, he gave a brief nod. "Yes. The robbery. We'll talk about that."

Good. Because right at that moment, the door opened and Casey returned with Alice, the blonde-haired, middle-aged woman who helped run the shelter. Noelle immediately stepped back, praying they wouldn't see the color in her cheeks or notice the way her hands were shaking.

Before moving out of earshot altogether, though, the detective said one more thing. Softly. For her ears alone. "But after we talk about that, we'll talk about whether you're wearing that incredibly sexy black bra."

Her pulse jumped as her heart skipped a beat. It took a few seconds for it to return to its regular rhythm as Noelle watched the detective greet her co-workers. And for a moment—just a naughty little moment—Noelle wished she *hadn't* gone for the white cotton today.

2

MARK SANTORI still couldn't get over his unexpected good fortune. Somehow, against the odds, he'd found a silver lining in this rotten Santa crime spree. And she was staring at him from a few feet away, looking just as sexy and uncertain—as interested and nervous—as she had the day he'd kissed her in a women's dressing room.

Her name was Noelle Bradenton. And she was the woman he'd wanted with instant heat and relentless lust since the moment he'd laid eyes on her.

"I think that's all I'll need from you two," he told the other shelter workers, who'd given him statements about this morning's robbery. Though he'd been focusing all his attention on his newly identified mystery woman, rather than her two coworkers, he had paid attention to their comments about the crime. As he'd suspected when he'd first heard about it, it was similar to a number of other cases that had plagued the city for the past two weeks.

Trying to kick off a nice holiday season for the needy families in their care, the shelter workers had contacted a party business in town. The place offered visits from costumed characters for private events. Noelle and her colleagues had hired a Santa Claus to bring in a little cheer early in the month—before rates for visits from the fat guy skyrocketed, as they would in another week or two.

The perp—who'd been so perfectly disguised as to leave no real description behind—had shown up, done his jolly job, then left with as much cash as he could stuff down his pants. If this case followed the pattern, when he visited the party company who'd employed the thief, Mark would learn the employee had quit, and that he'd given a fake name and references on his job application. It was become an all-too-standard scenario this holiday season.

Today was, however, the first time the thieves had targeted a shelter for women and kids. Somehow that made it a whole lot worse.

"You know," the young, red-haired one said, making no move to leave the cramped office, "maybe you should ask No-elle about her hometown. Seems to me if there really have been other similar robberies, someone ought to be investigating the place where Santas are trained."

Mark had no idea what the girl was talking about. Glancing at Noelle—the beautiful woman he would have pegged as an exotic dancer before he figured her for a social worker—he saw her glaring at the redhead. His curiosity was piqued. "Just where are you from?"

"That doesn't matter," she muttered.

"Maybe it does," he replied, meaning it. At this point, he'd consider any tip.

Sighing, the woman admitted, "I'm from Christmas."

Ahh, things suddenly made sense. Because Christmas, a small Illinois town about eighty miles from Chicago, was supposedly the Mecca for all things related to December 25. Their ads ran on the local TV stations, urging people to take a day trip out to enjoy some old-fashioned holiday fun. For only twenty dollars, people could have their greeting cards personalized by the big guy and postmarked from a town called Christmas.

Ugh. Sometimes it seemed as if old Ebenezer Scrooge had had the right idea.

One thing he recalled, though, that could be connected. The town did boast of a Santa training school the way Quantico might brag about the FBI academy. "Interesting," he murmured as Noelle's two co-workers stood to leave. "I think that may be important, Miss Bradenton." He wondered if she could sense the same anticipatory tension he was feeling about being alone with her again. "Maybe you and I should talk a little more."

She cast a glance toward her co-workers, who were already at the door. A flick of her tongue to moisten her lips told him she was nervous about being alone with him. That was amusing, considering a week ago, when she hadn't even known his name, she'd been kissing him like she wanted to taste his tonsils.

His breathing slowed, deepened, at the memory of it. There'd been such surprising intensity, not to mention a complete lack of inhibition or regret. Absolutely the only thing he'd regretted about last Friday was not handcuffing her to his side to prevent her from getting away.

Mark had feared he'd never see her again that morning and had scrambled to try to find her in the store. He'd even considered asking the sales clerk if she remembered whether the sexy woman with the long dark hair, the pale, angelic face, and the body of a Victoria's Secret angel had purchased anything. It'd been a long shot, but he had thought he might be able to track his delightful stranger down from a credit card slip.

In the end, though, Mark hadn't asked the clerk in the dress department. The gray-haired saleswoman had been scandalized enough at finding him almost on top of a nearly naked brunette in the dressing room. If she'd realized Mark didn't even know the *name* of the woman who'd given him a hard-on that had to be visible to families waiting in line to see Santa, she might have fainted dead away.

Santa. That quickly pushed erotic memories out of his mind and reminded him of the job at hand. Investigating a crime...not the body of the woman standing just a few feet away.

"So," he said once they were indeed alone in her small, cramped office, which was crowded with boxes of second-hand clothes, blankets, toys and books, "You're really from the infamous town of Christmas?"

She sat on the arm of a worn-looking sofa that stood under the front window. "I am," she murmured, appearing deep in thought as she glanced outside.

The view wasn't much to get excited about—just a run-down neighborhood of small, brick-front tract homes from the sixties, all looking much like this one. The front yard had a few leftover patches of brown grass protruding from clumps of rock and dirt. The winter sky—icy-gray and too bitter cold for any snow-bloated clouds—wasn't anything to smile about either.

The grayness seemed to match the atmosphere in this place this morning. According to the workers, the shelter currently housed three formerly abused wives and seven of their kids, ranging in age from three months to twelve years. They were all cramped into a row house that was virtually indistinguishable from every other one on the block. That, he figured, was the point. Hiding out in a small, slightly worn and nondescript house added a level of security for the women who'd fled from dangerous situations at home.

The thought of those dangerous situations—and of angry husbands trying to track down their wives—suddenly made him stiffen. He barely knew Noelle Bradenton, but the thought of her sitting in this place every day, exposing herself to a bunch of whacked-out, raging husbands, made him very, *very* uneasy. "Tell me about your hometown."

She spoke again, still staring outside. "I prefer not to even think about that place, or the miserable holiday for which its named. Besides, I seriously doubt Christmas is a hotbed of criminal activity."

Ahh, another Christmas hater, just like him. Wanting to lighten her mood, he asked, "No mischievous elves painting graffiti on the side of Santa's workshop?"

Rolling her eyes, she glanced over. "You think you're kidding...but in Christmas, believe me, that would be possible. There *is* a Santa's workshop and there *are* some slightly deranged residents who dress in green-and-red tights and little feathered caps throughout the entire winter."

She had to be joking. Which was good—perhaps he'd get a smile out of her before he left today. *And a phone number.*

"Still, the last crime I remember in Christmas," she continued, "was when old Mr. Hennessey was charged with indecent exposure because he forgot to zip his fly."

He grinned, getting an instantaneous picture of Noelle's childhood in a small hometown where everybody knew everybody. Whether she'd believe it or not, his upbringing had been pretty similar, even though he'd been raised here in Chicago. But his largely-Italian neighborhood had had all the rumors, gossip and idiosyncrasies of any small slice of Americana.

The Christmas angle was most likely a dead end, but he made a note to make a few calls, anyway. "So you have no other description of the thief?" he asked, managing not to smile. "He was just a fat guy with a white beard?"

He already knew the answer—her co-workers had given the full details—but he wasn't ready to leave. Funny that he was having such a good time questioning her when a few hours ago he'd been in such a foul mood after getting a call about yet another Santa robbery. It could be because every time he looked into her dark brown eyes, he pictured the way they'd grown even darker when she'd been in his arms, dressed only in some utterly sinful black underwear. Even now, the memory of her curvy body—so thoroughly hidden in the chunky sweater and long skirt she wore today—made his mouth go dry.

She crossed her arms, a frown tugging at her brow. "I wish I could tell you he had his real name tattooed just above the fluffy white trim of his red velvet suit, but he didn't. He was Santa. Top to bottom, just, Santa Claus."

Mark didn't let his amusement show on his face as he stepped closer and lowered his voice to a loud whisper. "I hate to tell you this, ma'am, but to my knowledge, Santa Claus doesn't really exist."

Her jaw dropped and she sputtered a bit. Then she began to chuckle, shaking her head in rueful amusement. "Aww, gee, you mean my folks have been lying to me all these years?"

Soaking up the warmth of her good humor, Mark leaned against the desk, watching her, trying to come up with more questions to ask. More reasons to stay. Frankly, he had all the information he needed and could have left ten minutes ago. But something wouldn't let him go…her smile, most likely. Not to mention the memory of those sexy black panties.

Forcing himself to shake off the image, he re-directed his heated thoughts. "I shouldn't have told you that. My mama's never gonna forgive me," Mark murmured.

"Why?"

"Well, when I was nine, she threatened me that if I ever told any little girls there wasn't any Santa Claus, I'd never get another G.I. Joe or Transformer in my life."

Noelle quirked a brow. "Wow, I've cost you a G.I. Joe?"

He shrugged. "Nah, my baby sister cost me a G.I. Joe."

"You told your baby sister there was no Santa?" She tsked and shook her head. "Very naughty, indeed."

"No, I didn't tell her, *she* told *me* the day she got suspended from kindergarten for beating up a third-grader on the playground. He was the one who spilled the beans about Santa and she came to me and my brothers to ask if it was true."

Noelle was grinning, looking amused and interested, even while Mark wondered why the hell he was talking about his family and his childhood. Maybe to keep his brain distracted and his mouth occupied so he wouldn't ask her what she was wearing under that boxy green sweater. *Black lace? Green silk? Nothing?*

He swallowed the thought—and the accompanying hunger—away.

"I'm still not clear on how G.I. Joe entered the picture."

Back to kid talk. Safe ground. "We all figured that if Mama found out *none* of us believed anymore, our piles of presents would get smaller and Christmas wouldn't be as special, so we covered for Lottie about why she'd gotten into the fight at school."

"Is this the sister whose dress you were buttoning up?"

Oh, man, she'd gone back to the dressing room. To their stolen embrace. The woman was *killing* him here. He still somehow managed a nod, saying, "She's the one and only Santori girl. The baby of the family."

"I think I'd like her," Noelle said. "But I still don't get why you lost your G.I. Joes if you didn't tell your mother that the Santa secret was out of the big fat sack upon his back."

Chuckling, Mark explained. "We drew straws, and I got the short one. I told our parents Lottie was fighting because she'd seen *me* fighting the same boy in my class. My mother decided I was being exposed to too much violence."

"Ahh, so long G.I. Joe. Did you get a Ken doll instead?"

"Worse," he muttered, remembering the disgust only a nine-year-old boy who'd been cheated of G.I. Joes could feel on Christmas morning. "I got stuffed Wembley and Boober Fraggles."

Noelle's smile widened into a burst of laughter. "Oh, no, you got Fraggle Rock dolls?"

God, the woman had a great laugh. It went perfectly with her beautiful smile and her lovely face. Not to mention the sinfully sexy body. All throaty and warm…a woman's laugh. A *sultry* woman's laugh. It rolled through him like potent whiskey and was thoroughly intoxicating. He wanted to drink that laugh down, to taste her. To savor her.

"Please tell me the bully your sister beat up didn't find out what you got for Christmas."

Forcing himself to focus on the light and amusing past instead of the hot and sexy present, Mark gave an exaggerated shudder. "Yow…I wouldn't have made it out of elementary school alive, even with four brothers, if that had ever gotten out."

Her jaw dropped. "Five boys, and one girl? Good grief, no wonder your sister was beating up kids on the playground."

That pretty well summed up his family dynamic, which was all the conversation he wanted to have about the Santoris. Frankly, he was much more interested in talking about *her.* Where she lived, whether she was single, and oh, that sexy black bra… "So are you finished your shopping? Got any more little black dresses to try on?"

Groaning, she closed her eyes and shook her head. "Please don't talk about that anymore."

"How can I not talk about it?" He stepped closer, knowing he shouldn't. They were in a public place—her workplace—but if he didn't touch her again soon, he was going to explode of sheer tension. "After all, I've been dreaming about it for the past seven nights."

Her eyes flew back open. Mark moved even closer, until he was standing over her as she sat on the arm of the couch. His pants brushed against her skirt, just a whisper of a touch that hinted at so much more. From his vantage point above her, he could see the wildly pounding pulse point in her neck. She was sucking in small, shallow gasps of air between lips that were parted and moist.

Hunger surged through him, heating his blood, bringing all his senses to life. He wanted to taste those lips, to share those breaths. He'd give a lot to kiss her again, wanting that kiss more than he'd wanted anything in a very long time. Except, perhaps, what would happen *after* he kissed her again... maybe even on that big, comfortable old couch where she was sitting.

But the door wasn't locked, and the house was far from empty. Plus, they barely knew each other. So he somehow managed to merely brush the back of his hand across her shoulder instead of sucking on her tongue the way he wanted to.

"You shouldn't talk like that," she whispered.

"I haven't said anything the least bit objectionable." Though, God knew he'd been thinking some downright salacious things. "So, tell me where you're going to wear that little black dress." *And what goes underneath it.*

Noelle tilted her head back and met his stare. Her mouth opened as if she was about to answer his question. But a child's laugh in the hall outside quickly reminded her of where they were. She moved down from the arm of the couch, lowering herself into the seat. "I don't think that's a good idea."

"Why not?"

He was not prepared for her blunt answer. "Maybe because you could probably have me *out* of that black dress in about five minutes flat, no matter where we were?"

Now it was Mark who sucked in a deep breath and whose pulse pounded. Not merely because he suspected she was right, but also because he didn't think he'd ever met a woman who'd been so incredibly forthright about what was happening between them.

Oh, something was definitely happening. Something hot and sexy, despite conversations about sticky-fingered Santas or childhood antics. They'd been dancing around the awareness—the attraction—but it was as thick and tangible as the air surging out from the heating vents on the floor beneath their feet. And it was twice as hot. "You say that like it's a bad thing," he murmured, knowing she could see the hunger in his eyes.

One of her fine eyebrows curved higher. "Are you always this aggressive with a woman you've just met?"

"Only if I've already seen her naked," he said as he sat beside her on the couch. Not close enough to make her nervous...but close enough to smell the sultry sweetness of her perfume. Damn, she smelled good.

"I was *not* naked."

"You were in my dreams," he said with a helpless shrug. "Believe me, it didn't require a whole lot of imagination."

Noelle was shaking her head as if she didn't know whether to laugh at him or smack him. Or perhaps even put her hands around his neck and pull him down on top of her.

He voted for option number three. And without giving it much thought, he leaned a little closer, fell a little deeper into the well of awareness swirling between them.

She leaned forward, too, almost as if not even realizing it, until her soft, dark hair—the same color as the hot coffee with just a hint of cream that he so enjoyed every morning— brushed his cheek. "You really should leave, Detective Santori," she said, her voice soft, almost shaky.

He somehow resisted the urge to nibble his way along her creamy-smooth jaw. "Have dinner with me," he urged, even though they both knew what he was really saying. *Have an affair with me.*

She was refusing before the last words left his mouth. "I can't do that."

Couldn't do dinner? Or a sexy affair? He hoped she was on a diet—not that she needed it—and wasn't doing the restaurant thing. Because as far as desire went, there was no doubt in his mind that Noelle was as hungry for him as he was for her.

Figuring it was probably time to make sure there were no genuine barriers before he launched an all-out assault on her reservations, he quickly covered the basics. "Are you married?"

She shook her head.

"Engaged? Spoken for?"

Another shake of the head, with amusement still making her lips quirk, as if she knew exactly what he was doing.

"A future nun? Bought into that 'no sex' Tantric stuff?"

Another negative turn of the head. "You didn't ask me if I was a lesbian," she said dryly.

Mark snorted a laugh. "Honey, after last Friday, that question didn't even enter my mind."

She didn't try to deny it. There could be no denial—she'd been a wanton, physical creature of pure sensation and desire in his arms last week and they both knew it.

So, she wasn't married or attached—thank God. And she sure as hell wasn't frigid. Which left nervous...not liking men too much…*vulnerable*. "A breakup within the past year?" he guessed.

Her quick gasp told him he'd hit pay dirt.

Ahh, here was territory he understood. A beautiful woman who kissed like a temptress and looked like pure sin wasn't going to take just *any* offer than came her way after a bad romantic breakup. She was unsure, tentative, just as anybody would be. Just as *he'd* been the one time he'd handed his heart over to someone, only to have it put through a meat grinder and handed back to him like a hamburger patty. "Okay, so how about a back-in-the-dating-game dinner?" he asked, trying to tease her into accepting.

She nibbled her bottom lip. "I wish I could…"

"But?"

Noelle shifted on the couch, turning sideways to face him, one leg curled under the other. With a look of pure resolve, she explained. "But I can't. You showed up here and introduced yourself and ruined everything you started last Friday in that dressing room." Her frown was accusatory.

"I *what?*"

She continued as if he hadn't spoken. "Now I know who you are, what you do and where you live."

He was *so* not following this conversation. "Okay…?"

"So," she said, "you just won't do."

Oh, he could do a lot. He could definitely do a lot, particularly because the more she threw up these adorably cute protestations, the tighter his pants grew, and the more he wanted to push her back on this couch and slide his hands up his skirt. He'd need about five minutes to give her a taste of what he could do. Then he'd need about five hours to finish *doing* it.

"Because," she added, though he'd almost lost track of the conversation, "I'm just not in the market for someone like you.

After what happened between us, I've realized that I'm in the market for one thing, and one thing only."

He could hardly wait to hear what.

Crossing her arms, she explained. "All I want is some nameless, anonymous sex with a stranger I'll never see again."

NOELLE SPENT the rest of the day Friday wondering what demon had taken over her mouth and made her spit out the bald, complete truth to Detective Mark Santori. She'd come right out and told the man she wanted a one-night stand—hot sex with a stranger.

What on earth the man must have thought of her, she had absolutely no idea. He'd probably either pegged her as a nutcase or a skank, and she honestly wasn't sure which was worse.

To give him credit, though, his reaction had been pretty cute. He hadn't been all shocked or judgmental. He'd simply grinned and offered to leave the city, change his name and arrange to accidentally bump into her at her earliest convenience.

Darn, the man was too charming. Too…*everything*.

That sexy self-confidence might very well have broken through her protective wall, but Casey had come back into the office with a typical minor emergency. Noelle had used the distraction to insist she had to get back to work. Her last glimpse of Mark Santori had been, once again, his gorgeous backside as he'd walked away down the sidewalk toward his car.

Oh, how she wanted to see that man walking *toward* her one of these days. *Naked*. Or…not. Because she didn't know how she could face him after what she'd admitted.

"You make sure you button up tight," Alice said as Noelle gathered her things to leave at the end of the day. Alice wasn't reaching for her coat because she was living here tonight. All the staff—Noelle, Alice, Casey and a fourth counselor, Eileen, who was on vacation this week—took turns rooming at the shelter. "It's like mid-February out there. At this rate, we won't have a white Christmas, we're going to have an *ice* Christmas."

Noelle wanted a green one, so she didn't comment.

"Noelle, I…I just want you to know, I…"

Seeing the tightness around her mouth and the way Alice kept her hands clasped in front of her, Noelle knew the older woman was still blaming herself for this morning's robbery. "It wasn't your fault," Noelle said firmly, not wanting the woman tearing herself up over it any more. "You have a good heart and a kind soul. Who the heck would think Santa Claus would steal money from kids?"

Alice's eyes grew bright and misty. "I'm going to go to the bank Monday and see if I can take out a signature loan."

Noelle's heart twisted. Her co-worker was a middle-aged divorcée whose entire world revolved around the children she interacted with here at work. She lived in a small apartment, had no family, no other source of income, and would give her last dime to anyone in need. That the thief could have caused such a nice lady so much pain was another reason Noelle wanted to string him up by his long white beard.

Reaching out, she gave Alice a quick hug. "Forget it. That's not necessary. We're going to get through this."

How, she wasn't entirely sure. But she was definitely thinking about it. Thinking about it so much as she walked outside into the frigid twilight air that she didn't see anyone standing in front of her until she was face-first with a big, broad chest. Fear and surprise made her gasp a startled breath. But even as a moment of panic flashed through her brain, his familiar, warm, spicy scent calmed her instantly.

"You might want to keep your eyes open when you walk," a low voice said, sounding amused.

Yes, it was him. Mark. And he'd obviously been waiting for her. "Did you forget something earlier?" she asked, tugging her wool coat tighter around her body for protection against the strong wind whipping down the street.

"Yeah," he murmured.

He spoke softly, and she felt the warmth of his breath on her cheek. When he didn't continue, she cleared her throat and asked, "What did you forget?"

A heady silence lengthened between them. Noelle peered intently up at his face, lit by the last remnants of sunlight and the flicker of lampposts beginning to come on as dusk settled on the street. Mark was watching her closely, as if unsure what to say.

In the end, he didn't say anything. He simply bent toward her, closer, until their lips met and melted together. Noelle moaned a little, even as she wondered how on earth she was letting this happen here, now. With *him*.

Mark didn't try to take her into his arms, didn't touch her, didn't cup her face with his hand or tangle his fingers in her hair as she suddenly longed for him to do. No. He simply kissed her sweetly, hungrily, letting his lips and tongue say everything that needed to be said…without using any words whatsoever.

She tilted her head, meeting every gentle stroke of his tongue with one of her own, tasting the warmth of his mouth and the minty flavor of his breath. Soon, she started to quiver and shake, but it wasn't from the cold. She wasn't cold at all…she was suddenly on fire. Burning up, dying for his touch, wanting to feel his hard body against hers without the impediment of their thick coats.

But he never drew her tightly against him. In fact, he never touched her at all, except with that incredible mouth.

Finally, when he'd finished speaking to her in the most elemental way possible, he slowly ended the kiss and drew away from her. Noelle almost cried at the loss of his warmth, his closeness. It had been a kiss…just a kiss…but she felt as if she'd just been made love to in full view of her co-workers and everyone on the block.

Funny. She really couldn't bring herself to care.

"What was that?" she managed to whisper when she could think again.

She could see by the puffs of air warmed by his breath that he was breathing deeply, slowly, much too calmly considering she was nearly out of her mind with surprise. Wonder. Desire.

Finally, he replied. "That was a reminder," he told her, his voice low and sultry. As sultry as the early evening shadows lengthening over the yard, creating mysterious hidden pockets of darkness.

She cleared her throat. "A reminder of what?"

"Of what got you thinking of this whole stupid affair-with-a-stranger thing."

Noelle couldn't say a word. Because it was as if he'd read her mind, looked right into her and seen the truth. Somehow, he knew that the reason she'd decided to go for it with a complete stranger was because of the kiss *this* particular stranger had given her in a dressing room last Friday. She'd alluded to it earlier, in her office, and he'd obviously put the pieces together and realized the truth: that *he'd* inspired her insanely wicked plan.

"So before you go off and find some nameless guy to give you a few hours to forget everything it is you're trying to escape," he added, "why don't you think about what made you want it so much in the first place?"

Then, without another word, he turned around and walked away, disappearing into the shadows of the evening until all that remained was the click of his shoes against the sidewalk. And soon they, too, were gone.

3

NOELLE HADN'T PLANNED on visiting Christmas to see her cousin and her new baby until mid-January, after the December insanity was over with. The town was bad enough the other eleven months out of the year, but in the weeks leading up to its namesake holiday, Christmas grew utterly unbearable. Besides, if she ran into Jeremy—her former fiancé—and his new wife, she might just throw up.

Still, here she was, in her car, about ten miles outside the town where she'd been raised. That was about fifty miles closer than she wanted to be. She'd already spied a dozen cutesy billboards that invited every passerby to stop in for some mulled cider and sugar cookies in front of a roaring, chestnut-popping fire. *Gag.*

"You're sure this isn't too big an imposition?" her cousin Sue asked, her voice sounding a bit hollow on Noelle's cell phone. But even with the bad reception, she could hear Sue's upset tone. Her cousin felt horrible at having to ask for Noelle's help, just as Sue's husband, Randy, had predicted she would when he'd called the previous night.

But family was family, and Sue was as close to Noelle as a sister. So she hadn't even hesitated in answering Randy's call for help. Besides, the call from Sue's husband had come at a fortuitous time. The idea of going home to Christmas for a few days had certainly distracted her from the hot cop who'd nearly had her sticking to the couch in her office just twenty-four hours ago. The one who'd also left her standing in a boneless, brainless puddle of confused woman on the sidewalk last evening.

"Noelle?"

"It's okay, Susie," Noelle replied into her phone, wondering why she couldn't stop thinking of the things Mark had said. Or the way he'd kissed her. *Both* times. Sexy, hot, playful and erotic in the dressing room. Moody, intense and sultry in front of the shelter last night.

She couldn't help wondering what kiss number three might entail.

"I hate this. I hate feeling so helpless," Sue said.

Her poor, frantic cousin had called three times since Noelle had left Chicago this morning to drive to Christmas. As if Noelle would begrudge her cousin—and closest friend—a few days help when Sue was having complications with her pregnancy. Helping out with the inn was the least Noelle could do.

"I promise," Sue added, "it should only be for a day or two until one of our moms can come up from Arizona."

"Don't sweat it. I can stay till Monday or Tuesday at least. Hopefully one of them will be able to get a flight by then."

"I think you mean one of them will be able to tear herself away from the studly seventy-year-olds hanging out by the shuffleboard court," Sue said, a hint of laughter in her voice.

Noelle laughed as well, picturing their mothers, who were loving their new retiree lifestyle at a planned community in hot and sunny Arizona. "Well, even if they can't, I can stay a few days into next week. I have some vacation time to burn up before the end of the year anyway."

That vacation time was supposed to have been used for her trip to St. Lucia, but she suspected more than ever that she wasn't going to need it. Because after the unsettlingly attractive Detective Santori had left her office yesterday, Noelle had spent the rest of the day scrambling for emergency donations—or promises of them—and had still fallen well short of what they needed for even the most basic of Christmases for the kids.

The community had been great, but it wasn't exactly an affluent one. Besides, there was only so much anyone could give during this time of year. The county Social Services Department had a budget tighter than Noelle's size eight jeans. And the mayor's office hadn't even returned her phone calls.

Thankfully, she might have the chance to ask the man in person, at next weekend's mayoral Christmas ball—the event for which she needed a little black dress. For the first time, she was glad she'd scored the ticket. She hadn't been looking forward to representing Social Services and mingling with the politicos and millionaires who attended the mayor's functions. Now, however, some personal contact with those millionaires could come in very handy.

Counting on some non-Grinchy millionaires was one recourse, but she also had to make contingency plans to come up with more money. Her vacation fund would help. January's rent money would, too. And heck, she could live on grilled cheese and canned green beans for a month.

Still not enough. Not for food, decorations, clothes, blankets and a few little toys for the children of the families they served. But she'd find a way, and it would *not* involve poor, guilty Alice having to mortgage her old age.

"I *really* do appreciate this, honey," Sue said, sounding a little more relaxed. "I know you hate coming to town at any time of the year, but this month is going to be hell for you."

No kidding. Her cousin knew that better than anyone, since she and Noelle had grown up together at the Candy Cane Inn, which had been started by their mothers. Unlike Noelle, Sue had never let the overdose of everything Christmas destroy her genuine enjoyment of the holiday. Maybe because Sue's birthday was in July, she wasn't stuck with a glaringly seasonal first name, her father hadn't walked out on his wife and daughter on December 26, and Sue hadn't been practically left at the altar last Christmas Eve.

Instead, Sue had developed a real love for their weird hometown and its weird people. So much so that when Sue's father had died eighteen months ago, and both their mothers had decided to retire and move to Arizona, Sue had offered to take over the inn. She swore she'd never regretted it. Neither had Randy, her husband of two years.

Nobody, however, had figured on a difficult pregnancy in the near future. Since Sue and Randy had saved Noelle from any feelings of guilt for not continuing the family legacy— allowing her to happily live her new life in Chicago—she was more than willing to help in whatever way she could. Even if it included a short trip back to hell.

"It's okay," Noelle repeated. "I had a sucky day at work yesterday, anyway, so the distraction will do me good."

It wasn't just the distraction from the robbery she needed. She also needed to put the image of Detective Mark Santori out of her mind for a couple of days. It might have been easier if he'd been arrogant, or a jerk. But he hadn't. He'd been charming and flirtatious, confident and assured in her office.

And then, God, during those strange, almost surreal moments outside on the front walk, he'd been so intense. Moody. Intriguing. Seductive. As if he'd left her office earlier in the day, stewed over thoughts of her hooking up with a stranger, and come back to remind her that nobody else was going to do.

She greatly feared his plan had worked.

No. It couldn't happen, not with him. It didn't matter that Mark was hot and sexy, cute and charming. Because he was too much. Too...too *close*.

Her lover needed to be someone far, far away. Because only by being absolutely certain she'd never run into whatever amazing stranger she chose to have her wild fling with could Noelle get as outrageously wicked as she planned to be.

And oh, she *planned* to get outrageous. Eight years worth of sensual fantasies were stored in her brain. Those fantasies had been building since her first lousy sexual experience with Carl Ritter after a winter dance in high school. He'd been the resident *stud* who'd turned out to be a *dud* when they'd done it in his father's golf cart, which was decorated to look like Santa's sleigh. To this day, whenever she kissed a sloppy, drooly kind of guy, she instantly visualized Mr. Ritter's makeshift sleigh, complete with eight plastic reindeer spiked on two long sections of rebar. From Dasher to Blitzen, they'd looked like tiny horses speared by Vlad the Impaler.

God, no wonder she hated Christmas.

Mark hadn't been a sloppy kisser. Far, far from it.

She sighed deeply, reminding herself to put him out of her mind. There were plenty of other men in the world. Men who could make her forget that all of her previous sexual experiences had ranged from mediocre to mildly interesting. Men who could give her the kind of mind-blowing sex she'd only dreamed about. Oh, how Noelle wanted mind-blowing.

All kinds of blowing.

But not with him. It didn't matter that she had already found someone who'd instantly made her fantasize about all the erotic things she wanted to do, because Mark was one man she just couldn't do them with. Because with Mark, her emotions would come into it...she knew it with an inexplicable certainty. At this time of year in particular, she knew better than to risk getting her heart broken again by any man. She only hoped this weekend away would be enough time for her to get that entrenched in her all-too-imaginative mind.

Somehow, though, she was afraid it wouldn't be. Which, she suspected, was exactly what the man had intended when he'd appeared out of the shadows, kissed the taste buds out of her mouth, then disappeared again.

And for that, she didn't know whether to hate him…or to simply beg him for more.

MARK HAD THE WEEKEND OFF. During most other weekends of the year, he'd probably have been hanging out with his folks. The Santori clan typically gathered at the family-owned pizzeria on Taylor Avenue every Sunday, as well as the usual drop-ins for a beer or a calzone during the week.

But this Sunday fell during the month of December. The Christmas season. Meaning Pop would be griping about money and reminiscing about holidays in the old country when an orange and a peppermint stick had seemed like a wealth of treasures. No one—not even Lottie the mouth—would remind Pop that he'd been born in Brooklyn. They were well used to him channeling his immigrant father.

Mama would be distributing the names for the family's Secret Santa exchange, arranging the "random" drawing to her own liking. Tony's four-year-old son would be bouncing off the walls on a pre-Christmas high that was more potent than ten pounds of Pixie Stix. Newlyweds Luke and Rachel would be cooing over their first Christmas together, and Joe and Meg would be cooing over their baby Marie's first Christmas *altogether*.

Painful.

Maybe if his twin brother, Nick, were in town it'd be bearable. But Nick was currently serving his third tour in Iraq with the 1st Marine Expeditionary Force. Mark was already worried enough about his ten-minutes younger brother without seeing his parents' dismay over not having their baby boy home for Christmas again. He couldn't stand to hear "Jesus, Mary and all'a da saints help us, what if a telegram arrives about our leetle Nicky?" coming out of his father's mouth one more time.

Nick was okay. Mark would know it if he wasn't…he'd just *know*.

To top it all off, if he was at the restaurant, he'd be hearing the not-so-subtle reminders from his mother and sisters-in-law that he should find a good woman and settle down.

He shifted in his seat as a quick thought flashed through his mind about a glorious brunette in black panties. He might not want to *settle* down, but he'd like to *go* down, that was for damn sure. And there would be no settling about it. Some seriously pleasurable oral sex was just one thing he wanted to do with Noelle Bradenton.

That was another good reason to get out of town. Being away from Chicago would keep him from doing something stupid like going by the shelter to see if Noelle worked on Saturdays.

No, man, forget it. He'd taken his shot and she'd turned him down. Yeah, she'd turned him down for a reason no man ever expected to hear from a beautiful woman—because she only wanted a sexy fling with a stranger, not somebody whose name she already knew. But a brush-off was a brush-off, no matter the reason.

So why couldn't he get her out of his mind?

Probably because she'd *admitted* she was looking for sex. And she'd admitted silently—in her kiss, in her smile, in the hitchy little sound she made in the back of her throat whenever they were close—that she wanted that sex to be with *him*.

Her body was screaming yes. Her mind was saying no. It was his bad luck that he was crazy-hot for a woman whose mind was winning the battle.

Going back to the shelter and kissing her one more time—just to determine once and for all whether their first kiss had been as incredible as he remembered it to be—had been a crazy idea, but one he couldn't shake. After he'd left her office and returned to work Friday, he'd thought about Noelle hooking up with some stranger, and he'd broken out into a cold sweat. But returning there and kissing her again...well, it'd been impulsive. Unexpected.

Fantastic.

"Hell, maybe I shoulda gone to the restaurant," he muttered. Because being surrounded by Santoris and their madness might be just the thing to make him forget about the brunette who'd cost him another night's sleep the previous night.

Nah. He'd rather torture himself with images of what he *wasn't* going to have than with the realities of his big, loud, nosy family. Jolly, happy Santori's restaurant was definitely a place to avoid during the holiday season. Which made this weekend's excursion pretty damned ironic. Because he was going to Christmas...Noelle Bradenton's hometown.

"You really think you're going to find something on this Wallace guy in some town that has gingerbread men statues outside City Hall?" His partner Harriet's gravelly voice was made deeper by cell phone static. The closer he'd gotten to Christmas, the worse the reception had become.

"Not saying it'll pan out," he admitted—to both of them. "But I have the time and it's not too far. Might as well check since nothing else seems to be turning up."

Harriet fell silent, obviously still not convinced he wasn't wasting his time. Mark was used to the reaction. His partner—

who was twenty years older and twenty pounds heavier than he—was a full-fledged pessimist.

She was also sharp as one of those stiletto-heeled shoes… which she'd never be caught dead in. And she'd taught him a lot in the two years they'd been partnered up. If the other guys in the squad had a problem with Harriet's gruffness and suspected sexual orientation, well, tough shit. Mark liked her, respected her, and valued her opinion. "You think I'm wasting my time?"

The woman grunted into the phone. "What do I know? Everything about this case is screwy. Who'd imagine a midget in an elf suit crawling through the heating ducts of Riley's Department Store to raid the jewelry cases in broad daylight, when the place was open?"

Not him. Particularly since the elf had then passed the stolen goods—worth at least fifty grand—off to the store's costumed Santa. The guy had breezed out with the stuff *literally* stuffed into his oversized red suit. "I guess he was inspired by that *Bad Santa* movie that came out a couple of years ago," he said.

She grunted. It wouldn't be the first time either one of them had seen some criminal inspired by Hollywood, TV or music.

"Keep me posted on what you do find out, okay?" Harriet said. "Hell, who knows? Maybe you could be onto something since that informant from 21st Street mentioned some kind of training grounds for thieves not too far from Chicago."

"Exactly why I'm going there."

"Just keep your head down…wouldn't want you to be clobbered by the hooves of any low-flying reindeer." Harriet's snicker made Mark chuckle and roll his eyes as he hung up.

When he pulled off the highway to the main road leading to Christmas, however, Mark stopped chuckling. Because this had to be a joke. He'd assumed everything he'd heard about the town, or seen in commercials, had been exaggerated.

It wasn't.

From the red and white striped picket fences in front of every house, to the stained glass Santa-and-his-sleigh window encompassing the entire front of the library, to the ropes of greenery draped along the rooflines of every building in sight, this place screamed holiday cheer. Not only screamed it, but batted it upside the head like a nail-studded two-by-four.

Cruising through the downtown area of Christmas, he noted the cutesy names of the stores. Jolly Jim's offered the latest and greatest in lighted ornaments. The front window display was a battlefield where tacky lit-up tin soldiers, snowmen, Santas and elves competed for space with smiling baby Jesuses and singing angels. Holly's Holly boasted the biggest selection of mistletoe in town. *Did mistletoe come in different varieties?* And Kris Kringle's diner had on special Whoville Roast Beast.

No doubt about it, he'd fallen through a black hole into the Nightmare Before Christmas. Or, in this instance, the Nightmare That *Was* Christmas.

A couple of hours of walking around the place confirmed it. If there was ever an entire town that needed to be locked into an enormous padded room, this was it. God, no wonder Noelle hadn't wanted to talk about her hometown…it was certifiable.

After his visit to the Institute of Rotudifical Purveyors of Goodwill—aka the Santa College—he decided the trip had been a wasted one. The owner of the place hadn't been in, and the woman he'd found in the office hadn't exactly been a font of information.

If it had looked as if the lead might actually have been important, Mark might have pushed her on the current location of the owner, some guy named Taggert. But he had to admit it…the trip out here had been more of a whim to get out of town for the day. His cop instincts hadn't been on alert and he had no solid information that had led him to his place. A couple of hours in Christmas was nearly enough to make him scratch it off his list of possible leads.

Besides, if something more came of it, he could always return on a weekday and tackle the dean of Santas during office hours. But for now, it was time to get outta Creepsville.

At least one good thing had come of his visit here: Mark was never going to complain about the crime or fast pace of Chicago again. Because anything was better than having undiluted joy and goodwill shoved down his throat whether he wanted to swallow it or not. At least in Chicago you could flip somebody off if they wished you a Merry Christmas when you weren't in the mood to hear it.

Yeah. A quick getaway was definitely in order. But as he drove down Nativity Avenue—one of the two main streets criss-crossing through the tiny town—he spied something out of the corner of his eye that made him reassess his plan. Actually, he spied some*one* who made him do that. Standing beside the lollipop light post on the porch of a place called the Candy Cane Inn was the most delicious-looking elf he'd ever seen.

An elf named Noelle Bradenton.

"WHAT DO YOU MEAN you've rented out my room?"

Noelle stared in shock at Randy, her cousin's husband, who stood behind the reception desk at the Candy Cane Inn, wearing a sheepish expression and a blush. Not unusual for Randy, who'd been the shyest boy in Noelle's class at Christmas High. Good thing Sue was the take-charge type, or fairhaired, tall and lanky Randy might still be twiddling his thumbs, trying to figure out a way to ask her perky ex-cheerleader cousin out. Instead, he and Sue were happily awaiting the birth of their first child, due just after New Year's.

Noelle still hadn't quite forgiven her cousin for that—foisting a holiday birthday on her baby. If and when Noelle ever settled down and started having a family, her legs were staying closed during the months of March and April…no way was any child of hers going to have to share his or her birthday with the savior of the world.

"I'm sorry, Noelle, this stranger just offered so much above our normal going rate I couldn't refuse. We really are trying to bring in as much as we can to pay for either Sue's mom or yours to fly up from Arizona for the rest of the month. And with a baby in the house, we know we're going to have to bring in fewer guests for a few months. So I guess when I saw a chance to bank a little bit, I grabbed it."

Noelle had just come from Sue's bedroom, where her cousin was on bed rest for the final few weeks of her pregnancy, so she knew what Randy meant. Still, she couldn't believe someone had come into the inn and laid down a boatload of money to rent the one remaining room—Noelle's old room—in the twenty minutes she'd been visiting her cousin.

"Who is this person who couldn't take no for an answer?" she asked, still wishing she'd stuck her luggage in her old room the moment she'd arrived, instead of leaving it piled by the back door in the kitchen. Randy might have had a harder time selling her bed out from under her if her panties had been strewn across it.

"His name's—"

"Not important," someone said, smoothly cutting Randy off before he could finish.

Noelle swung around, her heart pounding and her pulse racing. Because something told her she knew whose voice that had been, whose face she was about to see. The instant flood of moisture between her legs confirmed it.

"Oh, my God," she murmured.

It was him. Detective Mark Santori. The man she was dying to go to bed with but who she'd convinced herself she could never have. Somehow, he was here, in Christmas—in her childhood home—looking at her with heat and speculation and deep, intense interest.

"Good afternoon, ma'am," he said as he stepped across the foyer. He'd apparently been lurking around in the garland-and-ribbon-bedecked parlor. Probably wondering, as she often had throughout her childhood, why, exactly, the Virgin Mary was sitting on Rudolph the Red-Nosed Reindeer in one of the four nativities in the room.

"It's you."

He smiled lazily. "No, it's not. I'm someone you've never met, just passing through town." He shrugged his shoulders. "I'm not going to be here long, so absolutely no introductions are necessary."

Noelle's jaw dropped. She could only stare at him, wondering what kind of game the man was playing. At the same time, she was also wondered how on earth she'd had the strength to let him walk away from her last night outside the shelter without experiencing—at least once more—the delight of his mouth. Even now, if she closed her eyes and thought about it, she knew she'd be able to taste his tongue against hers, to feel the heat of his breath.

There was no use denying it, even to herself. She wanted him desperately, and no one else was going to do, especially after today. Her nights were going to be even more plagued with fantasies of the man. Because he looked so incredibly sexy, clad in a worn, soft pair of jeans. His dark brown turtleneck sweater emphasized the breadth of his chest and the width of his shoulders.

He wasn't wearing the leather jacket he'd had on in the store—and again yesterday at the shelter—so she was able to fully appreciate the man's amazing body. Good God in heaven, she could sleep all night on top of that chest and never roll off the side.

Wow. Just…wow.

"Do you two know each other?" Randy asked, looking back and forth between the two of them, confusion on his smooth face.

"No. We absolutely do *not* know each other," Mark answered, a small smile playing about his oh-so-kissable lips. "I'm afraid we are complete strangers."

Suddenly she got it. That spark of wickedness in his eyes told her so everything she needed to know about what was on the black-haired detective's mind.

He was offering her a chance, giving her the opportunity to take exactly what she'd sworn she wanted. A sultry interlude, far away from home with a perfect stranger. And he *was* perfect. Oh, most definitely.

How he'd come to be here suddenly didn't seem to matter. Maybe he'd followed her. Maybe he was investigating his case. Maybe it was pure chance. What mattered was that he was here. They both were. He was staying in her room, would be sleeping in her nice, big, comfortable bed. A hunky, naked man covered only by her thin pink-and-white percale sheets. Just like she'd dreamed about when she was a lusty teenager. It only remained to decide what to do about it.

The money moment had arrived, she had to put up or shut up. Whether he'd followed her here to Christmas, or this was all some karmic set-up, she was being handed the opportunity to indulge in the fantasies that had filled her head since the moment this man had stumbled into her dressing room.

She could take. Have. Indulge. Savor. Embrace.

Or she could chicken out and go to bed on the fold-out couch in the living room, tossing and turning through the night, picturing him right down the hall. All self-protective, keeping her heart guarded and her legs closed.

You can lose your clothes and still keep your heart under lock and key, a voice whispered in her head.

There really was no deciding. No hesitation at all. So with a slow smile and a slower nod, Noelle murmured, "Well, then, stranger, here's hoping your stay in our little town is something you'll never forget."

Their eyes met, their stares held. Somehow, just as they had when they'd kissed on the sidewalk yesterday evening, they exchanged a wealth of information—of invitation and acceptance—without saying a single word. They were both fully aware of the sexual promises they'd just made to one another.

Everything else seemed to fade away, including Randy who was probably still somewhere in the vicinity. But even he didn't seem to really exist in this new place—this place of heady, sensual delight that she and Mark had just created with nothing more than the silent acknowledgement of what was to come.

Mark was feeling the magical intensity of it, too. She could see it in the curve of his lips, the lazy sensuality of his small movements as he leaned a hip against the front desk. Understanding and a sultry kind of want shone in his green eyes. That only built the heat even more. "I somehow suspect I won't forget a minute of my stay here in Christmas," he whispered, his voice low and thick.

Though the lobby of the inn was warm enough, Noelle couldn't prevent a tiny shiver of pure anticipation, knowing she was about to embark on the kind of erotic adventure she'd always longed for but had never truly, in her heart of hearts, believed she'd have. Now, however, looking at the straight-from-her-fantasies man watching her with desire nearly dripping from him in waves, she knew everything she'd ever wanted was just a few short hours away.

And she couldn't help feeling that Mark Santori's stay in Christmas was going to be something *she* would never forget, either.

As long as she remembered her new mantra: arms—and other body parts—open, heart firmly closed.

4

RETIRING TO HIS ROOM that evening, Mark looked at it through new eyes, knowing it was Noelle's. The femininity of it—all soft and pink—would normally have made him turn and run, and not only because of the Martha Stewart–like décor. He also wasn't about to put someone out of their own room. So if he wasn't pretty damn sure she'd be sharing the bed with him tonight, he'd have given up the room as soon as he'd found out it was Noelle's.

But he *was* pretty sure she would be sharing the nice, big bed with him. And his whole body got hot and alert just thinking about it.

A man of few previous commitments, he'd still never considered sex as easy or casual. He'd had a couple of relationships—only one serious—and had never done the one-night-stand thing, unless a few wild college parties counted. So why he was ready to jump into a fast affair with a woman he'd met just a week ago, he really couldn't say. He didn't, however, have a single doubt that he wanted this. Wanted her. Wanted *them*. For at least this weekend.

Maybe it was the knowledge that they might have *only* this weekend that made him prowl anxiously around the bedroom. Probably wearing a horseshoe-shaped pattern in the pale pink rug, he paced around the three sides of the antique, four-poster bed. The soft pink duvet, combined with the white and pink wallpaper with rose-trimmed border, made the place look like something out of a romance magazine. The gentle lighting provided by one frilly, shaded lamp on the bedside table lent an intimate glow to the room, making it that much more alluring. Dreamy. It gave him a sudden glimpse into the psyche of the woman who was about to become his lover.

Noelle was a romantic.

He might not have expected it of the sweater-wearing social worker, but the woman he'd kissed in the twilight last night? Yeah. Absolutely. And she was woman he was waiting so very anxiously to see again.

Still, wanting desperately to go to bed with Noelle Bradenton didn't mean he was totally cool with this evening. Knowing what was going to happen between them should have relieved the tension and pressure of wondering. Instead, it put him on edge, made him wonder if they were being too deliberate. Because after the spontaneous combustion of their sexy, hot encounter in the dressing room, he wondered if a scheduled weekend of passion was going to be a letdown.

"Letdown, my ass," he muttered, knowing the sex was going to be phenomenal.

It wasn't the sex that was bugging him, he suddenly realized. It was what was going to happen *after* the sex, when Noelle breezed out of his life, satisfied and sated, never wanting to set eyes on him again. And as the moment drew closer and closer, he began to wonder if he'd made a big tactical error in offering to be Noelle's weekend stranger.

He didn't have a moment more to think about it, though, because a soft knock on the door signaled her arrival. Glancing at his watch, he realized it was a few minutes past eight. Something had made him think she'd come late at night, when the house was silent. That she'd creep through shadows, perhaps even slipping naked into his bed while he slept.

But no, it was relatively early and there were other lights on in the house. *So maybe she changed her mind.*

He thrust that thought away as he opened the door, not even trying to determine if that was a good thing or a bad one. The second he set eyes on her, however, he gave up his mental resistance.

Noelle had not had a change of heart about what she wanted—the smile on her lips confirmed it. And right at this moment, with her beautiful face lit by the soft hallway light, he couldn't think of a single bad thing about it.

"Hi," she murmured, her voice shaking a little. From nervousness, or excitement, he couldn't tell.

"Hi yourself." He stepped back and ushered her in, noting the shiny silkiness of her hair hanging loosely past her shoulders.

She'd changed her clothes and now wore a low-cut black sweater and cream-colored cords that hugged the body he'd been fantasizing about for a week. The glimpse of black lace peeking out from the shoulder hem of her sweater made Mark close his eyes for a second, remembering how amazing she'd looked the day they'd met.

Oh, no, she definitely hadn't changed her mind. The only question was: would he?

"My cousin is on bed-rest, and her husband spends the evenings with her in their private suite," she said, her voice still a bit thready and weak. "The other guests are all already in their rooms for the night, too." Noelle's hands were clasped in front of her waist, and she was babbling a little, another sign of her nervousness.

Hell, he couldn't blame her. This was…weird. Just, strange. They both wanted each other like a couple of horny teenagers, but weren't sure how to proceed. Just dive onto the bed, letting clothes fling where they may? Start with a conversation about the weather? Or something in-between.

Like maybe a date?

"This is...I don't know what to..."

"Shh," he said, feeling for her because of the visible embarrassment that made her eyes flare and her bottom lip disappear between her teeth.

She lowered her head, a curtain of thick, rich dark hair shielding her face. "I might have sounded pretty cocky, but I've never done anything like this."

"I know. Neither have I." Coming no closer, he sat on the padded bench in front of the vanity table, deciding to take things one step at a time. He'd be patient even if it killed him. Because in the end, the payoff was going to be fantastic—whether it occurred tonight or a month from now. "So if we're total strangers," he said with a smile, "are we allowed to talk at all?"

She lowered herself to the edge of the bed. "I don't know."

"How about we agree to steer clear of personal issues and find something else to discuss?"

Her bottom lip stuck out a little and she frowned. "As long as it's not about Christmas."

"The town, or the holiday?"

"Both."

"Another Christmas hater, huh?" When she nodded, he continued. "I guess we do have a lot in common. This is some hometown you have. I can see why you left."

"You mean you haven't suddenly developed a taste for gingerbread and turkey?"

"Gimme a pizza any day," he said with a shrug.

"Me, too. Chicago deep dish. They don't make it within a thirty mile radius of here. Mr. Lebowski owns the only Italian place, and he only serves thin crust. Says if you want bread, go to the bakery."

"My family makes the best deep dish pie in the city," he said, not even trying to be modest. "You'll have to come by Santori's and try it one night."

Her eyes clouded over and she glanced down.

Bad move. He'd stepped out of stranger mode and treated her like a friend. Or, even worse, a date. "So why don't you tell me why only a stranger will do?"

Her jaw dropped. "Well, if that's not personal, I don't know what is."

She'd misunderstood. He quickly clarified. "I don't mean I want to know about your romantic track record." Rising and smiling slowly as he stepped closer to the bed, he murmured, "I mean, why don't you tell me what wicked, sexy things you've been wanting to do that you could only make happen with a complete stranger, someone you'll never have to face again?" Maybe by talking about what was driving her, Noelle would relax and let them both figure out exactly what they wanted to happen here.

Sex, yeah. But Mark was beginning to suspect that sex might not be enough. And a single weekend definitely wasn't going to be. At least, not for him.

Moistening her lips with the tip of her tongue, she admitted, "I guess you just answered your own question, didn't you? About why a stranger is the perfect person to…experiment with?"

He swallowed hard, but didn't relent. With his jeans brushing against her slacks, he said, "You must have some really wild stuff in mind if you think you'll never be able to face your lover again once you're done." Dozens of vivid, evocative images flashed in his brain as he imagined giving her everything she'd ever wanted. He somehow managed to thrust them away, determined to push this issue with Noelle before either of them took things beyond the point of no return. "So tell me what you fantasize about? What erotic, outrageous, potentially illegal things do you want to do and never have to admit to in the light of day?"

She gasped, as he'd expected her to, at hearing her plan put in such bald terms. But he wasn't backing off. "Do your fantasies include domination? Do you want to be in total control, or completely controlled?" he lowered his voice. "I do have handcuffs with me."

Maybe, deep down, Mark was expecting her to back off, to rethink her weekend affair idea. And maybe, even deeper, part of him wanted her to. Because as much as he wanted her—and oh, Christ, did he want her—he wasn't sure he wanted her on *her* terms. He didn't know if he could stand being buried deep inside her body and not hearing her cry out his name—his *real* name—when he made her come. Or that he could share some of the most intimate, carnal moments of his life with someone who never wanted to see him again.

This stranger thing, he'd begun to realize, might not be a great idea.

"So?" he asked, hearing a slight taunt in his voice as he practically dared her to put up or shut up, "tell me every sensual, evocative thing you've ever dreamed of doing, but never figured you really would."

She tilted her head back and looked up at him, a warm flush of color rising in her cheeks. Her tongue flicked out to moisten her lips and he nearly lost his mind.

Mark swallowed, wondering if he'd just made a very bad move. Because instead of teasing her into a smile, he appeared to have taunted her into a seductress. "Noelle…".

"You smell good," she whispered.

"So do you." Unable to resist, he reached out and slid his fingers through her long, silky hair. Then he trailed a path down her neck and over her shoulder, until he was ever-so-lightly touching the lacy strap of her black bra. The warmth and softness of her skin only made him want to touch her more, and the sweet scent of her hair made him long to bury his face in it and absolutely inhale her.

"Do you *really* want to know what I want? What I'm absolutely dying to have?"

The purr in her voice was wickedly seductive. Mark's body reacted powerfully as the lazy interest that had kept him semierect all evening surged into full-fledged arousal. Noelle, still sitting beneath him, had to notice; she was practically face-level with his crotch. Her audible gasp nearly made him back off, but she stopped him by smiling a little and shifting on the bed. As if she was restless. As if she was wet. As if she was ready.

"I want *that*." She reached out and fried his circuits completely by letting the back of her hand brush against the length of his erection, barely contained by the zipper of his jeans. "I want every bit of that." She touched him again. Lightly, evocatively, tracing the full outline of his cock with her fingers and smiling secretly, as if pleased by whatever she'd discovered.

He had the feeling he knew why she was pleased, and looked forward to showing her just how much he had to give her.

When she leaned close, so that her lips brushed against the fabric of his jeans, he had to clench his fists. "Noelle…"

"You're right," she murmured. Then she breathed deeply, letting him feel the warmth of her exhalations through the denim. "There's so much I want to do. So much I've never done."

She sounded dreamy, sultry, and very, very hungry.

"What happened to conversation?" he asked through a very tight throat, wondering exactly when this situation had spun completely out of his control.

"It's overrated."

He decided she was right when she reached for his zipper and slowly began tugging it down. "Can I at least kiss you first?" he said, while still capable of coherent thought.

"Nuh-uh," she whispered as she finished unzipping, then unbuttoning his jeans. Leaning closer, until he could feel her warm breath through the cotton of his boxer briefs, she added, "When you kiss me, I get…distracted."

Distracted? Uh, yeah, he got that. He could barely focus on his own name, much less anything else, when he looked down and saw her sweet mouth so very, *very* close to him.

Her cool fingers traced his bulge again. Noelle's eyes went even darker with want as she stared at a spot of moisture on his briefs. "I want to taste you." That's just what she did, her pretty little tongue flicking out to scrape against the gray cotton so she could sample his essence.

"Holy mother of… You're killing me here," he muttered hoarsely.

She didn't stop. Instead, Noelle teasingly slipped her fingertips into the front opening of his shorts, almost cooing as she delicately brushed them against his dick.

"So warm and smooth." Her voice sounded wondering. "How can something so hard feel so incredibly soft to the touch?"

Another bit of his control flew out the window. "Noelle…"

"I'm a stranger, remember?" she whispered, never looking up, remaining focused on her sensual task.

Hell, he was lucky he could remember his *own* name at this point. And when she moved to let her tongue replace her fingertips, lightly flicking it against the little bit of skin she'd revealed, he realized he couldn't even remember that.

Unable to resist, he stroked her thick, dark hair, wondering how it was going to feel spread across his naked groin. It appeared he was going to find out very, *very* soon.

The strains of the hallelujah chorus filled his head for some bizarre reason, which almost made it seem he had heavenly approval to get as erotic and carnal as Noelle wanted him to. Gabriel himself couldn't have resisted the devilish woman who was driving him crazy with her slow, deliberate breathing and the light strokes of her fingers. Not to mention the delicate flicks of her tongue.

Then he realized something, and froze completely.

The singing wasn't just in his mind. It was coming from right outside the window.

SUE HALLORAN HAD THOUGHT being pregnant was going to be a breeze. No, the pregnancy hadn't exactly been planned and it had taken Randy a little while to get used to the idea that there was going to be a baby in their lives. Oh, he'd never been *unhappy* about it—if there was ever a man who was born to be a father, she'd married him. But Randy had worried himself into a state of panic within an hour of learning he was going to be a Daddy.

That state of panic had never fully dissipated. She'd finally gotten him to keep his more dire concerns to himself by screeching at the top of her lungs that it wasn't good for her *or* the baby to hear him muttering about toxic chemicals in drinking water and infants born with tails.

Randy was a worrier. A worst-case-scenario type of guy.

Sue was an optimist. A we-can't-do-anything-about-it-so-let's-just-forget-about-it-for-now kind of girl.

They usually balanced each other out pretty well.

Until now.

Because right around the time she'd gotten her sweet, protective husband to stop darkly muttering about the negative influence of C.S.I. on their unborn child—as if the kid was watching it through her belly button—she'd learned that there really *was* something to worry about.

Placental Previa. She'd immediately recognized the technical term when the doctor had named it Thursday. If she hadn't known it from her own cover-to-cover reading of the thirty-five pregnancy books Randy had bought the first month of her pregnancy, she would from her husband's frequent outloud reading from said books.

Randy, it seemed, had been right to worry. This *wasn't* going to be the free-and-breezy pregnancy Sue had assured her husband she was going to have. The pregnancy her mother, aunt, and friends had all assured *her* she was going to have.

Nope. She was one of the lucky 1 in 200 or so women who developed the condition that had caused some bleeding—not to mention pure terror—a few days ago. Which was why she had to remain in bed for the rest of her pregnancy and hope the relative lack of movement would keep the baby safely developing in her womb for at least another week or two.

Her stout, resolute, generous self knew it wasn't a hardship at all because there was nothing she wouldn't do to keep the baby safe. Heck, she'd stopped drinking anything with caffeine in it, stopped eating Snickers bars—her secret addiction—and had even stopped dyeing her shoulder-length hair, which had returned to its natural boring, sandy-blond color. So this should've been a piece of cake.

It wasn't. Because the bored, selfish part of her was whining.

It was so frustrating, being stuck in this bed when she knew there were a million things she had to do to keep the inn running and get ready for her maternity leave. Randy was a born innkeeper in terms of keeping their guests happy and comfortable. He'd fallen right into the role of host when he'd left his own family's local business to help her run hers shortly after their wedding.

Unfortunately, her husband had zero business sense. If she didn't get back on her feet and return to overseeing things, he would be letting anyone with a sob story, an empty wallet, and no credit card move on in.

"It's not just boredom and worry," she admitted aloud, talking to the baby, as she often did these days.

No. She was also grieving.

Though Randy didn't understand, Sue was truly grieving at the knowledge that she wasn't going to be able to have the baby naturally. Silly, she supposed. But after the doctor had explained everything—stressing that her baby was fine and, at nearly thirty-six weeks, could be delivered soon if necessary—she'd been almost *more* upset knowing she was going to have to have a C-section.

Her mother had thought it wonderful that she'd simply be able to schedule the delivery and avoid the whole painful labor thing altogether. "Great, Mom," she muttered again, considering the source. Her mother had often griped about how angry she'd been to learn during her own pregnancy that they no longer routinely put women out, then woke them up when it was all over with. Sue firmly believed that was why she was an only child. Her mother didn't like…messes.

Sue, on the other hand, had been looking forward to the entire experience, from water breaking to pushing. She and Randy had been A+ students at all the childbirth classes and they'd already rehearsed for the big moment when it was time to leave for the hospital. "Well," she whispered, "Daddy rehearsed. Mommy just nodded her head and laughed at him. But we won't tell him that, will we, Mia?"

This week she was calling the baby—whose sex she didn't yet know—Mia, after soccer player Mia Hamm. The kid's kicking abilities were astronomical. At six months, the baby had been Mary Lou, because she'd sometimes seemed to be swinging around Sue's internal organs like a gymnast on the high bars.

The point was, she'd worked hard to be ready to take on the biggest physical challenge of her life. *All for nothing*. She was instead going to lie in this bed for as long as she could stand it, then make an appointment like she was going to get her hair or nails done, and have her baby surgically removed from her body.

It wasn't fair, not for someone who'd worked so hard to be prepared. That sounded petulant, but frankly, with her whacked-out hormones, petulance was something she was feeling right now. Ten minutes from now, she'd be weepy. And tomorrow she'd be scared out of her mind again about the baby's well-being.

But for right now, petulance was doing just fine.

"Honey?" Randy said tentatively, peeking his head in the door to their room. He was probably still nervous to be around her after she'd nearly ripped his head off earlier when he'd offered to get her some decaffeinated tea or rub her feet. He wouldn't look directly at her, keeping his gentle eyes slightly averted. "You doing okay?"

"No," she muttered, sniffling a little.

He hurried to the side of the bed. "What is it? What can I do? Do you need me to call the doctor?"

She reached for his hand. "I'm fine. At least, as fine as I've been since I got sentenced to this bed. I'm just…bored. And lonely."

"I'll stay with you."

"Is everything running okay?"

He nodded. "Noelle's been a big help. She stepped right back into the thick of things, as if she never left."

"Poor thing," Sue murmured, knowing how much her cousin had sacrificed to come back here at this time of year. Particularly *this* year, when Noelle's former fiancé was walking around town with his new wife, who *so* hadn't had any baby. So much for Jeremy's story that he'd gotten some woman from out of town pregnant when he'd come to the inn last December 22 to cancel the Christmas Eve wedding.

She didn't know whether Jeremy had made up the pregnancy story or if he'd been lied to himself. Didn't really matter—either way, he deserved what he got. From what Randy said, Jeremy—who was her husband's first cousin—was *very* unhappy. Which, frankly, sounded like divine justice to Sue.

"She seemed okay when she got here," Randy said. "I know she was happy to see you."

Yes, she'd been happy. Noelle had hugged her tight, and laughingly compared Sue to a giant beach ball with a head, arms and legs. "I hate that we had to ask her to do this."

"But she is good company for you." He looked around, obviously just noticing she was alone in the room. "Speaking of which, I thought she'd be here with you. Where is she?"

Good question. It was after eight o'clock, the inn was quiet, and Noelle was nowhere to be seen.

"I'll go find her," Randy said, probably anxious to get out of here before she started crying again, or else threatened to throw him out the window for offering to plump her pillows.

Hormones. What a bitch. And very aptly named.

"It's okay," she said. "Let her be…she's worked since the minute she got here."

Before she could ask Randy to rub her feet now, because she was ready for him to, unlike twenty minutes ago when he'd offered, Sue was distracted by an unexpected sound. Voices, loud and jubilant, raised in song.

Her spirits instantly rose. "Is that what I think it is?"

Randy tilted his head to listen, then slowly nodded, obviously not sure whether this was a good development or a bad one. "Yeah, it sounds like the Christmas Carolers."

She clapped her hands together, suddenly feeling a lot better. The Carolers—a group of local performers who performed their well-rehearsed repertoire all year long—had come at a perfect time. They were just the reminder she needed that her favorite holiday was just around the corner.

But her happiness faded when she realized something: she couldn't go to the door to greet them. Nor could she offer the traditional hot cider and goodies that she usually did. "I won't be able to see them," she said, her voice hitchy. She sniffled. "I can barely hear them.

Randy rose to his feet, his sweet, kind face pulled into a concerned frown. Then he stiffened his shoulders and nodded resolutely. "Don't worry, honey. If you can't go to the music, well, the music will just have to come to you."

HEARING A TROOP OF PEOPLE marching past her bedroom door when her tongue was delicately stroking a man's rock-hard erection was one way to kill a mood. Oh, it didn't seem to kill Mark's—he was every bit as big and ready after he swung around to make sure the door was locked as he'd been when she was about to gobble him up. For Noelle, however, the desire to get wickedly carnal and suck on the man's sex as if it was one of those supersized candy canes shrunk just a tiny bit when she recognized the tune of "I Saw Mommy Kissing Santa Claus."

"What the hell is going on?" Mark asked, looking stunned and frustrated. Listening to the laughing voices and the singing in the hallway, he buttoned his jeans. Grabbing for his zipper, he tried to ease it up without injuring himself.

Noelle would have offered to help, but frankly, she didn't think she'd have the strength. The next time she touched that man's zipper, she wanted to be yanking it down to finish what she'd just about started. Not pulling it up and hiding all that yummy male goodness she could still almost taste on her tongue.

"Who are those people and why are they singing?" he asked, still watching the door in disbelief, as if expecting it to swing open at any moment.

Knowing the Christmas Carolers—who had to be the ones invading the inn—she wouldn't put it past them. If they'd known Noelle was in town, she didn't imagine even a locked door would have kept the merry band of miscreants out. "They're apparently going to serenade Sue in bed," she murmured, instantly realizing why Randy would have let the twenty-something strong musical group into the inn. "She's always loved them."

He gaped. "Are you telling me those are a bunch of carolers? Good grief, Christmas is three weeks away!"

Noelle geared up for his response to what she knew was going to sound crazy. "They're an organized musical choir— 'The Christmas Carolers'—and they perform all year round. In elf costumes."

Mark looked stunned. "You are shitting me."

"Nope, I'm afraid I'm not," she said with a rueful shake of her head. "From January through October, they go out one Saturday a month, rotating neighborhoods in Christmas, just to keep everyone mindful of the fact that they live in holiday hell."

His jaw fell open.

"In November, it's weekly," she explained, feeling his shock. "And starting December 1, they are out every single night of the month."

"How…un-holiday like," he sputtered, appearing really offended by the idea. "What's the point of having a special day if people are determined to take all the uniqueness out of it?"

Which was exactly how Noelle had always felt about the town's overdoing of everything related to the Christmas holiday. Funny that he'd so quickly and easily verbalized it.

He was still frowning. "Stores shouldn't have aisles full of wreaths and garland before Halloween. And there oughta be a law…no Christmas songs any time after January 5 or before Thanksgiving."

She totally agreed. "And *The Christmas Story* shows only once in December, not ninety-five times a day so we no longer even care if Ralphie gets his Red Ryder BB gun."

"Or if the Bumpus hounds eat the turkey," he said with a deep chuckle. He suddenly looked so boyish and cute that she wanted to pull him down beside her on the bed and kiss him to bits.

No kissing to bits she reminded herself. No. Only sucking, licking, biting, scratching and thrusting were allowed when it came to Mark Santori. No sweet, playful romping! In fact, they shouldn't be having this light, friendly conversation at all. He was supposed to be just her sexy stranger. Her lover— not her friend. Not her *romance,* that was for sure.

"I hear 'My Favorite Things,'" he muttered, shaking his head in disgust. "Who, I would like to know, decided *that* was a Christmas song? The song doesn't say red and green paper packages with strings, they're brown. Hell, they could have sex-toy catalogs in them for all we know."

Oh, no, he'd done it again—made her laugh by grumpily

saying something she'd thought a million times, though maybe not so descriptively. Still, their instant connection, the outlook, attitude and sense of humor...they made all kinds of strange, much-too-dangerous visions flash in her mind. Like the idea that maybe they were compatible in more ways than physically.

No, Noelle. You're going to have *him. Not* like *him.*

"I can't believe your cousin's husband actually let them in. Is he hard of hearing?"

Noelle rose to her feet, feeling selfish for leaving her cousin alone this evening, her first night here. How rotten she'd been to ignore Sue, just so she could go have wild, hot sex with a gorgeous, black-haired man she wanted to tie up and lick all over like a giant postage stamp.

Hmm. When looking at it that way, she seriously believed her cousin would understand.

But no way was she going to find out. This whole secret fling thing needed to remain a secret. Exposing it to the light of day would be putting too much emphasis on it. Too much importance. It needed to be completely casual and guiltless for Noelle to go all-out with her carnal plans and prevent herself from imagining that she and Mark would ever have anything more than sex.

Because they wouldn't. Period. Not as long as that little voice in her head kept whispering reminders of her painful track record with love.

"Sue must be feeling so left out of things," she said as she glanced into her mirror and tried to fix her wild hair. It still showed evidence of Mark's hands tangled in it.

Those *hands*. She wanted them touching her everywhere.

"So maybe someone could bring her a cake and a book of

crossword puzzles," he muttered. "Not thirty carol-singing nutjobs."

Oh, Lord, it was too late. She already liked this man. Maybe too much. That wasn't supposed to be part of the deal. "I'd better go."

Mark stiffened, eyeing her with disbelief. "You're kidding, right?"

"Sue and Randy will wonder where I am."

"That didn't seem to matter ten minutes ago."

Ten minutes ago. That'd been right around the time when she'd been licking at the moisture on his briefs, loving the musky, masculine taste, dying for a much deeper sample. She was still quivering, deep inside, at the memory of it.

That was just one of the things she'd never done—taking a man all the way to the edge and swallowing every bit of what he had to offer. And it was definitely something she wanted to do with her sexy stranger. *This* sexy stranger.

Of course, she'd never say that out loud, no matter how much he tried to get her to confess her most sensual, secret desires. Any more than she'd admit that she wanted his tongue licking her to the same explosive heights at exactly the same time.

Her legs shook a little bit and she had to close her eyes, having absolutely no doubt Mark would be delightfully daring. Unlike her ex-fiancé, Jeremy, who, when it came to oral sex, was like Randy Moss of the NFL—strictly a *receiver*.

Shaking off the images filling her head, she sucked in a mind-clearing breath. "Ten minutes ago there weren't thirty carol-singing nutjobs in the house. If nothing else, I have to make sure Marnie Miller doesn't swipe any of Sue's good Christmas china."

He gaped. "What?"

"They don't make the pattern anymore, and Marnie knows Sue has it. There's always fierce competition whenever somebody discovers an odd piece here or there and points it out to either of them. No china is safe when Marnie's in the house."

Crossing his arms in front of his broad chest, he leaned against the doorjamb. "So there *are* potential thieves here in Christmas?"

She immediately realized what he was talking about. Shifting in her uncomfortably tight pants, which had fit just fine before this man had gotten her all wet and swollen at the thought of making love with him, she shook her head. "Well, even with Marnie's sticky fingers, I do *not* believe this town has thieves who'd dress up as Santa Claus in order to steal from children. Just the kind who'll pilfer a sugar bowl or teacup, knowing it'll eventually be stolen by the person you took it from."

"So your cousin might someday steal to get her sugar bowl back?" He tsked. "I'm shocked."

"Aunt Leila, Sue's mother, started the whole thing twenty years ago. She publicly accused Marnie Miller of having no sense of originality because Marnie went into the city and bought the same pattern after she saw it here at the inn. Then, when Uncle Ken—Sue's father, who died a year and a half ago—accidentally knocked over the cake platter and broke it, Aunt Leila desperately tried to get Marnie to sell her hers."

His eyes were twinkling. "Don't tell me. Aunt Leila pinched it."

She couldn't help reacting to his good humor, liking the way his eyes sparkled that pale green when he was in a good mood. Not the dark forest color she saw when he was aroused. "So the story goes."

"A real Hatfield and McCoy feud, hmm?"

"Yep. And Sue is determined to keep up the tradition."

"I suppose it's safer than raiding each other's stills."

She nodded. "But don't even *ask* about the fruitcake recipe wars."

Mark met her stare, laughter spilling out of those succulent lips. Mercy, how she wanted a kiss…the kiss she'd told him he couldn't have for fear he'd distract her.

Kissing him would definitely distract her. Right now, Noelle couldn't afford such a distraction, not if she wanted to make it out of this room and to Sue's side before her cousin noticed she was missing and sent someone to find her.

"I should go," she whispered, trying to walk past him to the door.

Mark caught her arm. "Stay."

"I can't." The words were hard to get past her tight throat. "Someone might come looking for me."

"And I guess it wouldn't do to have someone finding you here, with me, doing—" he smiled slowly, lazily, sexily "—this and that."

Oh, Lord, this and that. How she'd love a little of this and a lot of that.

But Mark had nailed it—the last thing she needed was to have someone like Marnie Miller's chirpy daughter Millie—God, how her parents must have hated her at birth to saddle her with that name—come walking through the door in time to see Noelle doing *this* to Mark's *that*.

"Exactly," she said. He let her go and watched her walk to the door. With every step, she wondered if this had been fate. Maybe having their tryst interrupted was a good thing—maybe they both needed a chance to rethink this idea of having a wild weekend affair. It could very well be that they'd—she'd—made a mistake.

And maybe you need to see if your nose is growing, girl,

because you are lying to yourself if you think you don't want to rip off the man's clothes and dive on him.

True. She did. But unless she wanted the Christmas Carolers to burst in to serenade them with "Have a Holly Jolly Christmas" while she had Mark Santori's big juicy cock in her mouth, she really needed to get going.

She was shuddering as she unlocked the door, both at the mental image and the naughty, raw words she pictured whispering to him in the hottest of moments. She'd never been so daring—not even in her own mind.

Stepping into the hall, she reached back to grab the knob and pull the door closed behind her, but her hand, instead, grabbed a handful of Mark. A sizeable handful of Mark.

"Oh, jeez," she whispered on a moan as she glanced over her shoulder. Even her most innocent movements were betraying her.

He laughed, low and long, watching her face so intently, she realized she was blushing. "What are you doing?" she asked.

He looked down at his crotch. And her hand. "I think I'm being felt up."

Noelle yanked her hand away. "Sorry. That was an accident. I didn't expect you to follow me."

Stepping out and pulling the door closed behind him, he managed a nonchalant shrug. "I'm coming with you. After all, if I can't do *this*—" he nodded toward the closed bedroom door "—I might as well do…*that*."

5

When Noelle walked into Sue's bedroom and saw the delighted look on her cousin's face, she *almost* forgave the singing townspeople for interrupting her very intimate moment with Mark. Because for the first time since she'd arrived earlier today, Sue looked absolutely joyful. She glowed the way pregnant women were supposed to glow, with outright happiness and contentment.

Of course, Sue would; she loved Christmas. Noelle was the only Scrooge in her family. And a bunch of adults dressed in ridiculous elf costumes and jostling to outsing each other wasn't going to change her opinion about the holiday any time soon.

But Sue was entranced. Clapping her hands along with the junior choir members—who ranged in age from precious-in-tights four-year-old Holly Wannamaker to miserable-in-a-pointy-cap fourteen-year-old Cody Finnegan—Sue mouthed the words to "Jingle Bell Rock." Standing beside the bed, watching with a doting yet protective eye, was Randy. Whenever one of the little ones skipped too close to the bed, he or Noelle were there to gently scoot them out of the way.

But even as she got caught up in the chatter and the hugs and good wishes from her former friends and neighbors, Noelle's mind was in another place. And her eyes never strayed far from Mark, who watched the goings-on with a wry grin.

"So who's the hunk?" Sue whispered from the side of her mouth while also smiling at Marnie Miller, who was doing a solo rendition of "Carol of the Bells." The song didn't work very well with her singing all the parts herself, and Noelle feared the woman was going to pass out from lack of oxygen before finishing the last ding-dong, but apparently nobody had the heart to tell their leader that.

"He's *your* tenant," Noelle said, not meeting her cousin's eye. Hopefully Sue would leave it at that.

"And he's *your* stud-muffin."

A deep throat-clearing told them they'd been overheard. "Actually, I prefer hunk. Stud-muffin sounds too baker-ish," a male voice said.

Sue's face pinkened and Noelle almost laughed. Mark did have a way of moving quietly, catching people unawares. It was probably a cop thing.

He appeared amused by her cousin's assessment. "I'm Mark Santori," he said. "And you have a lovely home. Thanks for letting me crash in on the celebration."

Sue straightened her covers and smiled up at him. "You're most welcome, I'm glad you joined us. Have you met my cousin, Noelle?" Sue's eyebrows wagged up and down like a cartoon character's. "She lives in Chicago and she's *single*."

Oh, God, how Noelle wished Marnie's awful soprano voice would break the glass in the window and send a shard of it through her eyeball. Anything to escape the embarrassment of having her very pregnant cousin trying to pimp Noelle to a man whose underwear she'd been licking about twenty minutes ago.

"I'm afraid I won't be around long enough to make any serious acquaintances, so we'll just have to remain strangers," Mark murmured, his voice so smooth and his tone so even,

Noelle had to laugh. The guy was good, his subtle words obviously meant for her and her alone.

Sue looked confused, obviously seeing the spark between them, and probably wondering about Mark's apparent rebuff. "Well, if you want someone to show you around town, you won't find anyone more knowledgeable about Christmas than Noelle. Our great-great-grandfather founded it, after all."

He nodded with interest, glancing across the bed at Noelle. "I guess that means you just love the holiday season, hmm?"

She smirked. "Oh, it's the most wonderful time of the year, don't you know."

"I think I've heard that. Though I personally prefer St. Patrick's Day."

Grinning, she admitted, "Me, too. Irish coffee."

"Green beer."

"Red-nosed Irishmen instead of rosy-cheeked North Polers."

He shrugged. "But I think the leprechaun/elf thing is pretty evenly annoying."

The two of them laughed together, both caught up in their own silliness, especially since they were being serenaded by a bunch of oversized elves. Not for the first time, Noelle mentally acknowledged how much she enjoyed this man's wit. He was so easy to talk to, so easy to get along with. And so damned sexy she wanted to leap on him.

Looking at the other dozen or so females in the room, she acknowledged she wasn't the only one who felt that way. Practically every other female in the place—young and single, or arthritic and marked with liver spots—was looking at him the same way. She couldn't help stepping a little closer, staking her claim. At least for tonight. Because tonight was all she was going to have.

Sue continued to eye them speculatively until her attention was caught by the next of the Christmas Carolers soloists. A few others came over to gush over how beautiful Sue looked pregnant, and to ask a bunch of private, intimate questions that Sue either answered or evaded as she saw fit.

Once Mr. Stuart the banker began singing "Adeste Fideles," positively mangling the Latin lyrics, Noelle found herself standing in a quiet corner, with Mark right beside her.

"Is that really your old second-grade teacher?" he asked, nodding toward a white-haired old woman on the other side of the room who was glaring the fear of God right into poor, fidgety Chuckie Green.

Noelle couldn't suppress a sigh. "Mrs. Finkelstein. What did she say? Is she still telling the same old story about me pulling up my skirt to show everybody my pretty new Care Bears panties?"

"You wear Care Bears panties?" He shook his head mournfully. "Man, now I *really* wish we hadn't been interrupted."

Smirking, she replied, "Oh, yeah, well, you really missed out on something special."

His frown deepened. "Don't I know it."

Mark sounded very serious now, as if he, too, had been unable to completely put the intense moments they'd shared in her room completely out of his mind. If the Carolers hadn't shown up, they would probably right now be in the middle of something hot and crazy, and maybe even illegal in some states. Noelle's pulse sped up a bit, just at the thought.

"You know, my curiosity is going to kill me if we don't get out of here soon," he murmured, still watching the Carolers, who'd regrouped for another big chorus number.

"Curiosity?"

"Well, yeah." He glanced at her out of the corner of his eye, still leaning in nonchalance against the wall. "I mean, Cheer

Bear had the rainbow on her tummy, and Grumpy had the rain cloud." A tiny smile tugged at his lips. "I was really looking forward to seeing what was on Horny Bear's."

Noelle couldn't control the laughter that spilled out of her mouth. Her shoulders shook as she tried to snort the giggles away, seeing the attention they were getting from some others in the room. "You're twisted."

"Think that's why we get along so well?" he asked.

"Probably," she admitted. "Why do you know so much about the Care Bears?"

"Lottie, my sister. She was addicted."

"Me, too. I knew I'd like her."

Their shared laughter seemed to have dissipated the heavy awareness that had gripped them both a few moments before and Noelle suddenly realized she felt comfortable—warm—talking to him. "Now, what *did* Mrs. Finkelstein say?"

"Just that she hopes you aren't doing anything requiring any skill with mathematics because you're hopelessly inept."

Noelle resented that remark. How many seven-year-olds could do three-figure division? Mrs. Finkelstein was a Nazi; Noelle had always suspected it. "And may I ask why my elementary school teacher was discussing my ineptitude with you?"

"She thinks I'm your boyfriend."

The words caused her heart to trip a little bit in her chest. "You're kidding."

"Haven't you noticed?" Stepping closer he murmured, "We're being watched."

Trying to be surreptitous, Noelle glanced around at the familiar faces crowded into Sue's spacious room. She received a lot of smiles and even more knowing winks. "Oh, God, they *do* think you're my boyfriend."

He merely nodded.

Panic set in, making her heart race and her breath come fast and furious out of her mouth. She couldn't stand this—being stared at, talked about…laughed at. Not now. Not again. "Go to the other side of the room."

Mark responded with a droll lift of one brow that said he didn't believe she really wanted him to leave. "Make me."

The man was enjoying this…enjoying making her the subject of gossip all over again, just like she had been last year during her big wedding humiliation. Then again, he didn't know—he *couldn't* know—just what this was doing to her. "I can't stand to have everyone talking about me again, Mark. I mean it," she whispered, wondering if he heard the note of anxiety in her voice.

His hand on her shoulder told her he did. "What's wrong?"

She tried to keep a tight smile on her face, knowing by the heads bobbing together that Mark's innocent touch had sparked another flurry of whispers across the room. "Let's just say when I left here last year, I was the subject of a whole lot of gossip. I came back praying nobody would even know I was even in town and now they're…they're *talking* again."

Mark didn't remove his hand. Instead, he squeezed her shoulder and stepped close to her, as if lending his physical support. "Noelle, if people are looking at you it's because you're beautiful and charming."

She definitely didn't buy that one, used to everyone in Christmas considering her the serious, sarcastic, nondescript one compared to her vivacious cousin Sue.

"And if they're talking about you, did you ever think it's maybe because they're happy for you? Glad to see you, and think it's nice to have you back?"

No, it didn't. This was Christmas, and Noelle knew better. Her whole body tensing, she stepped away from him, wrapping her arms around her own waist. "Please, Mark. I can't do this. You don't understand, when I left here it was because of…"

He touched her chin, lifting her face and forcing her to meet his eyes. "Because of a man? The bad breakup you mentioned the other day?"

Swallowing, she nodded. "I can't stand the thought of my romantic life being fodder for the gossip mill again."

And finally he seemed to understand. Because with a simple, gentle brush of his fingers against her jaw, he stepped away and offered her a slight smile. "It was nice talking to you," he said with a nod. "I appreciate the background on the town. Now I'll let you get back to your party."

Without another word, he faded away, into the costumed choir, though he continued to stare gently at her from across the room. Noelle wondered if he could see the hint of regret she couldn't quite hide. And when he was sucked into a conversation with an attractive girl who'd been a few years behind Noelle in school, she definitely felt some regret. But she made herself focus on Sue and the impromptu party, trying to avoid looking at Mark as he socialized with the townspeople.

It wasn't easy… He was the tallest man in the room, and the broadest. His laugh was deep and distinctive, his manner relaxed yet powerful. His jet black hair caught the glints from the twinkle lights on the tiny tree in Sue's front window and everywhere, no matter where Noelle turned, she felt his intent stare following her.

Charming and friendly, Mark became one of the most popular people in the room within a very short time. All that was bad enough. But when Mark squatted down to get eye-level with a precious three-year-old who looked a lot like Cindy-Lou Who, Noelle felt her throat close tight.

Because there was no denying it: the man was wonderful. Friendly and funny, handsome and charming. The kind of man to love. Not the kind of man to *just* have an affair with.

An affair, however, was all Noelle could afford right now— all her tattered emotions would allow her to risk.

Maybe if it were a year from now she could put some of the unease and self-doubts out of her mind and risk getting emotionally involved with a man, rather than just physically. Perhaps even if it were hot and steamy July, she wouldn't be forcibly reminded of the way the holidays always seemed to bring her only heartache. But at this time of year, there was no way to silence the whispers of dread deep inside her that reminded her of the pain of losing someone she cared about. In the very distant past…or in the recent one.

Letting herself love someone was the equivalent of saying she was ready to be hurt again, willing to risk heartbreak one more time in her life. And Noelle was nowhere near ready to say any such thing.

Which left her wondering exactly what she was going to do later, when she was once again alone with the intoxicating man watching her from across the room. Because as of right now, she had absolutely no idea if she had the courage to go ahead with her seductive plan or not.

IF LUCK HAD BEEN ON HIS SIDE, Mark would have spent Saturday night making wild, erotic love with the incredible woman who'd literally had him in the palm of her hand—or on the tip of her tongue—the previous evening. But luck was a temperamental lady and she royally screwed him over. So he'd instead had a sleepless night and was now nursing a cold cup of coffee in the inn's empty dining room.

He should never have gone with Noelle to listen to those stupid singers. If he hadn't gone along, she wouldn't have grown self-conscious about the attention they were getting. Nor would Sue, Noelle's very pregnant cousin, have had the opportunity to *introduce* him to Noelle, effectively killing her "stranger" fantasy, as ridiculous as it seemed. And if she hadn't seen him chatting with the Carolers—dressed in matching silly green pointed hats, red smocks, and striped stockings—she wouldn't have come up with the loony idea that he was too *nice* to be her sexy, dangerous stranger.

Nice. Hmm…if he'd said what he *really* thought to the first man he'd seen in the caroler's getup—that the guy's chances of getting laid had shrunk with the hat and gone to subzero with the tights—she might not have thought so. His partner Harriet would argue it, too, as would the guys in the precinct. Not to mention the scumbag criminals he'd busted over the years.

But, deep down, Mark suspected it was at least partially true. Hell, how could he *not* be something of a nice guy? Being polite to women, respectful of his elders and treating others as he wanted to be treated were among the many rules he'd been brainwashed with since early childhood.

In a big Italian family with six children, treating others as you wanted to be treated wasn't merely a nicety to keep Mama off your back. It'd been downright necessary. Because as tempting as it might have been to take the head off his baby sister Lottie's obnoxious Teddy Ruxpin doll and shove a handful of marbles down its gabby throat, he sure wouldn't want her to retaliate by breaking the arms off his Optimus Prime Transformer. So he knew how to play nice when he had to.

He'd never, though, imagined that being nice on occasion would cost him a night of great sex. He could almost hear Teddy Ruxpin laughing at him now from that great flash-in-the-pan toy burial ground in the sky.

"Up yours, Teddy," he mumbled.

Draining the last of his coffee, he tossed his napkin on his plate, wondering if he should just leave. Ideally, his weekend of stranger-sex with Noelle Bradenton should have required a stay through Monday but now it looked like he might not need to. Because here it was Sunday at noon, and the closest they'd come to having sex was when she'd teased him with her wicked fingers and devastating tongue the previous evening.

"My, oh my," he whispered, sighing at the memory of it.

It seemed impossible that his seductive temptress had tensed up so much. In spite of her "too nice" excuses, he suspected her coolness was also caused by her memories of the bastard had hurt her so badly. If she'd left town because of the breakup, the relationship had to have been a serious one.

Mark would very much have liked to get hold of the man, not only for hurting Noelle, but also for making her skittish and nervous about letting anyone get close to her. He had no doubt that was the reason Noelle had come up with her sex-only idea, when what Mark really wanted to do was just spend time with her, talking, seeing her laugh. Determining if something special really was developing between them, as he suspected.

And having sex.

But, uh-uh. She'd shut the door in his face…literally.

"Shoulda sat your ass on the bed and never gone with her," he muttered.

Funny, though, unlike Noelle's reaction to their time with the boisterous singers of Christmas, Mark had actually enjoyed the evening, other than the no-sex ending. Yeah, the carolers were weird, but they also had a down-home friendliness. Despite what Noelle had imagined, she'd seemed to be a favorite in the room. She'd been sweetly animated, fussing over one elderly lady who was having trouble standing up and looked in danger of tipping over in her curly-toed shoes.

It *hadn't* been her old teacher. Judging by the looks Noelle had sent in that old bag's direction, the pinch-faced woman could have fallen face-first into a turkey's ass and Noelle wouldn't have tried to stop it.

But other than that, she'd been comfortable with everyone in the place until, noticing the fatigue on her cousin's face, she'd politely shooed everyone out.

Seeing Noelle in a natural, nonsexual setting had made Mark want her even more. Any doubts he'd had before she'd arrived in his room Saturday evening had disintegrated. He wanted her—mind *and* body—as he'd never wanted anyone.

For her part, the evening had had the opposite effect. He'd almost laughed in her face when she'd said he was too *nice* and wonderful to go to bed with. But she'd disappeared back into her cousin's room before he could argue it.

All because he'd been a good guy.

If only she'd known that throughout the damned chatty hour with the carolers he'd been picturing her naked and open to him in his bed, she might have reacted differently.

Noelle's abrupt change of mind should have sent up red flags, should have had him in his car heading back to Chicago by midnight. It hadn't. Because, as strange as it seemed, for the first time in four years, he began to think he could open up to a woman, let himself trust someone. Definitely let himself want someone. He wasn't ready to give up Noelle just yet.

Mark hadn't been sure he would ever be willing to give a woman the benefit of the doubt again. After his first experience with so-called "true love," he'd been as suspicious about women as he was about everyday perps. Renée, his former girlfriend, had loved him, all right…until he'd refused to help her cover up the fact that she'd been stealing money from her employer.

Having the wool pulled away from his eyes about the woman he'd planned to marry was bad. Though disturbed that she'd done something so intrinsically wrong, he'd forced himself to think she'd just made a mistake. He'd offered to help her, to make sure she got a good lawyer and was treated fairly.

Mark would never have bailed on her—at least not while she was still embroiled in legal troubles. As for afterward? Well, who knew? Even then he'd been wondering whether he wanted to have children with a woman whose moral code was so radically different from his own. But he hadn't reached that point yet and had offered to do whatever he could for her. With the exception of one thing: he would *not* lie.

Lying, as it turned out, was the only thing Renée had wanted him to do. The minute she'd found out he wouldn't, she'd accused Mark of having no heart, of being incapable of love. Then she'd gone a step further, hinting to the cops investigating her case—some of them his colleagues—that he'd been an accomplice.

She'd cost him an internal affairs investigation less than one year after he'd made detective. So much for true love. Thankfully, he'd been completely cleared, though he'd never forgotten the blot on his record.

Renée, who'd made a reparations deal to avoid jail time before leaving town, had also cost Mark his ability to love and trust a woman again. So why in the name of God was he already going so crazy over Noelle Bradenton, who'd made it perfectly clear the night before that she had no intention of following through on the sultry promises she'd made in his bedroom?

The possibility that she had led him on—that she'd been deceiving him—should have made him pack his bags already. But it hadn't. Because he deeply suspected the only person Noelle was deceiving was herself. She wanted him just as much as he wanted her. And he wasn't going to leave town until he at least got her to admit that much.

"Would you like some more coffee?" a soft voice said over his left shoulder.

He immediately recognized her voice, not to mention her delicately spicy cologne. "Yeah, gimme some," he growled.

She stepped closer, so he could see her beside him, and her eyes widened. "Excuse me?"

"Was that impolite enough?" he asked. "I mean, I'm not allowed to be a nice guy, right?"

She looked around the room to ensure they weren't being overheard. Impossible, since the place was completely empty. "I didn't mean it like that," she said, sounding weary. Noelle had smudges of shadow beneath her eyes, and her shoulders were a bit slumped, as if she hadn't slept well the night before.

Good. Hopefully her night had been at least as fitful as his. Though, lucky her, she hadn't had to contend with a hard-on that had made it impossible for him to sleep on his stomach. "What *did* you mean?"

She put the coffee pot down and lowered herself into the chair opposite him, perching her pretty, curvy butt on its edge. "I mean, well, it just seemed strange to be in that big family situation right after…right before…"

"Better than during," he pointed out, almost laughing as her pale cheeks pinkened.

She sighed heavily. "I couldn't pretend you were some dangerous stranger who kissed me until I couldn't even breathe in a Bloomingdale's dressing room after I saw you stand there for ten minutes politely listening to Frank Jones drone on about his hand-carved duck collection."

His lips twitched. "So where did I go wrong…dangerous strangers don't like ducks? Or nice guys don't kiss beautiful, half-naked strangers in dressing rooms, then dream for days about the way she looked in her lacy black panties?" He silently dared her to answer truthfully…to admit it was possible for him to be both.

Noelle's breaths deepened. From across the table, Mark could see the way her tight pink sweater highlighted her body's instinctive reaction to the memory he'd just put in her head. Very obviously. Mouthwateringly so. God, he couldn't wait to taste her, to suck one of her tight nipples into his mouth and stroke the curves of her perfect breasts. He shifted in his seat as his jeans tightened across his lap.

Mark leaned across the table. "Because it seems to me that I kinda broke at least one of those rules already."

"You like ducks?" Her voice was thready and weak.

"I don't give a rat's ass about ducks. I just know to be respectful of my elders." Reaching out to finger a lock of her silky hair, he brushed it back behind her ear. "I definitely am not a nice enough guy to give up the chance to kiss a sexy, half-naked stranger when she's looking at me, practically begging to be tasted."

"Oh, my," she whispered, her voice quivery.

Mark couldn't take it anymore, couldn't sit there and look at the juicy moistness of her lips without experiencing them again. So leaning even closer, he wrapped his fingers tighter in her hair and tugged her forward until their faces came together over his steamy coffee cup.

Then he kissed her.

Forcing her to part her lips for him, he silently demanded that Noelle let him explore the recesses of her mouth, enjoy the softness of her tongue and the sharp edges of her teeth. With a soft moan, she gave up any pretense and hungrily kissed him back.

The kiss was wet and deep, hot and arousing. She satisfied

him as the food had not. But even as he sated his hunger to taste her, he knew his other hunger—to have her, to touch her, to take her—was only going to grow.

When their mouths finally parted, Mark stared into her dark eyes, now wide and snapping with fire. "Enough of these games. You know what you want. And so do I." Leaning close again, so his lips brushed her cheek, he urged, "Come to bed with me, Noelle."

She sucked in a quick breath.

"I mean it. Now. Let's go before I pull you across this table and rip your clothes off."

Excitement made her pulse pound faster in her neck. "The dishes…"

"Fuck the dishes."

Noelle drew her hand to her throat, her breaths beginning to sound choppy. Mark suddenly realized *this* was exactly what she'd been wanting. She wanted to be overwhelmed and taken, not charmed and wooed.

Noelle wanted it passionate and fierce, hungry and maybe even a little bit coarse. Nice-guy stuff could come later…with sweet, slow, languorous lovemaking—the kind he so enjoyed. But for right now, she didn't want it sweet—she wanted it *wild*. And he was more than willing to let her have it her way…as long as he got to have her.

Pressing his advantage, he lowered his voice, letting her hear his throaty need. "Do you know what it did to me, looking down at you yesterday?" He took things a step further, dropping all pretense at seduction and letting her know exactly what he was thinking, in the most carnal way possible. "I thought I was gonna die when your pretty pink tongue flicked out of your mouth and tasted my cock."

"Oooh," she moaned, shifting a little bit in her chair. He'd lay money that she was drenched, and he could hardly wait to find out.

"Man, if I'd known it was going to kill my chances with you, I'd never have gone with you to your cousin's room last night." He laughed softly. "And do you want to know the truth about why I went?"

She said nothing, waiting expectantly, her excitement palpable.

"I came with you to hear those singers just so I could be near you. I wanted to watch you, maybe get close enough to smell that sweet musky scent of yours, knowing *I'd* put it there. That you were dripping with desire for *me*."

"Oh, my God," she said on a moan. Her mouth was parted, her breaths coming in short gasps.

"I was across the room watching you being friendly and sociable, so sweet and neighborly." He licked his lips. "And all the while I was picturing you flat on your back, your legs apart so I could see how glistening wet I'd made you. I was picturing you touching yourself, inviting me to watch while you showed me what you like."

She shuddered and moaned. Finally, in a shaky voice she admitted, "I want you so much."

"Right back at you."

"Your room. My room…our room," she said, her words choppy.

"Yes."

He stood and thrust his chair back, then reached for her hand, tugging her to her feet.

It was no surprise to him that Noelle was ready to pick up where they'd left off yesterday evening. Because she'd once again allowed fantasy to override common sense. Exactly as she needed to do, if his suspicion that she'd been alone for quite a long time was true.

He briefly thought again about the fool who'd let her get away—the man who'd hurt her enough to freeze her off men completely. A deep, selfish part of him had to admit to a sense of gratitude. Because Noelle was *his* now.

She wanted a stranger. He'd be a stranger. She wanted wild, wicked sex, wanted to fulfill her fantasies. He'd do that for her, too.

She thought she could explore her every deepest, dark desire with someone she barely knew. All because she believed there would be no awkward morning after. No embarrassment, no repercussions. And he was ready to give her everything she needed.

Except one little thing.

Disappearing the morning after? Well…that, he feared, was going to be impossible. She might not know it yet, but Mark was not about to let Noelle whirl back out of his life after only one weekend.

Especially if the rest of the weekend turned out to be as amazing as he suspected it was going to be.

6

—————

As Noelle stumbled to keep up with Mark in the race to his room—to *her* bed—she gave thanks that Randy had told her he was going to take a nap with Sue this afternoon. He'd looked so tired this morning, she'd told him she'd oversee the cook and the part-time maids as they cleaned up after breakfast and the check-outs. They were all gone now. Mark was the only guest left, and she planned to take care of him herself. *Definitely.*

"Is this place as empty as it seems?" Mark muttered as they strode, hand in hand, down the side hall toward the private rooms of the inn, where he'd been the only guest housed.

"Yes. Just us, Sue and Randy until at least four."

"Lucky your cousin's room is on the opposite corner of the house," he muttered.

She knew exactly what he meant. Sue and Randy's room was separated from hers by the kitchen, pantry, and private family room. There were lots of walls between them. Walls that would hopefully help block out any, um…noise.

Oh, how she wanted to make some noise.

"Stop," he muttered, halting mid-stride. She didn't know why until he pushed her back against the wall and crowded against her. "I can't wait to kiss you again."

And he did, trapping her there, stepping close so one of his legs slid between hers. Noelle whimpered as his mouth met hers in a frenzied kiss. Wrapping her fingers in his thick hair, she rose up on tiptoe, to line things up better. He shuddered in response as she rubbed wantonly against his erection.

Mark ended the kiss abruptly, pulling away from her. Leading her the few steps to her room, he pulled her inside it and kicked the door shut behind them. His eyes smoldering, he reached for the bottom of his long-sleeved sweatshirt. Saying absolutely nothing, he tugged it off and tossed it away.

Noelle's mouth went dry and her heart hammered like a piston. She'd always thought she preferred a leaner, elegantly built man—strong, with a graceful runner's physique.

Now she knew better.

Because Mark's thick, powerful chest and shoulders made every hormone in her body wake up and dance. He was broad and big, obviously a fan of pounding metal at the gym.

Licking her lips, Noelle watched as Mark stepped closer, his lids heavy and his gaze expectant. Glancing at his jeans, she murmured, "Are you going to finish?"

He shook his head. "I can't go any further. I need to keep something on. Otherwise I'm going to rush this and take you right here in the middle of the floor. And there's too much I want to do to you first."

Noelle's legs literally gave out. She dropped to the edge of the bed, wide-eyed and open-mouthed as Mark came closer, almost stalking her. The excitement roaring through her blood made it hard to think, hard to plan, hard to focus. She was charged up with instinct and hunger, wanting nothing more than to lie back and let him *do* things to her.

"Take off your clothes, Noelle." It wasn't a request.

She didn't even consider refusing. Kicking her shoes off, she unfastened her slacks, remaining seated on the bed. Mark watched from a foot away, the tightening of his jaw the only reaction as she pushed her khakis down and shimmied them past her hips and bottom. Within a moment, she was clad only in her pink sweater and a skimpy pair of pink panties—definitely no white cotton when Mark Santori was in the vicinity.

"Okay, your top, my bottoms, between the two of us, we're practically naked," she said nervously.

He stared at her bare legs. "Not nearly naked enough."

Stripping in front of a man required a level of trust that Noelle hadn't believed herself capable of giving anymore. Somehow, though, the appreciation—the hunger—in Mark's eyes gave her courage. She rose to her knees on the bed, licking her lips, watching him watch her.

Reaching for the edge of her soft sweater, she slowly lifted it, letting it scrape delicately against her tummy and her midriff. She heard his quick intake of breath as the edge of her lacy pink bra was revealed. That indication of his deep want gave her the confidence to tug the sweater over her head, carefully disentangling her long hair along the way. A second later the top was on the floor with the rest of her clothes.

She knelt on the bed, wearing just the lacy pink bra and panties she'd donned out of wicked instinct this morning. Mark stared at her, his eyes glittering, his mouth open. The way his massive chest moved in and out told her he was breathing slowly, as if trying to control an internal battle, seeking restraint.

She didn't want him restrained.

So without another word, she reached for the center clasp of the bra and flicked it open with her thumb. Dipping one shoulder, she allowed the strap to fall, baring one of her breasts. The chill in the room wasn't at all responsible for the tightness of her nipple, which puckered even tighter in anticipation of what was to come.

A quick glance at Mark confirmed his strong reaction. He couldn't take his eyes off her, not for an instant looking disappointed that she wasn't particularly buxom. "You're perfect," he growled, making her believe it.

A dip to the other side and the bra fell away. His hiss was the only sound in the room as he continued to look his fill.

Noelle's long, dark hair was hanging forward over one shoulder, curtaining her breast, and it slid across her skin as she shifted on the bed. The touch was surprisingly pleasurable. Evocative. So she moved again. "Mmm," she murmured, enjoying the sensation. She'd never imagined the eroticism of her own hair brushing against her sensitive skin.

She'd also never imagined the eroticism of revealing her body for the first time to a man. Because under Mark's obviously appreciative stare, she felt wanton and powerful. Beautiful and sexy. Something she'd never experienced before, when time, location or her own inhibitions had led her to seek out dark rooms and late hours for any sexual activity.

It's because he's your stranger. You can do anything and not feel a bit self-conscious about it.

The inner voice made Noelle smile and gave her confidence to go further. Further than she'd ever gone.

Lifting one hand, she began to touch herself. She let her fingertips trace a path over her hip, then slide across the indentation below her belly. Moving up, she caressed her own stomach and midriff, until her hand rested just below her breast. Parting her lips and closing her eyes, she began to stroke her nipple, which was still curtained by her own thick hair. The softness against her sensitive skin was delightful and she almost purred at the pleasure of it.

"Your hair is incredibly beautiful," he murmured, still standing at the foot of the bed. "Yesterday, when you were tasting me, I couldn't help imagining your head in my lap and all those dark curls spread across me."

Picturing it, she moaned. "It does feel good." She plucked at her softly encased nipple, rubbing it between two fingers. Her hair would slide just as easily over parts of Mark's body, and she smiled at the thought. "It's going to feel amazing softly draping between your legs when I'm sucking you." Her own eyes flew open as she realized what she'd pictured… more importantly, what she'd said *aloud.* "Oh, I didn't mean…"

Mark wasn't shocked. In fact, he was watching her with an expression of hungry anticipation. "I hope you *did* mean."

His approval gave her the courage to go on, to be wanton. Daring. So she slid her hand down again, touching herself the way she wanted him to touch her. *Soon.*

Noelle reached lower, until her fingers brushed the thin elastic at the top of her panties. She'd pleasured herself before—refusing to allow her ex-fiancé's betrayal to deny her of any sexual satisfaction at all. But she'd never done it while someone watched. Someone dark-eyed and intense, staring almost enraptured. But the way he'd spoken earlier in the dining room told her he wanted this. He'd fantasized about it.

The clenching in his jaw deepened as she dipped her fingers below the elastic, scraping them through her dark curls, then up again. He moved closer, until his legs touched the bed. "More."

She did as he asked, reaching deeper, to delicately touch her swollen clitoris. The rush of pleasure made her sigh.

"Take them off," he ordered. "Let me see you."

Feeling almost in a haze of sensuality, Noelle pushed the flimsy panties down, then crawled out of them, coming closer to the edge of the bed. Closer to *him.*

He didn't have to say what he wanted. Noelle knew. So, still silent, she leaned back and shifted her legs open…to let him see how much he'd already aroused her, just as he'd told her he'd pictured her doing.

"Perfect," he whispered, devouring her with his eyes.

"I'm already dripping and you've barely even touched me," she admitted.

"You're doing fine on your own," he replied, a faraway tone in his voice, as if he was totally mesmerized by watching her.

Reaching down again, Noelle touched herself, focusing more on the expression on Mark's face than she was on her own pleasure. When she let her fingers slide between the wet folds of her sex, his whole body stiffened.

She moaned. Or maybe he did. Probably they both did.

As if he couldn't endure any more, Mark reached for her arms, tugging her a little closer, so that the tips of her breasts almost brushed against the smattering of wiry hair on his chest. Almost…but not quite. The sensation was so delightfully torturous, she didn't know whether she wanted him to move that scant millimeter closer or not.

Holding her by the wrists, he lifted her arms and draped them over his shoulders. His skin sizzled to the touch and she could feel the flex and play of muscles beneath her hands—silk encasing steel.

Turning his head, Mark kissed the inside of her elbow, then slid his lips higher, pressing open-mouthed kisses all the way to her wrist. Lacing his fingers in hers, he pulled her hand to his mouth and delicately tasted his way across her palm, nibbling lightly on its fleshiest part.

When his tongue slid out to glide over the length of her middle finger, she realized he was tasting her, the essence of her, and liking it. That suspicion was confirmed when he drew her finger into his mouth and sucked, licking away any last bit of moisture from the intimate touches she'd given herself.

Noelle closed her eyes and dropped her head back, her hips arching forward a bit in response. "I want you naked."

He released her hand, only to move his mouth to her neck. His rough cheek scraped deliciously against hers as he kissed the hollow beneath her ear. "I want *you* on your back."

Again there was a hint of demand in his voice. She was helpless to resist. So without another word, she moved away and lay back on the bed. Bathed in the bright light of day streaming in through the sheers covering the window, she was cloaked in absolutely nothing...not even shyness.

Reaching for his belt, he unfastened it, then unbuttoned his jeans. Noelle watched, her pulse tripping over itself as he unzipped, but to her consternation, he stopped there. With the unfastened jeans riding low on his lean hips, he bent over her, surprising her with a sweet, delicate kiss to the inside of her ankle. As he had when kissing her arm, he moved with intoxicating slowness up the limb, delicately sampling her skin. He tasted the curve of her calf, nibbled at the indentation at the back of her knee.

All the deliberate attention was incredibly erotic. He wasn't ripping off his clothes and zeroing in on a few key body parts, as every other man she'd ever slept with had done. No. Mark was the soul of restraint, as if he could dine on her skin and be completely fulfilled. Stroking, blowing lightly. And oh, as he went higher, up her thighs, going back and forth between her legs to provide equal attention, how the tension increased.

She couldn't help wriggling, restless as she looked down at his black hair, stark against her pale body. "Mark..."

"Shh. You have the softest skin Noelle, did you know that? Delicate and smooth. I love the way it feels against my cheek."

His low voice and sweet words aroused her almost as much as his kisses and his touches. And when he moved even higher, maneuvering her legs apart to gain access, she took a deep breath and gave herself over to whatever he wanted to do to her.

She had a pretty strong suspicion of what that was.

"Oh, yes," she said on a deep moan, unable to help it when his silky hair brushed against the V of her thighs.

"Oh, yes," he echoed, his voice sounding as though it came from very far away. But she didn't have time to worry about that because his mouth was moving over her…there…oh, *there*.

Noelle's hips jerked up in response, wantonly demanding more than that fleeting brush of his lips on her swollen flesh. But as he'd done on his long way up her legs, he took his time. He brushed his lips against her curls, blowing on the swollen lips of her sex. Delicately licking at her clitoris, he then moved away to taste the delicate skin where leg met hip. When she was ready to lose her mind with the anticipation, she moaned, "Please, *please* I need more."

With no warning whatsoever, Mark opened his mouth on her, licking deeply into her wet folds and Noelle let out a tiny scream. He didn't notice, continuing to make love to her with his tongue. His hands remained on her thighs, holding her still. Suddenly, as if wanting to deepen the carnality, to bare her completely to his hunger, he lifted her legs over his shoulders. The position tilted her even closer to his waiting mouth and she saw him stare down at her—glistening and open to him— and smile.

That was when sanity deserted her completely.

"Say my name when you come," he demanded, not bothering to look up to get her response. His self-confidence was so damn sexy she nearly came just at the sound of his voice. She was already incredibly close. And when he covered her clit with his tongue and slid his finger into her wet opening, she did exactly what he'd asked for, climaxing and crying out his name.

Mark moved up her body and caught the last of her cries with his mouth, kissing her deeply. Noelle caught her own taste on his lips and was both shocked and titillated. No one had ever pleasured her quite *that* intimately before and her whole body felt inundated with new sensations.

"Would you please take off your jeans?" she asked, as she greedily ran her hands over his thick shoulders and arms.

"Nuh-uh."

She groaned in frustration, then in delight as he began doing that wickedly delicious slow sampling again, this time to the top half off her body. Her neck. Her collarbone. Her earlobe. The hollow of her throat. And finally—thank heavens—her breasts. When he sucked deeply on her nipple and moved his hand between her legs again, Noelle felt another orgasm wash over her, and rode it out with a moan.

It rocked for several long moments, during which she barely noticed Mark removing the rest of his clothes. But when he reached across to the bedside table and grabbed a condom from the top of it, she had a chance to study him all over.

She almost came again.

"Please hurry," she said as she stared at all that big, male heat that was about to fill her to the brim. He was rock hard and thick and while there were a million wicked things Noelle had fantasized about doing, right now all she wanted was the most basic. Him. Inside her. Now. *"Please."*

"You begging me now?"

"You bet I am and my patience is almost gone."

His throaty laugh warned her not to push him too hard, or he'd keep torturing them both. She clamped her lips shut.

"Got anything else to say?" he asked, looking down at her.

She shook her head.

"You sure there's nothing you want to tell me…no secret desires you want to beg me to fulfill?"

Oh, if only the man knew all the secret desires she still wanted him to fulfill. But this one was the most pressing, so she simply responded by lifting her hips in blatant invitation.

"Tell me, Noelle," he ordered, not giving her what she wanted. Pressing his lips to her neck he gently sucked her there. "Tell me what to do to you and how to do it."

She blew out an impatient breath. "I had kinda hoped you'd know how."

Her insult bounced right off him. "Beyond that. Come on, honey, I know there are things you want to do," he said. "Things you're dying to try. And the first one is so very…very easy. All you have to do is open your mouth."

She licked her lips, casting a quick glance down, wondering if the condom was a flavored one. Mark laughed softly. "I don't mean *that*. I mean you need to *say* it. To say what's on your mind, no matter how sexy or erotic."

"I'm afraid to distract you," she said, almost whimpering.

"I'm not easily distracted." He eased closer, his hard chest brushing her nipples, his hips between her legs.

Noelle parted her thighs wider, wrapping her calves around him, trying to tug him close. She might as well have tried to move a building. He remained just out of reach and she almost shouted in frustration. "What do you want from me?"

His rough cheek scraped her jaw and he nibbled on her earlobe. Lower, his erection teased at her wet flesh, dipping close enough to get a taste, then moving just out of reach, increasing the frenzy. "I want you to say it out loud. Say all the wild, wicked things you've never said to a man. Because that's what you're dying to do, isn't it? To scream. To get loud. To get a little down and dirty."

It was. Lord, it was. Carnal images and naughty words filled her mind, but couldn't quite leave her lips.

"I can start, if you want," he said, still whispering, his lips still close to her ear. "I want to fill you up, Noelle. I want to feel how tight and wet you are. I want you to squeeze my cock dry when I eventually let myself come."

She jerked, feeling a sizzle of reaction shoot through her body, just at the words.

"I want to make you moan and shake." His whispers continued to float over her sensitized skin, even as his body hovered just out of reach. The wiry hair on his chest teased her nipples and his breaths caressed the tender skin at the nape of her neck. His strong legs were tangled with hers. And teasing her with the promise of what she was *not* yet getting, was the thick rod she wanted him to plunge into her. "I want you to scream for it."

A low moan built in her throat and started to rise. Because she *was* ready to howl and scream, to demand and to take. Throwing her head back and keeping her eyes closed, she tangled her hands in Mark's hair and pulled him to her throat. She whispered an order, told him what to do, and was rewarded both with his satisfied groan and his mouth sucking her nipple. Hard and sudden. *Amazing*.

"More," he ordered. "Tell me more." He punctuated his demand with a quick, short thrust inside her, over so fast she barely had time to appreciate the ecstasy of it.

That taste of what was to come snapped the last of Noelle's restraints, leaving her nearly incoherent with need. Wrapping her legs tightly around his hips and thrusting upward, she gave him the raw carnality he wanted. Which was, as he'd somehow known all along, what *she'd* wanted as well. "Give it to me, Mark. Please take me, do me, fuck me *now*."

He shuddered with triumph, but didn't revel in it. Instead, he gave her what she'd begged for, plunging into her in a deep thrust that left her howling. "Yes, yes," she moaned, thrusting up to meet his deep strokes. "Harder. Faster. More."

She'd never felt this way, certainly never lost control of herself—of her inhibitions—enough to act the way she was now. Somehow, though, she couldn't bring herself to care. Because he was big and powerful and filling her so deeply she had to gasp at the shock of his possession.

They moved together, fast and wild, but even as the frenzy intensified, as thought disappeared and instinct took control, she noticed the care Mark took to never hurt her. He held himself on his powerful arms, riding her hard but never crushing her with his weight. He watched her face, kissed her over and over. Growling erotic things in her ear, he told her how good she felt and how much she pleased him. Mark used coarse language that would make her blush in the light of day but was perfect now, in the heat of the greatest passion she'd ever known.

Yet, always, she knew he'd stop if she needed him to.

That certainty—that security—was enough to allow her to completely let go of any lingering concerns or misgivings. So she gave herself completely over to him, holding absolutely nothing back. Until they were both breathless, panting and shaking, and finally, crying out in deep, mutual satisfaction.

"YOU GOT LAID."

Sue stared at her cousin, seeing by the immediate blush rising in Noelle's cheeks that she was right. She almost clapped her hands, delighted the other woman seemed to have moved on with her romantic life at last.

The two of them were alone in Sue's room Monday morning, sharing a few quiet moments and a cup of tea. Randy was doing some work in the baby's room and the rest of the house was nearly deserted. There had only been one guest the night before, and judging by the way the man had been looking at Noelle Saturday night, she'd venture a guess that he'd been the one to put that satisfied look on her cousin's face. "Admit it. You got some."

"Sue!"

"Don't *Sue* me, sweetie. You think I don't know why a woman walks in that spread-legged way first thing in the morning? Wow, I miss the days of doing that because of something big going in instead of something enormous feeling like it's about to fall out."

Noelle snorted a laugh. "I can't believe you said that. You know, they say unborn babies can hear everything around them."

"Auntie Noelle got some, honey," Sue said, laughing as she stroked her big belly. "And judging by the way she keeps fidgeting, she got a *lot*." She kept on laughing, glad for the distraction. Her cousin finally having a sex life again after that rotten Jeremy Taggert had practically left Noelle at the altar last year was definitely a welcome distraction. "Tell me everything. It's him, right? That big, hunky guy who's staying in your old room?"

Noelle pretended to be busy stirring some sugar into her cup of steaming hot tea. "You're imagining things."

"Oh, right. Like I can't see those red marks on your neck."

When her cousin's hand instantly flew to her throat, Sue smirked. "Aha."

"Tell me I don't have any hickeys."

"No. But there's definitely some red marks. Better put on a turtleneck before my mom gets here." Hearing the dejected note in her own voice, Sue thanked Noelle's suddenly active sex life for another reason. It gave her something else to think about other than the impending arrival of her mother, who was coming here to "help." Which translated roughly to "coming here to drive Sue insane." Randy might argue that she already was, at least lately, but he hadn't seen anything yet. Her mother had this incredible ability to find anyone's vulnerable spot and rub and abrade it until it turned them into an absolute lunatic.

"Tell me all about him," she said, shifting a little on the mound of pillows to get herself nicely situated for a good long sex gab. "How'd you meet? How long have you been dating?"

"We're not dating," Noelle said, her voice sharp.

"Okay, how long have you been sleeping together?"

Noelle quirked a brow. "So you don't *care* that we're not dating?"

"Why should I care?" Sue asked, meaning it. "You obviously like him enough to go to bed with him, so whether or not he buys you a steak first really doesn't matter, does it?"

Her cousin said nothing for a long moment, looking surprised.

"Oh, please, you think you're the first woman to have a purely physical relationship, do you? There's nothing wrong with great sex without strings." She rubbed her tummy and smiled ruefully. "Just as long as you know it can sometimes *lead* to strings."

"You and *Randy?*" Noelle said, eyes wide. "My God, I figured him for a virgin until your wedding night."

Sue smirked. "Ha. How on earth did you think he ever got me to go out with him in the first place? We hooked up at a party in senior year and he was just, so…mm…*good*…"

Noelle's hand flew up, palm out. "I don't want to hear about it."

"You started it. I'm just saying, sex for its own sake can be lots of fun, but it isn't always as easy as it seems at first."

Running a weary hand over her brow, Noelle murmured, "I've already figured that out. I thought it would be easy, but I'm already wondering how I'm going to go back to Chicago tonight, knowing I'll never see him again."

It was Sue's turn to gape. "You mean it was bad? You're not going back for seconds?"

"No, I'm not going back for seconds." She hadn't answered the first part of the question, but Sue kept quiet, because Noelle wasn't finished. "This was just a fling, a present to myself. Sex with someone who's practically a stranger. No chance of a broken heart that way."

Sue nibbled her bottom lip, hating to hear that resigned tone in Noelle's voice. It reminded her of the way her cousin had been last year, when Jeremy had broken their engagement a few days before Christmas last year. *Sorry, Noelle, I knocked up some slut from another town, so the wedding's off. Sure has been fun dating you for the past three years. Oh, and have a Merry Christmas and a fun reception—hope the cake's good!*

The pig.

Funny, on that day, rather than appearing enraged, Noelle had looked…worn out. Fatalistic. As if somehow she'd been expecting the betrayal, and was already steeling herself against ever letting it happen again.

Frankly, it had reminded Sue a lot of the way Noelle had looked when her father had walked out on his family so many years ago. Her cousin had reacted in a similar fashion both times…curling up inside herself as if she was never going to let anyone close enough to hurt her again. Jeremy the penishead had apparently finished the job of crushing whatever was left of Noelle's hopeful nature.

But maybe Mr. Studly with the chest as broad as the continental divide could help her get it back.

"I'd better go," Noelle said. "I have to get the house immaculate before your mom shows up."

"But you haven't given me any details," Sue said with a frown. "I want to talk about the sex."

"Well, I don't."

"Oh, come on," Sue said, punching down one of her pillows, "sex is a great distraction and I need something to distract me."

"Sorry," her cousin said with a smirk, "I'm only interested in sex if I'm actively participating in it."

"As you actively participated last night?" Sue asked airily.

Noelle grinned and admitted, "Yes, you nosy nudge."

Finally her cousin looked secretly satisfied like a woman *should* look after she'd had a night being done by a centerfold-quality hunk. "Well, I can't actively participate and I am bored out of my mind, so give me some details. Is he thick in other places besides that big chest?"

Noelle primly curled her fingers together in her lap. "Look, I know you haven't had sex in a long time, but I don't particularly like to kiss and tell."

"A long time? Hell, we were doing it up until last week. My midwife told me ejaculate could help soften up the cervix for labor." She patted her tummy. "Had to get pretty creative in terms of positions, but it was lots of fun."

Noelle's hands flew to her ears. "I don't want to know this!"

Once her hands were down, Sue continued. "Poor Randy, he felt awful, thinking our sex life might have caused the problems I'm having."

Her disgruntled frown fading, Noelle leaned forward on her chair, her elbows on her knees. "You feeling okay? A little...better about things?"

Sue knew what she was asking. Noelle was the only one to whom Sue had *really* broken down about her misery regarding the baby's delivery. "I suppose," she said, not really meaning it. "It seems so selfish to be upset about it, doesn't it? Most women would probably think I'm crazy to be sad that I'm going to miss the whole agony of labor and the pushing thing."

"Most women didn't see you train for the Chicago minimarathon by running in the snow for two winters straight," Noelle replied, her voice soft and understanding.

She was right. Sue had always worked hard and trained hard to accomplish any goal she set for herself, the tougher the better. Which made this complete helplessness that much more infuriating. "I don't want to think about it right now. But I really do want to hear some juicy sex details."

Noelle rose and shook her head. "So read a hot Harlequin romance novel."

Sticking her lip out in a pout, Sue said, "Come on, I'm dying of boredom here. Throw me a bone."

"Get Randy to rent you a naughty movie."

Sue smirked. "Rent? Puh-lease."

Noelle raised a curious brow.

"Go check out the top shelf of my closet."

Her cousin obviously understood and quickly shook her head. "No, thank you."

"Oh, come on, if you're only having stranger sex, and this weekend was it for you and the hunky hottie, you're going to need a lot more than porn to get through the next few weeks. You're going to need to go right to that sex toy shop on Michigan Avenue and invest in a dildo. A *big* one."

Noelle was groaning, rolling her eyes and laughing all at the same time as she walked out the room. But Sue wasn't laughing. Her cousin had grabbed a wonderful experience and enjoyed the heck out of it right here, in Christmas. But she knew Noelle. Come tomorrow, at home in Chicago, her cousin would retreat back to her sweater-wearing, man-distrusting, social working self. Which was a damn shame.

So without thinking too much about it, Sue quickly came up with a few ideas to help Noelle out, just as any good cousin-and-best-friend should do. She'd need Randy's assistance, but her husband was so eager to please these days that she didn't think he'd mind the loss of one or two of their "special" movies. She could do some Internet ordering for the other goodies she had in mind.

As for the method of delivery? Well, that was easy. She had a built-in Chicago delivery man right here…Mark Santori. He would, she felt sure, be happy to bring a few "thank-you" gifts to Noelle.

And one day, hopefully, Noelle would be saying some thank-yous of her own.

7

DURING THE DRIVE BACK to Chicago Monday afternoon, Mark had a lot of time to think about the incredible twenty-four hours he'd just shared with Noelle Bradenton. They *had* been incredible. Amazing. The most intensely pleasurable sexual experiences he'd ever enjoyed.

After their wild, fast and furious session yesterday morning, he and Noelle had parted for a few hours so she could get some work done at the inn. She'd promised to come back that night. With time on his hands, Mark had walked around the town a little more, his mind still on the holiday thieves. But he'd found no smoking gun, or even a hint of suspicion during his travels. His cop luck was running on empty in this case.

His luck *had* returned in another way, though, because Noelle had been as good as her word. She'd slipped into his room at ten o'clock the previous night and the two of them had started all over again. This time, *Mark's* way.

He didn't think he was ever going to have enough of kissing that woman. Or of stroking her soft, smooth skin. Or burying himself inside her tight, heavenly body.

Or, as it turned out, of just holding her hand and talking to her. This morning, after breakfast, he'd gotten her to show him around Christmas, despite the cold. She'd grumbled about it, and had kept up a running monologue of hilarious stories about the antics of the town's residents. Mark had been more fascinated by the way the brilliant sunlight shining down from an icy-clear blue sky made her dark hair come alive.

He'd also been fascinated with the little details she'd revealed about her life. From what he could gather, Noelle and her cousin felt closer to each other's mothers than to their own. Noelle's father apparently lived on the other side of the country and hadn't seen his daughter for years, but that was about as much as he could get her to share about him.

All in all, she was every bit as charming, vivacious and irresistible in the daylight hours as she'd been during the long sexy night.

Which made it damned frustrating to think she was going to stick to her plan to keep their fling strictly a one-weekend, out-of-town event. When he'd left the inn shortly after lunch, he'd asked her to have dinner with him later in the week and she'd turned him down flat. Even a deep, wet kiss goodbye hadn't changed her mind.

Okay, her voice had shaken, and her nipples had been hard under her sweater when she'd rejected him the second time. And she'd looked as if she was going to fling herself on him when he whispered that he hadn't done nearly as much with her as he wanted to. But she hadn't relented.

Fortunately for him, however, he had a couple of really good excuses to see her again. First, he was working on the shelter theft case and would have a legitimate excuse to go see her again. Second, Sue had given him a package and asked him to deliver it to Noelle back in the city, to thank her for her help, saying her cousin would have refused to accept it if Sue had offered it herself.

And finally, Mark wasn't going to let her get away. Period. He hadn't been joking when he'd said there was more he wanted to do with her. Much, much more.

Not the least of which was having a burger and maybe going for another walk…in *his* neighborhood, this time.

As for sexually? Oh, yeah, there were a lot of sensual pleasures he'd like to share with Noelle Bradenton. Just thinking of them—imagining her beautiful body bathed in the glow of a crackling fire on the thick rug in his apartment—aroused him all over again.

"Okay, enough of that," he muttered under his breath, shifting in the driver's seat of his car. He was pulling into the city and the last thing he needed was to crash because he couldn't get his mind out of his pants. Or Noelle's. Being near his own precinct, he couldn't stand the thought of getting creamed by a semi. How humiliating if a bunch of guys he worked with watched while he was pried out of his car with the jaws of life, a massive hard-on blocking his escape.

The image was enough to get his body back under control.

Figuring he'd stop in to see the folks before heading home to his apartment, he cruised down Taylor Avenue and parked in the alley behind Santori's. His brother Tony's SUV was there, as was Pop's Caddy. So was Joe's pickup.

He smiled, finding comfort in the familiarity that he sometimes took for granted. Funny, this weekend had reinforced to him how very much he did like his own world. His weekend in Christmas had started out like a trip to looney-land, but by the end, he'd been seeing some of its family-oriented charm. Enough to make him want to see his own family, if only for a beer and a little conversation.

"Markie!" his mother cried as he walked through the front door into the restaurant. He hadn't gone through the back because if Pop saw him first, he'd have been grilling him for any gory details of his latest cases. Then Mama would find out he was in the building and hadn't come to give her a kiss hello, and she'd whack him in the head with a spoon or something.

"Where you've been?" she asked, coming out from behind the front counter to greet him. As usual, she was wearing a dress—he'd seen his mother in pants, but never in the restaurant. She'd no more wear anything other than a dress to Santori's than she'd go to Sunday mass in a bikini.

She grabbed him for a quick bear hug, then thunked him on the head with hard flick of her index finger. "You disappeared this weekend. You were supposed to be here for the Secret Santa drawing."

Mark sighed heavily. Catching Joe's eye from across the room, he saw his older brother laugh. They'd all gotten their fair share of thunks in their lives. Since Joe had produced the family's first granddaughter, however, he was currently one of Mama's favorite people.

"Sorry, Mama, I had to go out of town on a case."

"And you forget to call your family?"

"Leave him alone, Ma, or he'll walk back out the door and I need the big lug to help me haul the old stove to the dump." This came from Tony, his oldest brother, who ran the restaurant for their partly-retired father. Being partly retired meant Pop stayed in the back, drinking Chianti and cooking—with Tony's help—and Tony dealt with all the day-to-day business crap. The arrangement seemed to suit them both just fine.

Tony, swaggering, as he usually did, was wearing a white apron, smeared with tomato sauce, which strained over his beefy chest. He took the "oldest child" title and ran with it whenever possible, bossing everyone around. But there was no one in the world Mark would rather have at his back in a brawl than his big brother Tony. Except, maybe, his partner, Harriet. Or, he supposed, his twin, Nick, who'd learned how to kick some serious ass in the Marines, despite being of leaner build, like Joe and their other brother, Lucas.

Standing by the counter, he looked around the room, breathing everything in. The sights were the same. The smells were the same. The voices were the same, and they all appealed to him like nothing else in the world.

This was his life, the one he'd always known. His friends, his co-workers, his job, they'd always come second to this place, this world.

So why, he wondered, did the loud, bustling restaurant—jammed with red-faced Chicagoans downing pizza, spaghetti and wine—suddenly seem so empty? Why did his eyes instantly scan the place, seeking a familiar head of rich, dark hair, when he knew with absolute certainty that she couldn't possibly be here?

"Who is she?" Tony asked as he walked by, carrying a brown bag full of take-out food to Mama, who stood behind the front register. Fortunately, she was ringing up the purchase for a customer and hadn't overheard.

Mark shifted and jammed his fists into the pocket of his leather jacket. "Don't know what you're talking about."

Hearing a snicker from behind him, he realized he was outnumbered and surrounded. Joe, the second oldest, said, "You might as well give up, little brother. You've got that 'where the hell am I and who was that woman who blindsided me' look on your face."

"Yep," Tony said absently as he waved to a group of newcomers to shut the front door against the bitter outside air. "You're suckered, all right."

Suckered. Maybe he was. It seemed too soon; he'd only known Noelle a couple of weeks. But he already felt as if he knew her better than anyone else in her life. She'd never believe it, but he already had a pretty good idea of what made her tick. What made her sad. What hurt her. What excited her. What she cared about.

And what she most cared about, aside from her very pregnant cousin, were the women and children at the shelter where she worked. Which suddenly gave him an idea. A very good idea.

Looking around at the customers, many of whom had been patronizing Santori's for twenty years, he realized there was one more reason he could stay in touch with Noelle. Not to mention do something really nice for some people who truly deserved it. So without giving it much more thought, he looked at Tony and said, "Do you have any of those big empty mayonnaise jars in the storeroom?"

Tony nodded. "Sure. Why?"

Smiling, Mark put his hand on his brother's shoulder and led him toward the back of the restaurant. "Because I need your help filling one up for some kids who really need a little Christmas miracle."

THOUGH SHE WAS BUSY catching up on work after having taken a couple of days off, Noelle realized on Thursday that she was lonely. Very lonely.

She missed her family, that was all. To her great surprise, she'd really enjoyed going home and spending a couple of days with Sue and Randy. Their excitement about the baby had been catching, and she could hardly wait to meet her godchild, who would hopefully be named something other than Sugar Ray. Sue had been considering the name, saying the baby was using her internal organs for punching bags.

Aunt Leila's arrival had been a special treat. Though she knew her aunt drove Sue nuts, Noelle had always felt very close to the woman. Aunt Leila's stories about retired life in Arizona had made them all laugh, even Sue, who gave her mother tips on trying to pick up some of the white-haired old guys in her square dancing class.

All in all, her trip home had been relatively painless. She'd avoided going outside into crazy-town, for the most part, other than her Monday morning outing. And she hadn't seen any slugs—aka Jeremy. She'd even allowed herself a smile or two when dealing with Mrs. Miller and the rest of the Christmas Carolers, who'd made Sue very happy for a while.

Yes, the long weekend had been okay. Even fun. *That* was why she felt lonely, despite being surrounded by people in the shelter, and *only* that.

"Bull," she whispered under her breath.

She missed *him*.

She shouldn't have. She didn't want to. But there was nothing she could do about it. After being back in Chicago for only forty-eight hours, she missed Mark Santori desperately.

Because the weekend hadn't been simply painless and fun. It had also included the most erotically charged moments of her entire life.

"It wasn't supposed to be like this," she muttered as she sat behind her desk at the shelter, doing some paperwork late Thursday afternoon. "A fling, it was just supposed to be an anonymous fling." Never to be regretted. But never to be repeated, either.

So why was she dying for an encore?

"I'm heading out," a voice said from the doorway.

Looking up, she saw Alice, whose weary expression probably matched the one on Noelle's face. They'd been beating the pavement or making phone calls all day, trying to drum up emergency donations for the Give A Kid A Christmas program. Lots of people were kind and sympathetic…but most of those same people had already given out their holiday donations and weren't in the position to offer much more than their heartfelt sympathy and best wishes.

"Any good news?" Alice asked, looking hopeful.

Noelle nodded. "Actually, there is. That close-out store downtown, Super Dave's, offered to let us come in at noon on Christmas Eve and buy any leftover toys at fifty percent off the sticker price."

Alice smiled a little. "That *is* good news. Their prices are already really low."

"Exactly."

If only they had the cash to pay even those discounted prices.

We will. Somebody was going to cough up the cash—either the mayor and his rich buddies, or the shelter workers themselves. They'd get it done.

"Well then, I'll see you later. Don't forget the three L's tonight," Alice said.

The reminder was a typical one. Whoever was on overnight duty at the shelter was reminded to look, listen, and mostly *lock*. There had never been any serious incidents here, at least not in the eleven months Noelle had been on the job. But that didn't mean they didn't occasionally hear threats from some angry man trying to track down his wife and kids in the Chicago social services system.

After Alice was gone, she went back to her notes, hearing the voices of the children through the wall adjoining the playroom. The older ones were home from school and their little siblings were ready for some serious playtime with their big brothers and sisters. Just like any normal home...only these kids had had lives that were far from normal.

"Damn," she muttered, still so frustrated about the money. Frustrated about a lot of things.

It might have helped if she could really focus on raising that money, rather than on the man who'd burst into her life the day after Thanksgiving. But it was practically impossible to forget him. Mark Santori had taken up residence in her mind. The real problem was, she wanted him to continue taking up residence in her body.

If only she could be certain he wouldn't take up residence in her all-too-battered heart.

Still, physically she ached for him. Desperately. Sometimes, she wasn't sure whether she would have been better off never going to bed with the man, thereby never knowing what she was missing. Most times, though, she just gave thanks for what she'd gotten and wished like crazy that she could keep getting it.

Like Oliver Twist, she wanted to hold out her bowl and ask for more.

But fortunately—or unfortunately—Mark had taken her at her word and hadn't contacted her once she'd arrived back in Chicago. So much for Sue's prediction that the man would find it impossible to resist her charms and would be battering down her door, refusing to take no for an answer.

"He took no for an answer a little too easily," she muttered, knowing she had no right to be disgruntled, but feeling that way anyway.

"Who took no for an answer?"

Jerking her attention toward the door, she felt her heart start to thud as she recognized the broad-shouldered man standing there. His green eyes twinkled with amusement, as if he knew exactly who she'd been talking about.

Noelle sucked her bottom lip into her mouth, knowing her cheeks were turning pink. "Uh…just talking to myself."

He didn't let it drop. Walking into the office, he shut the

door behind him, then strolled over to lean on the edge of her desk, towering above her. "That's the way rumors get started."

"Huh?"

"My Great Aunt Rosa started talking to herself and the next thing you know, Uncle Santiago had the parish priest over to do an exorcism."

She couldn't help laughing. Despite all her efforts to convince herself she only felt lust for Mark Santori, deep down, she knew she also really liked him. Probably too much. That realization gave her the strength to shake off her laughter, swallow hard and busy her hands with the paperwork on her desk. She'd remain all business if it killed her. "What can I do for you, Detective?"

He tsked, shaking his head in disappointment. "No kiss hello?"

She cast a quick glance toward the closed door. "Definitely not."

He frowned, his shoulders slumping as much as such a big pair of shoulders could slump. "Guess that means the oral sex is out of the question too, huh?"

Laughter spilled across her lips even as her panties moistened a little bit at some very hot memories. She still hadn't gotten to do all she wanted to do because Mark had remained true to the holiday spirit—wanting to give rather than receive. "You really arc bad."

"I'm a middle child. Can't help it."

Unzipping his jacket, he took it off and tossed it over the arm of the couch. Looked as if he was planning to stay a while. *Uh-oh.*

"Are you here about the, um, robbery?" she asked, hoping he'd say yes. Hoping he'd say no. Wishing like hell she knew what she was hoping.

"In a certain respect."

"Do you have any leads?"

Mark's negative shake of the head wasn't much of a surprise, though it was a disappointment. "No, but since yet another store has been hit, I know these guys aren't giving up. Which means they're going to screw up and I'm going to nail them."

She didn't doubt him. The certainty in his tone left no room for doubt.

"I do have a bit of good news. I don't know how much it'll help, but I have a donation to make." He dug into his pocket and took out a bank envelope, of respectable thickness. "I told my folks about what happened here, and they've had a big collection jar on the front counter of the restaurant for the past few nights. It's not a whole lot…yet. But I'm hopeful for more."

Noelle's jaw fell open. She hadn't been sure what to expect when Mark walked through her door—seduction, bossiness. Self-assurance maybe. But not this. Not a considerate, thoughtful gesture that had absolutely nothing to do with the wild, sexy fling they'd shared a few days ago.

And everything to do with that nurturing kindness she'd suspected in the man from very early in their relationship.

We're not in a relationship she reminded herself. If only she could convince herself of that.

"Anyway, it's a drop in the bucket to what you need, I'm sure, but there's more where that came from."

"You're serious?"

"Absolutely."

Shaking her head in disbelief, she said, "Why would you do this? Go out of your way like this?"

Mark sat on the chair in front of her desk, leaning back and kicking his long legs out in front of them. Clasping his hands over his chest, he tented his index fingers and shrugged in complete nonchalance. "It's not exactly out of my way, Noelle.

Anybody who heard about some kids getting scammed at this time of year would want to help."

Ha. So he thought. Noelle knew better—she still couldn't get anyone from the mayor's office to return her damn phone calls.

"Have you thought about going to the media?" he asked.

"Of course I have. But we try so hard to keep a low profile here. The last thing I want to do is draw the spotlight on this place, have reporters show the building or the neighborhood, something that might reveal our location." Glancing toward the door, she added, "There are some unpleasant people out there who would really like to find out where we are."

Mark sat up, dropping his hands onto the arms of his chair. His fingers clenched, growing white with tension. "Has someone been threatening you?"

Shrugging, she explained, "It goes with the territory, nothing specific. But my point is, I really would like to try to do this quietly, without bringing the press into it. So while I do appreciate your efforts, I hope you've been keeping them low-key."

"Completely anonymous," he said. "The sign on the mayonnaise jar just says some needy kids were ripped off and are facing a pretty sad Christmas, and the Santori family is collecting donations. Absolutely nothing else."

She nodded, relieved, though she'd expected as much. Mark was too good a cop—too good a man—to endanger her or any of the families here by revealing too much information. She trusted him…more than she would ever have trusted some nameless reporter who wanted to play up the schmaltz angle of poor, tragic children, and might put the story ahead of the safety of those same children.

"Well, in that case, thank you very much. It's deeply appreciated."

Before Mark could respond, the door to Noelle's office burst open and four-year-old Ginger ran in. A wild child with a mop of red curls surrounding her pale little face, the girl was one of their newer residents. "Hide me!" she shrieked.

Noelle merely raised a brow, watching Ginger dive behind the sofa. When not even a wisp of a carroty curl remained in view, she focused her attention on the door, where she knew whoever was "it" in the game of hide-and-seek would soon come knocking.

She didn't have long to wait. Mickey, a six-year-old with big gaps where his front teeth used to be, popped in. His eyes were wide and innocent in his adorable brown face, and he appeared to have been shoved from the outside.

"Can I help you?" Noelle asked, trying to keep the laughter out of her voice.

He stammered something, then raised his voice to whisper, "Is somebody in here?"

"I'm in here, Mickey," she replied, not wanting to give Ginger away. As the newest in the house, the little girl had been keeping to herself until today and Noelle wanted to encourage her to have some fun.

The boy angled in, sliding to the side and bending to peek around Noelle's desk, as if expecting to see Ginger's red curls behind the chair. "Um, okay."

"I'm here, too, bud," Mark said with a low laugh. Once he had the child's attention, he made a big display of pointing behind the couch, giving away Ginger's position.

A huge, gummy smile creased Mickey's face, and he darted around Mark's knees to find Ginger. She reacted with a shriek, then tore off out the door, Mickey hot on her heels. They were both gone sixty seconds after the girl had entered the office.

"Wow. Is that how you spend your days?" he asked, good humor evident in his voice.

"Pretty much."

"You must like kids."

She nodded. "I do."

Mark rose from his chair. "So, were you planning on having a bunch of them with that asshole who broke your heart?"

Noelle gasped, almost flinching at his bald statement. Mark didn't look the least repentant, he merely waited patiently for an answer to his intrusive question. "How did you…"

"Your cousin gave me a few more details about why you left Christmas to come here."

Sue. Noelle made a mental note to ream out her cousin, after the baby was born, of course. "Well, she's obviously got a big mouth and too much time on her hands."

Mark sat on the edge of the desk, his big body towering over her again, making her feel all small. Feminine. Vulnerable. "I told her to give me the guy's address so I could go over and beat the shit out of him. Either that or shake his hand. I haven't quite decided which I want to do more."

Her jaw dropped. Leaning down, Mark brushed the tip of his index finger down her chin, and across her lips, gently closing her mouth. "Part of me wants to pound him into a pulp for hurting you. Another part wants to thank him for not making me an adulterer."

Once again, he'd shocked her into speechlessness. All she could do was sputter. "Wha…huh…"

"I mean, if you'd been married when we met, I would've been doing some serious breaking of the Ten Commandments. I've always done okay at that whole no-coveting thing. But you, honey, would have been enough to make this former altar boy turn into an unrepentant sinner."

FOR THE FIRST FEW DAYS after Noelle had left the inn to go back to Chicago, Sue waited impatiently to hear from her. She was dying to know what had happened when Noelle got her "thank-you present" from her hunky new man. Staring at the phone, she willed it to ring, knowing Noelle would be responding sooner or later.

That the response would include some ranting and raving was a given. Sue had, after all, wrapped up an X-rated video and given it to Mark to hand-deliver to her cousin in Chicago.

Hopefully, though, after the ranting and raving was over, Noelle would admit to some wild reunion sex. Wild reunion sex had been the plan all along…the reason she'd quietly given Mark Santori the package Monday, asking him to deliver it in Chicago when he got home. The guy had practically salivated at the excuse to see Noelle again, never knowing, of course, what was in the wrapped package.

His reaction had told Sue he was in no way ready to go along with Noelle's silly one-shot, weekend affair idea. No. The man was hung up on Noelle. Very hung up. And he was just the type to bring her cousin's heart back to life, as he'd obviously done with her libido.

The realization made her whistle a little as she nibbled on her toast, idly staring toward the foot of the bed, trying to see her toes. It was impossible, of course, and had been since the sweet little fairy butterfly in her stomach had morphed into Jabba the Hutt somewhere around month six.

No toes. All she could see was the mound of stomach beneath the pale pink sheet and the white cotton blanket.

"Knock, knock," a voice said one second before the door to her bedroom pushed in. "Look who's here!"

It was Randy, and one glimpse at the nervous smile on his face instantly put Sue on alert. Her husband's voice had that high, nervous-sounding pitch that said his gaiety was fake.

That could mean only one thing: he knew darn well Sue wasn't going to be happy to see whoever was following him into her bedroom Thursday afternoon.

Scary. Because given her vocal complaining about her boredom, her husband would have to figure *any* company would be good company. She almost held her breath, wondering if her mother was about to enter the room to tell Sue why the colors she'd picked out for the nursery were all wrong and she'd repainted it.

"There's our girl! And how's my little grand-niece or nephew?" a boisterous voice said.

Randy's uncle Ralph strode over to the bed, his jowly face shaking and his bulbous nose glowing as red as one of the forty-eight Ruldolphs lining the lawn in front of the Christmas Courthouse. The man rouged his nose, she just knew it, in keeping with his image as the jolliest guy in town. She supposed in his line of work—as a self-proclaimed dean of Santa Claus U, as the locals called it—he figured he needed the makeup. Personally, she thought it made him look like a ruddy street drunk rather than a jolly St. Nick. But who was she to judge.

"Hello, Uncle Ralph," she murmured, hiding a sigh.

She wondered why Randy would have been nervous about his uncle dropping by, because the older man came around a lot. Every time he did, Sue made a point of mentioning Noelle and how fabulous she was doing, just to make sure everybody remembered that Sue's first loyalty was to her cousin. Because Ralph was the father of Jeremy Taggert, Noelle's faithless ex.

If she wasn't mistaken, the last time Ralph had dropped by had been a little over a week ago, just before Sue had had her bleeding scare and been taken in for an emergency doctor visit. Before her world had gone all screwy.

That particular morning, Sue had been on the phone with Noelle during Ralph's visit. She'd made sure to raise her voice when talking to her cousin about how well things were going at the women's shelter, wanting Randy to know what a fabulous, generous woman his mealy-mouthed son had lost.

She hadn't been faking. Sue was genuinely amazed at the way Noelle had put her social services degree to good use after quitting the inn. Her open-heartedness in caring for the children in her care was an inspiration, and Noelle's Give A Kid A Christmas program was one of the most worthy causes Sue had ever heard of.

Which reminded her…she definitely needed to send her cousin a contribution. She'd promised to do so that very day, until her health scare had thrown everything up in the air.

"We thought you could use a little company," Ralph was saying. Sue tuned back in to the conversation at the word "we," instantly going on alert. Glancing again at the door, she held her breath, praying it wasn't Randy's wife, come to try to peddle the cheap house-decorating crap she sold from a catalog and her monthly at-home parties.

But it was worse. Much worse. When she saw who walked into the room behind him, she knew why Randy had been nervous. Because the couple standing just inside the door was the *real* reason for Randy's unease.

Jeremy Taggert and his whiny wife stood there, obviously as unhappy as Sue was about this forced meeting. A quick glance confirmed their discomfort—Jeremy's sneaky, cheating rat face was pale and pinched. The wife—Lydia, Linda, something like that—had both her arms clutched around one of her husband's, as if afraid to let him leave her side.

Sue almost smiled, liking that her reputation still preceded her. No, she hadn't gotten into any fights in, oh, a good eight years or so…not since high school. But it was nice to think she could still put the fear of God into a whiny, man-stealing tramp like this one.

She supposed the meeting was inevitable. Frankly, she considered it a miracle that she'd managed to avoid coming face-to-face with the couple in the past year, since Randy and Jeremy were cousins. Obviously, Uncle Ralph had decided that Sue's inability to leave—or to throw a punch in Jeremy's general direction—made it a good time to effect a reconciliation.

For the sake of the baby, and Randy, she supposed she should let it go, be all adult and maternal and stuff. Turn the other cheek, live and let live, let bygones be bygones…yadda yadda yadda.

Then she thought about the tears on her sweet cousin's face, and the way Noelle had moved away from town rather than have to live here and be the object of gossip and laughter. And figured, screw it.

So with a smile of pure malice she said, "Why, hello, Jeremy, how very funny to see you. After spending this past weekend with Noelle and her gorgeous, hot-stud boyfriend, I was wondering when you were going to show up here to find out every little bit of gossip you could."

8

ON SATURDAY THE BITTER COLD snap that had gripped Chicago for the first ten days of December finally eased and the temperature rose back into the double digits. They were low ones, but at least Noelle could look out her poorly insulated front window without her face turning blue and her lips sticking to the glass.

She lived on the third floor of an old warehouse that had been renovated into several apartments. Though her place wasn't in the greatest part of town, it did have a ton of space and beautiful wood floors that she'd fallen in love with at first sight. Best of all, it was hers. All hers.

With the money she'd saved by living and working at the inn since graduating from college, she'd been able to buy herself a few nice pieces of furniture for the move to Chicago. A big, overstuffed couch covered in fabric as soft as broken-in denim dominated the living area of the apartment. A cute café table and two chairs were perfectly adequate for her tiny kitchen.

She had a few plants, a few paintings on the walls, a decent stereo system and absolutely nothing that could be described as garland, greenery or candy-cane striped. The colors red and green had been stricken from her decorating inventory. Because after living in a place with cherry-colored carpeting and forest-green walls for her entire childhood, she never wanted to see those colors first thing in the morning again as long as she lived.

Thank God Sue had done some redecorating after taking over the inn.

Yes, she loved her apartment, just as she loved her new life in Chicago, which, to be honest, was something she hadn't expected when she'd moved here eleven months ago. At that time, leaving Christmas had seemed more about running away. Now, she was happy to acknowledge, she knew it had been the best thing she'd ever done.

"So pfft to you, Jeremy," she thought, still laughing over the way Sue had told her she'd put Noelle's ex-fiancé in his place. Funny how little it bothered her to hear his name when just a few weeks ago she'd thought for sure she was still mourning the breakup. Someday, she was going to have to sit down and evaluate just why that was.

Noelle's rapidly numbing toes quickly pulled her mind off the confusing past to the here and now. They also reminded her of the one drawback to wood floors: they didn't provide much warmth in winter. Though she was accustomed to wearing fuzzy socks at all times, which served another purpose—built-in dusting—right now she had only the flimsiest, silkiest stockings covering her feet and legs.

Silkiest. Slinkiest. Sexiest. Yeah. She was dressed pretty much like a hooker waiting for a client.

"You should really change," she ordered her reflection, which stared back at her from the full-length mirror in her bedroom. "You have a perfectly respectable black bra and control top black pantyhose in your drawer."

The sultry seductress in the black lacy lingerie merely smiled, knowing she was not going to change. Not when for the first time in a very long time, she felt really good about how she looked. Right now, Noelle felt worthy of being looked at—confident in her ability to incite a sinfully sexy guy into a wild frenzy of lust.

The very thought of Mark—of his desire for her—made her thighs shake. The chill in the air might have brought goosebumps to her skin, but the steamy hot thoughts in her mind were making her whole body warm and liquid with want. Knowing she could probably see her breath if she stepped into her bathroom, she also had to admit that deep down she felt hot. Steamy. Absolutely on fire with hunger for the man she'd sent away yet again just two days ago.

Unable to resist, she cast her gaze to her bedside table, thinking about what was safely buried in the drawer. Beneath the coupons and beauty tips she'd clipped from magazines, and the mafia-worthy letters demanding that she renew her subscription to book-of-the-month club or else, was her very naughty secret, *The Lust and the Fury*.

She still couldn't believe Sue had sent her a porn movie, and she especially couldn't believe *who* she'd sent it with. Thank God she hadn't opened the package until Mark had left the other day.

Noelle hadn't watched the movie, though she'd been intrigued by the title, and the, um, well-endowed people on the cover. The blurb on the back that said the movie had been written and directed by a woman. Targeting lovers, the film supposedly had a story to go with all the boinking.

Nevertheless, she hadn't watched it, and she'd given Sue a serious talking to on the phone about needing to mind her own business. Still, she had to admit to a certain curiosity. The damn thing was practically singing a siren's song from across the room, daring her to go even further with her wicked rebellion from nice social worker to wild temptress.

If only she had someone to watch it with.

Sighing deeply at the thought, she pictured *him* with her, watching erotic images in the dark. His jaw would clench, his whole body would be rigid with want and hunger. He'd be big and hard, not letting her put up any barriers, refusing to leave her with any inhibitions at all.

Looking at her reflection in the mirror, Noelle could almost picture him standing behind her, staring as well. Breathing deeply, she studied herself through his eyes, knowing he'd first see her as the stranger he'd met in a department store dressing room a couple of weeks ago. Only the black lingerie she wore right now was even more sultry, more wicked, than what she'd been wearing that day.

The black lace bra not only scooped up and pushed out, it was also made of a sheer lace that did almost nothing to hide the dusky shadows of her nipples. Her new black panties were the skimpy thong type, which seemed appropriate with the thigh-high black stockings.

"Yeah, a call girl," she whispered. "If only you had the guts to call."

There was no doubt about who she wanted to call, who she'd been *dying* to call back into her life since Thursday afternoon when he'd surprised her at work. Mark had made it clear that day that he wanted to pick up where they'd left off in Christmas. After making his stark declaration about her being enough to tempt him into sin, he'd asked her to come home with him.

She hadn't done it.

Oh, sure, she'd been tempted. And if she hadn't been on duty at the shelter for the night, she might have been weak enough to give in to the heat that had blazed from Mark Santori's stare.

He wanted her—desperately—even after he'd already had her last weekend. Probably more so.

She shouldn't be so surprised. After all, didn't she want him just as much? Still, something in her marveled at the realization that the intimacies they'd shared at the inn hadn't turned him off in the least.

He wanted more. Much more. And so did she.

"But he's not a stranger," she reminded herself. He was not just a sexy, nameless guy she could fool around with again before putting him out of her mind forever. Because the more he came around, the more he showed up with money for needy kids, or a wink and a laugh and yet another request that she at least let him buy her a cup of coffee, the more she fell for the man.

Yeah. Fell for. As in, falling for. As in caring about. *As in just give me a rusty knife and start cutting into my chest right now.*

"Nuh-uh," she told herself, spinning away from the mirror and marching over to her bed. "No caring about allowed. Sex is all you can handle right now, missy." Sex with anyone *except* Mark Santori. Which meant she really needed to stop thinking about how nicely his big strong hands could cup the cold cheeks of her backside and warm them up.

Slipping on the little black cocktail dress she'd found the day after Thanksgiving—*after* her encounter with Mark—she focused only on the evening ahead of her. The mayor's holiday party was a fancy affair, being held at a downtown hotel, and the most important people in local government would be there. As would many wealthy invited guests.

One lowly social worker normally wouldn't be noticed by anyone, but tonight Noelle planned to be noticed. She would take any chance she could to ask for donations, whether the inattentive mayor liked it or not.

And maybe by keeping her mind on her job, and the crisis at the shelter, she'd be able to forget about Mark Santori and the look of deep regret he'd given her before walking out of her office—and her life—two days ago.

THE BLACK TIE, COUNTRY-CLUB set was not at all Mark Santori's thing. If given a choice between spending an evening rubbing shoulders with snotty people who considered him worthy only of writing tickets or arresting indigents, and downing some beers with the guys at a bar close to the precinct, he'd choose a cop's night out any time.

Except for tonight.

Tonight he had a vested interest in this party. One that had made it worthwhile to put on the penguin suit he'd bought last spring when yet another one of his brothers had leapt headfirst into matrimony.

"We're so glad you decided to come after all," said Rachel, his petite new sister-in-law. She, Mark and Mark's brother Lucas were walking together into an opulent downtown hotel Saturday night. "I was so afraid there wouldn't be any other friendly faces. With Lucas having to play nice with the muckety-mucks, I wouldn't have had anybody to talk to all night."

Rachel, a sweetheart of a southerner, looked a little nervous, as if not yet used to being in the limelight as the wife of a prominent member of the District Attorney's office. Slipping an arm around her waist, her husband gave her a smile of reassurance. The adoring look on his face had been there for months, ever since Luke had gotten out of his engagement to a piranha in Prada to hook up with his former fiancée's dressmaker.

"You'll be fine. You're the most beautiful woman here." Then, raising a wry brow and looking at Mark, he said, "And believe me, he may look innocent, but I know my brother. He's up to something. There's a reason he came here tonight."

As an attorney, Luke had that confess-or-pay-the-penalty thing going on big-time, and his stare challenged Mark to come clean. But Mark was a cop. He didn't knuckle under to lawyer tricks or intimidation. Not even when they came from his own big brother who was, without a doubt, one of the best things to happen to Chicago law enforcement since Eliott Ness and his untouchables.

"Can't a guy say yes to an invitation without somebody having to alert the media?" he said, maintaining a look of complete innocence.

Rachel tossed her blond curls and took his arm, shooting her husband of seven months a glare. "Of course he can. Ignore your brother. He's just grumpy because there's going to be another man at the party tonight who looks almost as good as he does in a tux." Patting Mark's arm, she added, "And it was really nice of you to come on your parents' behalf."

His parents, as popular local business people and major donors to the current mayor, received the holiday invitation every year. But Mama and Pop had never shown any interest in attending, offering up the tickets to anyone else in the family who wanted them. Lucas got his own invite these days, and usually nobody else was interested.

Until now, this year. When Mark had taken them up on the offer.

There was no doubt in his mind about his real motive for attending tonight's function. It was all about Noelle. Because two days ago a little birdie named Casey, who worked with Noelle at the women's shelter, had told him she was going to be attending tonight's party.

A part of him—the reasonable part who'd learned in his years as a Chicago detective to analyze every situation and draw the most obvious conclusion—had told him to just forget it. Forget *her*. They'd had their fling, she was satisfied, and it was time to cut the strings. Just the way she wanted to.

But the part of him who could still close his eyes and feel

the smoothness of her cheek against his own, and smell the faint scent of orange blossoms in her hair, simply couldn't let it end. Not yet. Not when he was still battered with emotions if he so much as whispered her name.

"It's so pretty," Rachel murmured, looking around with wide blue eyes at the decorations gracing every inch of the lobby.

From the front desk swathed with thick ropes of gold-tipped garland to the twenty-foot tree covered with glittering red and gold ornaments, the hotel screamed professional decorator. It was as if someone had lifted a magazine photograph out of *Southern Living* and brought it to life right here in one of Chicago's nicest hotels.

Somehow, though, Mark found himself looking around for a nativity set, wondering if he'd spot a stray Rudolph carrying the Virgin Mary to Bethlehem. He found himself almost missing the quirky charm of the Candy Cane Inn, so completely at odds with the elegance of this place. If given a choice between the two of them, he frankly thought he'd rather be back in Christmas. At least there everyone was honest about trying to cash in on the goodwill of the holiday season, unlike tonight's event, when the mayor pretended to be hosting a party when, in truth, he would be stumping for campaign money.

But a certain sexy brunette wasn't at the Candy Cane Inn back in her hometown—she was here. In fact, if he wasn't mistaken, she was right *there*.

"Excuse me," he murmured to Luke and Rachel, skirting around the edge of the elegantly dressed crowd in the ballroom. He wanted to stay out of her way for a little while, so he merely kept an eye on her thick head of dark hair, caught up in a sophisticated mass of curls and loops, as he stayed on the sidelines.

Passing a waiter carrying long flutes full of sparkling

champagne, he instead asked a bartender for a club soda. Beside him, a sophisticated blonde in a floor-length bloodred gown gave him a smile and a once-over. Ignoring her, he moved to a shadowy corner, sipping at his drink as he surveyed the room.

All around him, women in glittering, jewel-toned gowns and men in dark tuxes just like his own laughed and chatted, talking about holiday plans and gift exchanges. Not to mention, of course, those last minute tax shelters they needed to find before December 31.

Not one of them, he felt quite sure, knew a thing about the kids Noelle worked with, who weren't going to have much of a holiday season at all. Nor did they probably know much about the holiday events *he* experienced each year…the desperate thieves stealing radios and video games right out of display cases in the stores. The brutal accident scenes caused by selfish bastards who downed their eggnog and rum toddies, then went out and wrapped their cars around light poles. Or, even worse, innocent people.

But he'd be willing to bet they knew a thing or two about that crushing feeling of being alone on Christmas Eve. More than one of the suicides he'd worked during the holidays had been leapers from some of the richest condo buildings in the city.

"Pretty pessimistic," he muttered, trying to focus on the festive atmosphere, not his own jaded attitudes about the holiday season.

The crowd shifted a bit, enough so he finally got a better look at the woman whose dark curls he'd been following with his eyes. And oh, what a look. Because now, seeing her from head to toe for the first time this evening, he had to admit Noelle looked utterly amazing.

She wore a black dress that should have been perfectly normal and acceptable, but for the fact that it was skin tight and revealed her mouthwatering curves. Even from here, he could see the creamy smoothness of her throat and her chest, revealed by the low scooped neckline of the dress. The short, puffy sleeves left most of her slender arms bare, and every time she moved, he was reminded of Noelle's innate gracefulness. He'd bet she was a good dancer. Because God, she was good at lovemaking. A natural, with perfect rhythm and even better instincts.

A good bit of Noelle's long legs, covered with silky black stockings, were revealed by the short dress. Mark took a moment to appreciate them, remembering the way they'd felt wrapped around his hips when he'd made love to her.

He could have stood there studying her from afar for another hour, but when he quickly realized he wasn't the only one admiring her, he straightened and tossed back the rest of his drink. Because another man—a gray-haired guy in a tux too tight for his frame—was standing a few feet away from Noelle, doing whatever he could to look down her dress.

Mark strode across the ballroom, ducking and weaving to avoid bumping into any of the people in his path. But when he reached Noelle and the man, who was speaking intently with her, he hesitated. Noelle's expression was intense—too intense for casual party conversation. When he overheard her mention the words "donation" and "needy kids" he knew exactly why the Christmas-hating social worker had decided to come to this party tonight.

"Well, I'm quite sure we can come to some arrangement," the gray-haired man said, his tone suggestive. "Why don't you give me your number and I'll be in touch so we can work something out."

That was about all Mark was going to stand by and listen to. Stepping around the man, he murmured, "Good evening."

Noelle gasped, and she made a small O with her mouth.

"Miss," he continued, pressing his advantage while she was caught unaware, "I know we are complete and utter strangers. You don't know my name and I don't know yours and after tonight, we'll probably never see each other again. But I simply have to ask—will you dance with me?"

Noelle began to smile, then to laugh softly, even as her eyes widened with excitement and understanding. She knew exactly what he was saying, understood the wicked way he was reminding her of the passionate weekend they'd shared. She also knew he was asking her to repeat it.

The older man she'd been talking to cleared his throat, but Noelle completely ignored him. Extending her hand, she said, "Well, thank you, sir, I'd love to dance."

Taking her hand in his, Mark led her to the small dance floor where several couples were swaying to the Christmas music being played by the small band on the stage. Normally, he wouldn't consider "Winter Wonderland" to be a great song for slow dancing, but the way the ancient musicians with their matching bow ties played, it was just about perfect. Then again, any excuse to hold Noelle in his arms was very much appreciated.

"You look beautiful," he murmured against her hair as she melted into his arms.

"So do you," she replied. "What on earth are you doing here?"

"Just passing through. I'm a complete stranger at a party, remember?" he said, his voice low and intense. He did not want Noelle to start thinking about this, to start remembering all the reasons she thought they couldn't see each other anymore. He just wanted her to go with it—to go *for* it—as she had last Sunday.

She started to speak again. "But…"

"Shh," he ordered.

Though close enough to feel the warmth of her skin, and see the way the fine hair on her temple moved under his breath, he somehow managed to keep himself under control. Because that close-but-so-far-away feeling, more than anything, would drive Noelle wild.

One of his hands tightened the tiniest bit on her waist, while with the other, he laced their fingers together. Their bodies remaining separated by a thin strip of air, so that his trousers brushed her leg and their shoes nearly touched. The front of Noelle's sexy black dress scraped lightly against the jacket of his tux, tantalizingly near, but an eternity farther apart than he wanted to be.

They moved, slid, and swayed, ignoring the other dancers around them, and the changing of the song. And every movement, every dip, every note and every step built the tension and the desire. Soon, Mark could think of nothing else but having her again.

Still leading her in the dance, he began to angle them across the floor, toward the rear of the ballroom. When they were close enough to an exit to avoid unwanted attention, he tugged her with him toward a closed door nearly hidden by the fabric-draped walls. Ignoring the small "private" sign, he opened the door and led her into a dark, shadowy corridor, obviously intended for use by the wait staff.

"Where are we going?"

"To the closest private place," was all he said.

She picked up the pace, hurrying, almost stumbling in her sexy, strappy high heels. Her speed was all the answer he needed about whether Noelle was as desperate for him as he was for her.

"Here," she whispered, twisting at the brushed metal handle of another closed door. It opened, and this time she led the way, charging into the darkness without a second's hesitation.

He followed her, immediately realizing by the smell of lemony polish and cleanser that they were in some type of housekeeping closet. *Good enough.*

Pushing the door closed behind them, he felt around on the wall until his fingers brushed against a light switch. "Watch your eyes," he ordered as he flicked it on.

A weak bulb flashed to life over their heads, flickered once or twice, then stayed on to bathe them in a small amount of light. But it was enough—enough to see they were completely alone in the supply-stacked closet. Enough to see the desire dripping off Noelle in waves.

"I want you so much," she whispered hoarsely before grabbing him by the shoulders and tugging him close.

He covered her mouth with his for a deep, hungry kiss, cupping her head in his hands and letting his fingers drift between her loosely upswept curls. Her lips parted immediately, her tongue meeting his in a hungry feast of tasting and licking.

When Noelle reached for the jacket of his tux and pushed it off his shoulders, Mark didn't even hesitate. He let it fall, then stood back enough to allow her to unbutton his dress shirt. Once it had joined the jacket on the floor, Noelle looked at his chest, licking her lips appreciatively. "My God, do you have any idea how gorgeous you are?" she asked. "You're like a big, beautifully wrapped birthday present I get to open and play with and not have to share with anybody."

He noticed she didn't say Christmas, and laughed softly. "Well, I want to unwrap my present, too."

Reaching around her back for the zipper of her little black dress, he began to tug it down. Though he was not feeling the least bit patient, he was careful not to tear it. They'd have to get out of here eventually, and her hair tumbling out of its style would be enough to explain.

She stepped closer, sliding her arms around his neck, kissing him again, tilting her head for a tighter fit of their mouths. He would have liked to dance like this, connected from head to toe. Naked would be good, too.

As the kiss ended she murmured, "I've been dreaming about you every night."

"Ditto."

"I've been wanting more. So much more." Sucking on his bottom lip, she nipped at it lightly, letting him know just how wild she was feeling.

"Tell me what you've been dreaming of doing, Noelle," he asked as he finished unzipping the dress.

"Oh…this and that."

Her sultry smile told him exactly what kinds of *this* and *that* she meant. He couldn't help thinking back to last Sunday, when they'd indulged in so many hours of sensual pleasures.

"Which *this* did you like best?" he asked, watching as she lowered one shoulder, then the other, to let the dress fall.

When he saw the sexy black bra she was wearing, though, he forgot about his own question. Smiling at the way her breasts pushed up and over the lacy hem, he lowered his face to bury it in her curves. He licked at the seam of her cleavage, marveling again at how soft and smooth her skin was against his cheek. Breathing in her scent, he kissed the top curves of each breast. Then, sliding his tongue beneath the fabric, he licked hungrily at one practically exposed nipple.

"Mark!" She twined her fingers in his hair and held him tightly against her chest, forceful, taking the pressure and intensity she wanted.

Unable to wait, he jerked the bra out of the way, lifting her breast to his eagerly awaiting mouth. Catching her nipple between his lips, he sucked hard on it, feeling the way she sagged against him in response. Her tender flesh pebbled harder against his tongue as he suckled her, and her little whimpers of delight urged him on.

Reaching down, he pushed her dress to the floor and moved back to let her kick it out of the way. When he saw her skimpy panties and thigh-high black stockings, he almost erupted out of his pants. "Keep those stockings on when I'm inside you," he growled. "I want to feel them when your legs are wrapped around my waist." Then, before catching her mouth in another carnal kiss, he added, "And my neck."

Licking at his mouth, she reached down to unbutton his pants, then lowered the zipper. Her startled gasp told him the moment she realized he was wearing nothing underneath.

"Naughty," she murmured, brushing the tips of her fingers across his erection in a teasing caress.

"Hey, they don't make sexy, lacy underwear for men. Commando's about as racy as a guy can get."

She laughed softly, but the laughter quickly faded as he pressed into her palm, dying for her cool touch. The temperature in the small closet increased, growing steamy hot, as she ran her fingers up and down his shaft. He groaned, wanting—needing—more.

"Tell me what you want," she ordered, as if knowing he was nearing the end of his rope.

"I want you." *More than anything in the world.*

She kissed his neck, nibbling at the skin beneath his ear, whispering something soft and suggestive. Dropping her hand lower, she cupped his balls in her hand, handling him lightly, delicately, her touch sending pure heat rushing through him.

"Be more specific about what you want," she whispered. "Just like I was last weekend."

Last weekend. Oh, yeah, she'd definitely told him what she wanted, over and over again.

But this was different. Mark had enjoyed giving her pleasure, had totally gotten off on seeing Noelle let go of all her inhibitions and become a slave to her own body's desires.

He wasn't so sure he wanted to let himself do the same thing, however. Not just losing control, but he also didn't want to push Noelle into anything she didn't want to do.

"Do you want me to lick you here?" she asked, squeezing him lightly, running the tip of one finger along the seam of his nuts, to the base of his dick.

He shuddered and moaned. Dropping his head back, he said nothing, waiting, instead, for her to make her move.

She didn't. Instead, she continued to toy with him, caressing, not grasping. Teasing, not squeezing. Until he thought he was gonna lose it. "Noelle…"

"You have to say it," she whispered against his neck.

"You're killing me."

"*Say it,*" she ordered as she sucked on his earlobe, licking its edge. "Beg me for it, and I'll make you very glad you did."

He could no longer resist. Thrusting his hands into her hair, he tugged her mouth to his, whispering, "Taste me, Noelle. Suck me," just before covering her lips and kissing her deeply.

She didn't let him distract her for long. Once he'd given her the ravenous plea she'd asked for, Noelle seemed determined to drive him utterly wild. Pulling her mouth away mid-kiss, she slid down his body, her bare breasts scraping a hot path over the sweat-slickened skin of his chest and stomach. Her mouth followed suit.

Cushioning her knees with Mark's jacket, she knelt in front of him, staring at his engorged cock. From above, he watched her, anticipation making his whole body tense and anxious. The low lighting made her hair come alive like a mass of dark, sparkling embers, and cast shadows across her cheeks. But even in the dimness, he could see the smile on her face. And the way she licked her lips.

"God," he muttered, tensing in preparation for what was to come.

Then she moved her mouth to his erection and licked at him. Lightly. Delicately. Tantalizingly.

Mark leaned back against the closed door, wanting to close his eyes and enjoy. Wanting to watch her even more.

Her tongue traced a line of fire from the moist tip of his sex down the thick line in the back. Shuddering, Mark drew in a few choppy breaths as she delicately sampled the base of his shaft, swirling her tongue over his tight balls.

"You're killing me," he muttered, clenching his fists at his sides to try to maintain some kind of control. "I don't know if I'm going to be able to take much of this."

It was true. He'd enjoyed oral sex before, but no one had ever made him feel this incredibly good. Her mouth was magic, her tongue divine. Not content with merely tasting him, she also had her hand on him, her fingers teasing and caressing him into near incoherence.

But he had to admit it: watching her was almost the best part of all.

Noelle wasn't going to allow him to stop her. "Don't die yet, darling. I'm just getting started," she whispered as she kissed her way back up. Without warning, she covered the bulbous tip of his cock with her lips and sucked him into her mouth.

He groaned, deep in his throat, and dropped his head back, wondering if it was possible to die from an overdose of pleasure. Her soft mouth was incredibly good…warm, welcoming, moist. He had to admit, it was almost as delightful as her sweet, wet heat had been last weekend, and he hadn't dropped dead then. Which meant he was free to enjoy every bit of what Noelle wanted to do to him now, didn't it?

"Mmm," she murmured as she sucked him deeper, then pulled away. Again. And again. She freed him long enough to whisper, "You taste so good, don't you dare ask me to stop."

As if.

She returned to her task, sucking hard again while she used her hand to toy with him between his legs. Looking down at her, Mark couldn't resist tangling his fingers in her beautiful hair. Rubbing the silkiness against his bare stomach, as he'd fantasized about doing a week ago, he savored the sensations battering him from all sides. Soon, even that required too much effort, and he gave up all thought and existing only for the pleasure of her mouth and hands.

The tension built, began to spiral, and he recognized the signs of his own impending climax. "Enough," he muttered through a tight, thick throat, though the words nearly killed him. "You're going too far, sweetheart."

He tried to pull away, tried to tug her up so he could finish this in the proper way, in the proper place. Noelle, however, wouldn't let him. Reaching one arm around to clasp her hand tightly on his bare ass, she held him there. She began to tug him close, then push him back, setting the rhythm she wanted until he was literally making love to her mouth.

"Noelle!" he barked when the tension reached the breaking point.

His demand had no impact whatsoever. Sucking him so deep he thought he was going to die of sensation, she demanded all he had to give. Mark was powerless to resist, incapable of stopping. And soon, to his shock and incredible delight, she devoured him right through his soul-shattering climax.

9

IF THE SOUND OF PASSING VOICES outside the cleaning closet hadn't shocked both of them out of their erotic cloud, Noelle would probably have her legs wrapped around Mark's hips right about now, letting him drive her into sexual oblivion. But the voices *had* passed by, and they'd both realized just how much they were risking intrusion on their private interlude.

So instead of being pounded into with raging passion, she was currently standing in front of a mirror in the bathroom, trying to make some kind of coherent style out of her wild, messy hair. Not to mention wishing she had a toothbrush.

It wasn't that she hadn't loved every bit of what she'd done to Mark—she *definitely* had. She just would have liked to freshen up a little more than was possible in a ritzy hotel bathroom.

Noelle smiled at the memory, her knees almost growing weak when she gave herself over to the visual images of what had just happened. She wanted to sigh with wicked satisfaction just thinking about the sensations—his taste, his smell. The helpless sounds of pleasure he'd made. The look of uncontrollable ecstasy on his incredibly handsome face.

Oh, yes, she'd absolutely adored her most daring sexual adventure yet. Almost as much as she'd adored the wild things Mark had made her feel with his mouth last weekend. Now, there was just one more step. Next time, they'd have to put the two activities together at the same time, so she'd be able to check a certain number off her sexual fantasy list. And probably lose her mind in the process.

"Next time?" she asked her reflection as she carefully brushed her formerly done-up hair into a loose bunch of curls.

The thought startled her. She'd thought after last weekend that there would never be a next time. Yet tonight, she'd given in to that same intense longing she'd felt for Mark since the moment he'd stormed into her dressing room the day after Thanksgiving. Now she was already anticipating another sensual interlude.

So much for her plan to have a one-shot affair with a stranger from far far away. Mark wasn't a stranger. He was a strong, sexy, amazing guy who happened to live close by and wanted her like mad. Almost as much as she wanted him. So she'd be crazy not to let him indulge her with every naughty fantasy she'd ever imagined, wouldn't she?

Noelle was a lot of things, but crazy wasn't one of them. These barriers she'd tried to erect between them were obviously powerless against the overwhelming attraction they felt for one another, tonight had proved that.

So why not just go for it?

Go for an all-out sexual affair, limited by nothing—not distance, not conventions, not insecurity or fears of being hurt. While taking whatever fabulous moments she could with Mark, always, in the back of her mind, she'd absolutely *force* herself to remember it was temporary. Just a fling. History told her she just wasn't the kind of woman who men truly fell in love with…or stayed with. But Mark *wanted* her for now. So why shouldn't she take a slightly more risky approach and just have a wonderful time with him while she could? It'd be her Christmas present to herself since it was pretty unlikely she was going to get to fly off to St. Lucia this year.

In the past, sex had come after emotion, after a few dates at the very least. She'd never gotten it right and had always ended up alone.

This time, the sex had come right off the bat. And as long as she kept her emotions out of the equation, she might just have the experience of a lifetime.

She could live a fantasy during this supposed season of miracles and finally have the kind of holiday season she'd given up hope of ever having: a truly magical one.

"You should go for it," she told her reflection.

"Oh, you *definitely* should go for it if it makes you look that happy," a voice said.

Shocked, Noelle turned and noticed another woman standing in front of a make-up mirror in the far corner of the ladies' room. Noelle hadn't noticed her arrival, probably because she was so intent on repairing the damage to her hair and makeup.

The woman, a young blonde who'd been touching up her lipstick, straightened and offered Noelle a broad smile. "Sorry. I just recognized the look and couldn't help commenting."

"Recognized the look?" Noelle asked, incredibly embarrassed. Had she put her dress on backward? Torn a stocking?

The blonde walked over, her sapphire-blue cocktail dress bringing out the vivid blue of her eyes. She was a very pretty woman, soft-looking, with a nice smile and a curvy figure.

Without a word, she reached up and fiddled with Noelle's hair. "You missed a bobby pin," she said, pulling one free of Noelle's dark curls. "And you might want to put a little makeup on your neck, if you have some."

Noelle felt heat rise to her face.

"It's just a few red marks," the woman said, sounding comforting rather than judgmental or amused.

"I don't have anything except lipstick," she said, cursing her handbag—a teeny black velvet wallet pretending to be a purse. Panicking, she whirled around to look at herself in the mirror.

Without a word, the other woman opened her own pocketbook and retrieved a small tube of cover-up. Twisting off the top, she squeezed a little bit onto her fingers, then dabbed it on one or two red spots on Noelle's throat. Noelle finished the job of blending it in. When they were finished, their eyes met in the mirror and the two of them exchanged a quick smile as they surveyed their efforts.

"Not bad at all," the woman said. "My name's Rachel, by the way."

The blonde had a slight southern accent that implied immediate warmth. She looked so conspiratorial about helping her cover up evidence of her mid-party make out session that Noelle could take no offense. "Thanks Rachel. I'm Noelle. This is so embarrassing," she said. "Can I make it out of here, do you think?"

The woman nodded. "Men won't notice anything except how beautiful you are. And women will either be too jealous of your looks to suspect anything, or else they'll recognize the signs and reminisce about some wicked stolen moments of their own somewhere."

Noelle laughed softly, liking the other woman's soft-spoken charm. "You sound like you speak from experience."

Casting a quick glance around the room to ensure they were the only ones around, Rachel explained, "My husband and I snuck into an empty courtroom during a luncheon honoring a retiring judge last month."

Noelle lowered her voice, too. "Nice to know adventures still continue after the wedding. Have you been married long?"

The woman shook her head. "Just since May. But knowing my Lucas, we'll be sneaking into empty courtrooms when *he's* the judge retiring."

The look of complete adoration on the stranger's face as she talked about her husband brought another smile to Noelle's lips. It appeared Sue and Randy weren't the only married couple who had found a way to keep their marriages rock-solid yet also spicy and exciting.

Funny, looking back, Noelle realized she'd never even thought she might have that kind of relationship with Jeremy. Whether he'd cheated and dumped her or not, she'd just never pictured the two of them being wildly daring and sexually happy for the rest of their lives. Comfortable, quietly happy, yes. But blissful? Well, she'd never expected it for herself.

Which, she suddenly acknowledged, had been a damned shame.

She deserved bliss. Even if it was purely physical—not emotional—bliss. So she was going to grab at it with both hands and see just how many fabulous memories she could make with Mark Santori before the thrill wore off and they went their separate ways.

Just until Christmas, she reminded herself. She'd have a magical holiday yet. That should be long enough to quench the raging fire between them. Yet not long enough to get Noelle's heart involved in the equation.

It had to be. Because if she thought there was a chance she could truly fall madly in love with the man, she wouldn't have the courage to go through with this affair. Not when she knew, deep down, that if she couldn't keep a boring twit like Jeremy Taggert satisfied the duration of their engagement, she'd *never* be able to do it with a to-die-for sex god like Mark Santori.

A little voice in her head whispered that she *already* had feelings for Mark—confusing ones, intense ones—but she ruthlessly gagged it.

Patting her hair one more time, Noelle offered Rachel another nod of thanks. "I think I'll be okay."

"Your secret's safe with me," Rachel said. Then, with a mischievous wag of her brow, she added, "And, of course, the man who put that look on your face. I imagine he's hovering around outside, waiting to drag you back into some dark corner again."

Hmm…frankly, Noelle would rather be dragged back to her apartment. Or to Mark's. "I hope you're right," she murmured, seeing the way her eyes sparkled in the mirror.

"Want some moral support, honey?" Rachel asked as she turned toward the door.

"Thanks," Noelle replied, following the other woman.

Right before they exited, however, Rachel paused and reached into her handbag. Without a word, she pulled out a pack of mints, offered one to Noelle, then winked. "Just in case you, uh, wanted one."

Noelle had the feeling her face was about the color of a pile of bricks when they emerged into the ballroom. But thankfully, Rachel didn't seem to notice.

Someone else did, though. "You okay?" a low voice asked.

Glancing over, she saw Mark standing a few feet away, watching her closely.

She nodded. "Better than okay."

He stepped closer to take her arm.

"Get me out of here, Mark. Take me home," she added, her voice low and full of promise.

His eyes flashed with heated understanding and a sultry smile widened his sexy lips. "It would be my pleasure."

But before he could do it, Mark suddenly noticed the woman who'd been standing a few feet away…Rachel, who'd helped Noelle in the bathroom. "Uh…oh…Rach?"

Noelle glanced back and forth between her lover and the blonde, who was staring at them with outright merriment dancing in her eyes. "You two know each other?"

Mark nodded, shifting a little as if suddenly uncomfortable in his tux which, to Noelle's great relief, showed no evidence of dust, furniture polish or knee prints. "More important, do *you* two know each other?" he asked.

"We just met," Rachel said, obviously very comfortable teasing Mark. "I was helping Noelle hide the evidence of her passionate interlude."

Oh, Lord. Noelle suddenly wanted to sink into the floor, picturing the worst. Rachel was beautiful and funny and charming, and obviously knew Mark very well. With Noelle's luck, the blonde was his ex-girlfriend or something. Which suddenly made the friendly little southerner a lot less appealing.

"Who had a passionate interlude?" a male voice asked.

"Oh, great, this just keeps getting better and better," Mark muttered with an audible sigh.

A tall, lean man, with hair a shade or two lighter than Mark's and a pair of somewhat familiar green eyes joined them. He slipped his arm around Rachel's waist, and she leaned into him.

Noelle would bet this was Lucas. The future amorous judge.

"Mark's been holding out on us," Rachel said. But, true to her word, she didn't reveal what had happened in the ladies room. "It appears he does know someone at tonight's party. I think he has a very close friend here."

Cornered, Mark nodded. His expression apologetic, he turned to Noelle and said, "This is my brother Lucas and his wife, Rachel."

Ahh...now the eyes made sense. They were so much like Mark's, the only strong similarity as their builds were very different. Lucas was lean and wiry, Mark muscle-bound and broad.

The other couple greeted her warmly, Lucas also giving his brother a not-too-surreptitous nod of approval. Then a heavy silence descended upon them. Because the next natural thing for Mark to do would be to tell them who Noelle was—and how he knew her. Only, he didn't do it. Instead, he watched her intently, as if unsure about what she wanted.

Noelle suddenly understood why. It was the whole stranger thing. He was still playing her game, following her rules, giving her an out if she chose to play down their relationship and walk away from him and his family.

The realization made her heart melt a little. Because it was just one more reminder that beneath the tough-guy cop exterior was a very thoughtful man, indeed.

Offering Mark's handsome brother a smile, she extended her hand. "I'm Noelle Bradenton." Then, with a silent, sincere look of gratitude at Mark, she added, "And yes, your brother and I are very...close."

But not as close as they were going to be over the next couple of weeks. Which sounded pretty damn good to her.

IF MARK HADN'T RECEIVED A CALL from Harriet late Saturday night about another robbery by a guy in a Santa costume, he probably would have ended up taking Noelle home and not leaving until Sunday. Or Monday. Or next year.

But while every sexual instinct he possessed had been dying for exactly that—to finish what they'd begun in the housekeeping closet—in the days that followed, he decided it was a good thing he hadn't.

Oh, he still wanted her, ached for her, actually. He also, however, realized something had changed. Their relationship had shifted, crossed the invisible line Noelle had drawn in her mind. They'd come to a new understanding during the mayor's party. Sometime between the wickedly erotic encounter they'd shared in the closet, and when they'd run into Lucas and Rachel, Noelle's perception of what they could and couldn't be to one another had altered.

She wanted more than random, wild sex without strings or repercussions. No, she hadn't come right out and said it, but she hadn't needed to. It was understood.

Finally letting her guard down, Noelle was opening up, giving them both the chance to enjoy what was happening between them, other than sex. For his part, Mark definitely was enjoying everything they did together. He hadn't felt this good about a woman in…well, forever. She occupied his mind constantly, and his dreams even more, until by the end of each day he felt like he had to hear her voice or explode.

They'd even taken a step back in the timeline of a typical relationship, returning to the beginning and actually going out for dinner Sunday night. Though the evening had been full of good food and good conversation, in the back of his mind, Mark couldn't help thinking about the contradiction of going on a first date with a woman who'd already given him the best blow job he'd ever had in his life. He still shifted in his pants at the very thought.

Yet somehow, even though Noelle had met him Monday for lunch, Tuesday to shop for decorations and goodies for the kids at the shelter, and Wednesday for a drink, he'd managed to keep things pretty platonic between them. Despite the dark hunger in her eyes, which he was certain matched his own, Mark had somehow kept their physical contact strictly above the waist—mainly by meeting her in public places.

With no closets.

He knew the restraint was bugging her, and it was about to kill him. But he also knew something else: Noelle was risking a lot by opening up and letting him into her life. So she deserved to know he wanted to be in *every* part of her life. Not just her bed.

"You know, we're really lucky this latest guy let his little brain override the common sense in his big one," his partner, Harriet, said as they rode in her car to his family restaurant Thursday afternoon. Mark had lent his own car to his sister Lottie for the day, and planned to meet her at Santori's to get it back.

"I know," he replied, still thinking over the most recent robbery. "He was sloppy, telling that cashier his real name was Jerry when his paperwork said it was Herbert."

Having seen the cute cashier from a local grocery store—which had been ripped off by someone hired to play Santa at their grand opening Saturday night—Mark had the feeling he knew why the guy had messed up. The clerk was sexy and stacked. Fortunately, she was also observant. Remembering not only the name the perp had used when trying to pick her up, she'd also seen past his costume to note his dirty-blonde hair, hazel eyes and young-looking, boyish face. She'd even agreed to come down to the station and look through books full of mug shots to see if she could nail the guy. They'd had no luck yet. But Mark remained optimistic.

"I appreciate you driving me down here," he said as Harriet pulled onto Taylor Avenue.

"Hey, for your dad's pizza, I'd drive a lot farther than this." She stared straight ahead. "Besides, it worked out okay. Once I knew I was driving you here, I made some plans. I'm meeting a friend here for dinner." She paused. "A special friend who I've been, uh…seeing."

Mark raised a brow. Though he and Harriet were incredibly close in a lot of ways, this was the first time his partner had initiated a conversation about her private life, and she sounded nervous about it. Not surprising. For someone who loved to dig and pry into other people's personal business, Harriet was very close-lipped about her own. That was one reason most of their co-workers figured she was a lesbian. Well, that and the fact that Harriet never wore anything but dark, mannish suits—even to social events—and she made no effort to put a dot of makeup on her square face or color her rapidly graying brown hair.

Mark cleared his throat. "Well, in that case, maybe I'll stick around to meet your…friend."

"Yeah," she said, still not meeting his eye. "I guess that'd be okay."

Frankly, Mark didn't know and didn't care what the woman did in the privacy of her bed. She was a great cop, and she'd been a real friend. Especially because she knew him better than just about anybody else at the precinct.

Harriet, in a strange twist of fate, had been one of the cops investigating his ex-fiancée a few years back. And when Renée had implicated Mark, Harriet had been the one to pull him aside and give him a heads-up that the rat squad was going to be coming after him.

"So, your close-legged girlfriend gonna show up tonight?" she asked, looking secretly amused.

He should have expected the question. Harriet had been ruthlessly nagging him all week for details on his latest relationship, somehow knowing he'd lost his head over an incredibly sexy woman. But he had to admit, the close-legged thing caught him by surprise. "What the hell do you mean?"

Harriet snickered. "You think I don't know you well enough to know when you're getting it…and when you're *not?*"

Christ. He so didn't want to be having this conversation with a woman he sometimes thought of as a mother figure.

Especially since his own mother still believed all her unmarried children were virgins.

"So tell me who has you on a string. Is it that social worker from the shelter that got ripped off?"

Mark could only gape at her from the other side of the chilly car, which wasn't much warmer than the air outside. Harriet didn't seem to notice the temperature and hadn't even reached for the heater switch. "How did you know?"

The woman gave him a sympathetic look out of the corner of her eye. "You came back that day looking like somebody had just given you the greatest Christmas present you ever got. And every time the case comes up, you get the same look on your face."

Yeah, he supposed he did, and the realization made him grin. He wondered how Noelle would like being compared to a Christmas gift. Given her dislike of the holiday, he figured maybe he'd better call her a birthday present, as she had him last Saturday night. In the closet. When they'd....

"Here we are." Harriet parked the car, apparently not noticing the glazed-over look of lust Mark figured had to be on his face. He wiped the look off, not wanting any intrusive questions from anyone in his family. Particularly not his sister, who had the instincts of a bloodhound and the tact of one, too.

Following Harriet into the restaurant, he shook off the cold and shrugged out of his coat. Though he knew his partner didn't care, habit forced him to play the gentleman, so he took Harriet's coat as well. Walking across the crowded foyer, he hung them both among a number of others on a rack in the corner.

Suddenly, he caught a familiar scent, and it wasn't tomatoes or oregano. Mark stiffened, instantly on alert as a sweetly spicy fragrance filled his head. Somehow, his body had recognized the sweet smell before his brain had identified it.

It was perfume. Noelle's perfume.

He quickly quashed the excitement that had made his blood surge a little faster in his veins. Because another woman had to be wearing it. Noelle wouldn't be here—he knew that much. He'd been trying to get her to come to the restaurant for the past two nights, but she'd refused. Sure, they'd gone out; she'd agreed to spend time with him doing something other than licking each other into mindless pleasure. But she hadn't quite been ready to meet the folks.

Already steeling himself against the disappointment, he turned around. And found himself looking into a pair of very familiar brown eyes.

"Hi," she said softly. She nibbled her lip. "I, uh, wasn't expecting to see you here so early."

"I had to pick up my car from Lottie," he said, still stunned to see Noelle standing in his family's restaurant. And looking positively beautiful.

She wore a long, winter-white coat, which made her lush brown hair shine more vibrantly than usual. Her black cords clung to the curvaceous legs he'd been picturing in those thigh-high stockings for days.

How in the name of God had he resisted her since Sunday night, when now, surrounded by dozens of people—including his partner and his family—he was dying to push her back against the wall and kiss her lungs out?

"I wasn't expecting to see you here at all," he finally said, filling the intimate bubble of silence that had descended between them in the loud room.

"It was an emergency," she explained. "A major pizza craving."

Confident in his words, he said, "Well, honey, you've come to the right place. I wasn't kidding when I said my father makes the best deep dish in Chicago."

"Perfect. Because that's exactly what she's dying for."

He paused. "She?"

Nodding, Noelle slipped her heavy coat onto a hanger and hung it beside Mark's, then turned to face him. He had a hard time even remembering what he'd asked when he saw the way her red sweater plunged between her perfect, shapely breasts. Damn. He was going to have to stand here for a minute or two or else risk his partner—and his mother—seeing the bulge in his pants.

"Yeah. Sue is desperate for some Chicago deep dish."

Her pregnant cousin had a craving. That helped pull his attention off Noelle's mouthwatering cleavage.

Okay, pregnant women were known to have cravings. But what that had to do with Noelle being here, at Santori's in *Chicago,* when Noelle was eighty miles away in Christmas, he had no idea. "Umh…we don't deliver that far," he said with a small grin.

Sighing, she admitted, "I do."

His eyes widening, he stared at her in disbelief. "You mean you're driving an hour and a half to deliver a pizza?"

"It's for a good cause. Baby FloJo is really hungry and I think I told you the only Italian place in Christmas only serves thin crust."

"Yeah," he said, indeed remembering her comments about the restaurateur who'd compared deep dish to *bread*. The guy must have been born in New York. Then he focused on the rest of her statement. "FloJo?"

Stepping out of the way of a beefy guy trying to squeeze past them to the coat rack, Noelle moved even closer to Mark. Close enough for him to inhale that spicy, delicious scent of hers. And to feel the warmth of her breaths on his cheek. "Sue says the baby's using her kidney as a starting block so she's obviously a runner."

He nodded, almost hearing her cousin's complaints. "And you're really going to drive a pizza out to her?"

"Randy's meeting me halfway."

"That's still pretty far."

"I know, and knowing him he'll drive too fast to get back to her quickly." Shrugging, she shook her head, sending waves of that dark hair swirling, one of them brushing against his cheek. Upping the awareness again.

There went another minute or two here in the corner for some serious cooling-off.

"I told Randy I'd bring it all the way there, but he was adamant that I not drive all the way to Christmas and back by myself."

He wondered if she realized she'd just given him an opening, a perfect excuse to spend another evening with her. The hint of color rising into her cheeks—which he'd bet had absolutely nothing to do with the cold air blasting inside every time someone opened the door—told him she had. "That wasn't a hint."

"I know. But I'm taking you anyway."

She put her hand on his chest, her touch frying his circuits as always. "No, Mark, I can't let you…"

"Forget it, Noelle." He covered her hand with his own and squeezed it. "If you're making a pizza delivery halfway across the state, I'm going with you."

Though her mouth opened as if to argue, after a second, Noelle closed it again. With a small smile, she said, "Thanks. That'd be wonderful. I guess I'd better place my order."

"I can promise speedy service," he said with a wink. "I have an in with the owner."

Glancing toward the front of the restaurant, he caught his partner's curious stare. Harriet was looking Noelle over and nodding her approval. Hopefully as a friend and sister-figure. Not as a, um, competitor.

Knowing he couldn't stand here in the corner when his partner was waiting for him, and his mother would be appearing at any moment, he took Noelle's arm. Unable to resist the softness of her delicate sweater, and instantly picturing how good it must feel against her even softer skin, he rubbed it lightly. He led her to the counter, where Gloria, his sister-in-law, was busy taking phone orders and writing down the names of customers waiting for tables. Santori's was a family affair. Every one of them had waited tables here during their teen years, and Tony's wife was a regular fixture in the place now.

"Hi," he said, raising his voice over the chatter of the customers waiting to be seated. "I need to get a couple of pies."

"You gotta wait your turn. We're kinda busy in case you didn't notice," said Gloria, sounding impatient. Then she looked up and saw him there and her face widened into an enormous smile. "Mark! Hey, dollface, how you doin'?"

He leaned over the counter to kiss her cheek. "Good. You?"

"I'd be better if that brother of yours wasn't such a lunkhead." Though she hadn't yet realized he was with Noelle, Gloria did spot Harriet. "Hey, how *you* doin?"

"I guess you remember Harriet?"

Gloria nodded, sending her shiny black hair, puffed up in a do-wop style that looked like something out of a fifties movie, bobbing. Gloria was old school from head to toe. "Sure I do. Good to see you again." Then she gave Mark a hard stare. "Your rock-brained brother is gonna give himself a hernia," she said, her voice loud, as always. "You tell him to stop schlepping tables around here every time he decides he wants to rearrange the room because heaven *knows* he won't listen to me. After all, who am I? Only his wife, that's who."

Glancing around, he noted the slight changes in the restaurant's layout. Every three months or so, Tony got a bee in his bonnet and moved things around. He said he did it to keep things feeling fresh and new. In truth, he did it because it riled Gloria up and he positively lived to tease his wife into one of her passionate meltdowns. Mark had the feeling Tony liked making up after those fights.

In fact, even now, his brother was watching from just outside the swinging doorway to the kitchen, having heard every word Gloria had said. Giving Mark a grin and a wave, he ducked back into the kitchen before she could whirl around and catch him.

"I'll talk to him," he said, knowing it was hopeless. Who was he to interfere with the machinations of a good marriage? Tony and Gloria had a great thing going and despite their occasional eruptions because of their matching stubborn personalities, seemed to be truly happy. They were raising two spoiled, passionate, dark-haired boys to be just like them.

Before Gloria could go off on a rant about her husband, Mama walked out from the back room. Spying Mark, she beelined to the front counter, hugged him, then stuck her index finger in front of his nose. "You get your secret Santa gift yet?"

"Uh…I forgot about it and never found out who I have."

Bad move. His mother lifted her eyes heavenward and said a prayer for her forgetful son. But at least she didn't whack him. Then, looking around the room to ensure his future victim—er, gift recipient—wasn't in earshot, she said, "You have Rachel."

His new sister-in-law. Wonderful. Like he had any idea what to get the newest member of their family. "Come on, Ma, gimme Nick instead. I know you pick who everybody gets."

Fisting her hands, she put them on her hips and glared. "So the two of you can each go out and buy your own presents like you did that year you wanted the electric guitar and he wanted the stereo? I don'a think so!" Her all-knowing nod told him she wasn't finished. "Is good luck, you know. For the next son to buy a holiday present for his older brother's new wife. Just ask Joey."

Mark had no idea what his mother was talking about. But before he could ask, he heard Noelle chuckling. How he'd forgotten the woman he'd been sporting a hard-on for for the past three weeks was standing right behind him, he had no idea.

"*You?* An electric guitar?" she asked, as if someone had said he'd once danced with the Chicago ballet.

"I was going through a Jimmy Page phase," he admitted with a shrug.

"Are you any good?" Her lips still twitched with amusement, as if she already knew the answer to her own question.

"Nuh-uh," he admitted. "Tony told me if I tried to play 'Stairway to Heaven' one more time, he was throwing my guitar in front of the L train."

"He's lucky he didn't derail it," Gloria said.

Noelle's lips disappeared inside her mouth; she was obviously biting them to keep from laughing. Mark, meanwhile, was busy looking around at the three other very important women in his life: his partner, his sister-in-law, and Mama. Talk about trial by fire—he only hoped Noelle would still want to see him after this evening was over.

All three women were eyeing him and Noelle with expressions ranging from casual interest to pure speculation. But there was still time for damage control, if he acted quickly. Or if his brother Tony popped his head out of the kitchen again and distracted Gloria. Yeah. A big giant Italian blow-out would get everybody's attention off him and Noelle.

Unfortunately, Tony didn't show up and the silence continued for a long moment, until his mother said, "Did I raise you in a barn with no manners? Are you going to introduce us to your friend?"

Damn. No escape. He had to handle this now, before his mother put her hands on Noelle's hips to measure their suitability for child-bearing. "This is a very good *friend* of mine, Noelle Bradenton," he said, giving the women of his family, and Harriet, a hard stare, demanding that they not say anything outrageous. "Noelle, meet my mother, Rosa Santori, my sister-in-law Gloria, and my partner, Harriet."

His mother obviously didn't take the hint to behave. Throwing her hands into the air, she practically sang, "Hallelujah, our Markie finally has himself a new lady friend, I'd almost given hope after all'a these years. A nice girl she is, too, uh? I can tell these things."

Oh, Christ, here come the hands.

"Come here and let me see you better. She's so pretty! Such dark eyes, dark hair. You are Italian, I know it. I can tell this, too."

She might as well have stood on a table and shouted because everyone in the place had heard and was looking at them. Out of the corner of his eye, Mark could see Harriet's shoulders shaking with laughter. Too bad he wasn't going to be able to pay the woman back in kind tonight. Unfortunately, even if he introduced Harriet's "special friend" to his mother, he didn't suppose she'd get the underlying significance and embarrass the hell out of her, like she was doing to her own son.

Hoping the image of a sick relative in need would move Mama's thoughts in another direction, he quickly said, "We need to place an order so we can bring some food to Noelle's cousin, Sue, who can't get out of bed."

Bingo.

"Oh, dear!" Mama immediately made the sign of the cross. "I'll add her to my prayer circle. What is wrong with her?"

"She's on bed rest for the remainder of her pregnancy," Noelle explained.

Yow. Bad move. Because now his single-minded mother was smiling in that knowing way, which said she was about to say something embarrassing. Again. "Pregnancy? And are you happy for your cousin? Do you like *bebès?*"

Noelle, who obviously could read his mother like a book, nodded, giving Mark a mischievous look. "I do. Very much."

That was all the answer Rose Santori needed about whether Noelle was a good match for one of her sons. Her wide smile was accompanied by a shout for someone to get Pop out of the kitchen. When no one moved quickly enough, she stalked off herself, muttering something about dark-haired grandchildren.

Thankfully, before Mark had to look Noelle in the eye and admit that yes, he was part of a maniacally insane family, his partner, who always had his back, stepped in to cover him. "I think I see *my* very good friend."

Pure curiosity winning out over a desire to stay out of Harriet's private life made Mark turn and look around the room, Noelle still close by his side. Most of the tables were filled with whispering couples or laughing families. At one booth near the tropical fish tank, he did see a woman sitting by herself. But the petite blonde looked a little too simpering to be Harriet's type.

"Right over there," his partner said, nodding toward a table about halfway to the kitchen. She almost sounded nervous, which was when Mark realized his opinion really *did* matter to Harriet.

Determined to display no overt reaction to his partner's coming-out moment, he followed her stare and saw…a guy.

A shy-looking, middle-aged guy who wore glasses and had thinning light brown hair. "*That's* your special someone? *Him?*"

Harriet frowned darkly. "Yeah. Why? What's wrong with him?"

Immediately back-pedaling and cursing the day he'd ever listened to gossip and innuendo, he said, "Nothing. Not a thing. Everything's fine. He's looking at you like he can't take his eyes off you." Which was the truth.

His brusque partner's cheeks actually pinkened. "Thanks." Then, clearing her throat and casting a quick look at Noelle, she shot right back. "It's catching."

Turning around in time to catch Noelle watching him with lazy, lethargic hunger in her eyes, he had to acknowledge his partner's instincts.

"What can I say?" Noelle asked with an unapologetic shrug. "You look good to me. Really, *really* good."

"Ditto," Mark said, surprised by how great he was feeling right now. Such a big change from a few weeks ago, or, even the past few years.

As he'd told Harriet, everything *was* just fine. Better than fine. Because surrounded by family, with Noelle standing beside him, Mark suddenly recognized the strange lightness that had been making him smile for stupid reasons and almost actually look forward to this holiday season.

He was happy. Really happy—with his professional life, and his personal life—for the first time in as long as he could remember. And he didn't have to think too hard to figure out why. It was because of the beautiful woman standing by his side.

Which, in his opinion, was right where she belonged.

10

WHEN RANDY TOLD SUE that her cousin had insisted on driving a few deep dish pizzas all the way to Christmas just to make her happy, Sue started to cry. Talk about a guilty conscience…all she'd wanted was a freakin' piece of pizza, for heaven's sake. How had it turned into this massive drama?

"I'm sorry, honey. I thought you wanted it!" Randy said, sitting gingerly on the side of the bed, careful not to touch her. Sue was beginning to feel like a piece of rare china. Or a leper.

"I did want it," she explained. "But it was bad enough when I thought she was going to drive out and meet you halfway between here and Chicago. Now I'm going to lie here worrying until she arrives, and I'll worry even more when she makes that long drive back tonight all by herself."

"But she's not going to be by herself."

Sue's tears dried instantly. "What do you mean?"

"I mean," her husband replied, looking relieved that she'd stopped the crying—at least for this thirty-second interval—"that she's driving down with that guy, Mark, who was here last weekend."

"Yes!" Sue said, clenching her fist and punching it into the air. "I *knew* the video would do the trick."

Randy tsked and shook his head. "Are you ever going to learn how to stay out of other people's business?"

"No. I'm about to become a mother. It's part of the job."

"One of these days you're going to get yourself in trouble." He gave her one of those disapproving frowns that always made her hot instead of anxious. "Someday you might be punished for your nosiness."

"Stop getting me turned on," she said with a disgruntled huff. "You know it's going to be weeks and weeks before we can even get back to the basics, never mind the whips and black leather."

Randy laughed deeply, aware she was teasing. He'd never in a million years do anything that might hurt her, and they both knew it. Even if she asked him to. Which, frankly, she never would. Despite her saucy words, Sue wasn't into pain, which really should have made her feel better about the whole avoiding labor thing. But it didn't. She was still very unhappy about it.

"Will you hold me?" she asked softly, needing his touch. Since she'd been ordered to bed, her husband had been sleeping on a cot a few feet away and she missed him dreadfully.

Carefully scooting closer, Randy slid one arm behind her back to cuddle her. As if aware of his presence, the baby gave a good strong kick. Sue not only felt it, she could see it. So, apparently, could Randy. "I think he's saying, 'Send down that pizza.'"

"Or 'Go, Auntie Noelle!'"

Sighing even as he pressed a gentle kiss on her temple, Randy said, "Would you like me to go get you some ginger ale to go with your dinner?"

Thinking it over, Sue pursed her lips and shook her head. "Nuh-uh. I think I want some…grapefruit juice."

He was too accustomed to her cravings to react with so much as a bat of an eye. "Uh, don't have any, babe. I'm going to have to make a run to the supermarket. Or else ask your mother to."

She curled both her arms around one of his. "My mother's not here. She went over to Marnie Miller's house for dinner."

"Hope they hid the tea caddy."

Sue snickered.

"I'll be back in a few minutes. You'll be okay that long, won't you?"

She didn't let go of his arm. "Don't leave me. Can't you call someone and ask for a favor?" Not even attempting to hide the mischief in her voice, she continued. "Say, doesn't your cousin work part-time at the grocery store during the holidays? Maybe he could swing by with some juice on his way home."

"Su-ue…" he said, drawing out her name like Ricky saying, "Lu-cy."

She said nothing, just staring unblinking into her husband's eyes with a silent plea. Until Randy started to grin, then to chuckle. "What the hell, Jeremy always was an asshole, even before he screwed up Noelle's life last year."

Throwing her arms around her husband's neck, Sue gave him a big kiss. "Have I told you today how much I love you?"

He nodded. "Right in between when you told me you were never having sex with me again because of your stretch marks, and the time you said if I even thought about looking at another woman while you're laid up, you'd crush my head with the plaster snowman on the front porch."

Holding him close, she breathed in his familiar scent, tasted his warmth and his kindness, feeling his love for her roll off the man in waves. That love, and the love she felt for him in return, had been the foundation of her entire adult life. "I do, you know. I love you so much." Lowering her voice, she took his hand and pulled it to her belly, to feel as the baby rolled over beneath her skin. "And we're going to be so happy with our beautiful little gold medalist."

Randy nodded and kissed her eyelids, delicately stroking her stomach. "Yes, honey. I know we are."

NOELLE HAD SPENT A LOT of quiet time with Mark Santori since the day they'd met, in varying situations. Some sexual, some not. But this was, she believed, the first time they'd simply sat together in utter silence, holding hands in the dark.

While waiting for the three pizzas they'd ordered—wanting to be sure Sue had enough to last her—they'd spent a half-hour socializing with Mark's family. The entire group had welcomed Noelle into the fold, each brother or sister-in-law who'd walked in the door going through the whole introduction stage all over again. Noelle had almost asked Mark's sister, Lottie, a striking young brunette, if she'd ever found the right dress the day after Thanksgiving. But she figured that would open up a whole new conversation, one she wasn't quite ready to have with Mark's mother sitting nearby.

None of the Santoris had been able to hide their surprise that she and Mark were seeing each other, which made her really curious about Mark's romantic past. She sensed there was a story there. Maybe tonight, during their long ride when he couldn't get away or evade her questions, she'd find out more.

Though she knew he'd been worried, she really liked his family. The Santoris were like something out of a TV sitcom. Or a wacky reality show. They'd all—she hoped—liked her, too.

One thing was sure—everybody in that family felt free to say exactly what they were thinking and ask nosy questions. She'd been asked so many times how she liked children that when Lottie voiced the query, Noelle had been unable to stop herself from muttering, "Medium rare."

Lottie snorted some huge belly laughs that drew the attention of everyone in the place. "I like this one," she'd said to Mark. "Don't let her get away."

Don't let her get away.

How nice it was to imagine, for a moment at least, that she and Mark really did have something he'd fight to hold on to. That the warm way she'd been welcomed into the family fold tonight had been indicative of a real relationship, something solid and tangible and real.

But they didn't have that, not really. Deep down, even when she'd been going on romantic dates with him, she'd been constantly reminding herself that this was only temporary. She and Mark were in it for the short term, not the long one, because Noelle was nowhere near ready to risk her heart for anything more. Not when she knew, deep down, that she just didn't have that lucky forever-love gene, any more than her mother had. And she'd be a fool to forget it.

"What are you thinking about over there?" Mark asked after they'd ridden silently for an hour.

"About your family."

"Sorry about that," he said, shifting uncomfortably in the driver's seat of his large car.

"I liked them." Then, remembering what had happened when Lucas and his pretty blond wife, Rachel, had arrived, added, "I can't believe how generous they've all been. Do you know how much that check your brother wrote to the shelter was made out for? Just between the donations from your family's restaurant and what I was promised at the party the other night, we might be able to salvage Give A Kid A Christmas after all."

Maybe her vacation, too.

For some reason, the thought didn't make her smile the way it would have two weeks ago. Because suddenly the idea of jetting off to the Caribbean all by herself on Christmas Day didn't sound nearly as appealing as sitting next to Mark in a booth at his loud family restaurant. As for finding a handsome guy on the beach? Well…she knew without a doubt that she'd be comparing any half-naked beach gigolo with the fully clothed gorgeous hunk of man sitting next to her in the car.

"I'm really glad," he said. "Whatever Lucas donated, I'm sure he can afford it. Plus, I know there'll be more—Rachel went to the back room as we were leaving to get a mayonnaise jar for her bridal shop, which is right up the street."

Noelle merely shook her head, still stunned by the generosity of these people who were basically strangers to her, and to the kids at the shelter.

"By the way, my brother Joe asked me to find out if the house is going to be empty at any time on Christmas Eve. Are you doing anything with the families that day?"

"Why?"

Mark glanced at her, his eyes glittering a dark jade under the headlights of an oncoming car. "He's going to bring a crew of his guys out to build a big jungle gym in the back yard. With a half-dozen of them, they can knock it out in an hour."

"You're kidding me!"

"Oh, it's true. Joe's been in construction since right out of high school. He sponsored a Habitat for Humanity house a year or so ago and got that sucker built from foundation to curtains in nine days."

Noelle shook her head at yet another example of the goodness of people—strangers—who'd seen something bad and gone out of their way to try to make it good. "How can you hate Christmas with a family as wonderful and generous as yours?"

He shrugged. "In my line of work, I don't often see a lot of evidence of the holiday spirit in December." Then he posed a question of his own. "How can *you* hate Christmas when you so obviously love children, and you're so good with them?"

She didn't answer for a moment, wondering how to respond without sounding silly. Wondering which reason, of all the ones she'd told herself about why she hated the holidays, wouldn't seem petty and childish?

It wasn't hard to answer—there was really only one. There always had been. "My father left at Christmastime," she admitted. "I haven't seen him since."

He sat up a little straighter. "I didn't know."

"I was nine. And after that, well, my mother didn't exactly look forward to the month of December."

"Must have been hell living where you lived."

She couldn't prevent a humorless laugh. "You've no idea. I think she was determined to stay in Christmas as some kind of self-inflicted punishment for the failure of her marriage."

His voice low, he said, "Or maybe she just wanted to stay where she'd once been happy."

Yeah, she supposed that was possible, too. Sometime in recent years, Noelle had begun to understand her mother's behavior, and the decisions she'd made. They even got along well now…from a distance.

"Anyway," she continued, "up until that point, I'd always considered Christmas *my* holiday, since my birthday's Christmas Eve."

He glanced over in surprise. "Really? So you've got one coming up soon."

She nodded. "Yes. And even though I always complained about having to share my big day with the lamb of God," she added dryly, "I always secretly loved it. It made me feel extra special. Like Christmas—the holiday and the town—were all celebrating me every year, too."

He was quiet for a moment, obviously thinking it over.

Mark quickly understood, coming to the correct conclusion. "Until *that* year. When Christmas became about loss and heartache, your mother's sadness and your own sense of hurt and abandonment."

Noelle shouldn't have been surprised at how quickly he'd figured her out. She knew the man was incredibly intuitive. Still, the warm concern in his voice soothed her, surprised her. Comforted her. "Yes."

He wasn't finished. "And because you'd wrapped yourself in with the whole Christmas experience, let me take a wild guess and say deep down, you somehow blamed yourself for your father leaving?"

This time, Noelle wasn't just surprised at Mark's perceptiveness—she was outright shocked. Her breath caught in her throat and she stared at him, wondering if the man had somehow opened a window into her psyche and glimpsed a part of Noelle that she'd never *ever* shown to the world. "How did you…"

"It's not unusual for the kids to blame themselves," he explained.

Noelle knew that. In her job, she saw it all the time, and she understood it. *Now.* As for then? Well… "I was too young to really understand."

"Of course you were. But not too young to avoid grabbing the blame and heaping it on your own head when you were just a kid caught in a bad situation."

Noelle sat quietly for a long moment, letting Mark's assessment sink in. He'd said aloud something she'd never admitted, even to herself, despite having lots of experience with kids from broken homes. She'd just never put it that baldly before in reference to her own life.

Bringing her hand to his mouth, he pressed a gentle kiss

on her fingers. "You were a little girl, sweetheart. And you know now why you felt the way you did about Christmas."

"Sure." She nodded, letting her hand, still enclosed in Mark's, drop to his powerful leg.

With a grunt he said, "Which is why it bites that you let the dickless wonder you almost married screw the holiday up for you even more."

Noelle couldn't prevent a gurgle of laughter at Mark's vivid description and disgusted tone. "I guess I don't need to tell you much about that situation. Sue obviously filled you in enough for you to get a good picture of my ex and how I reacted to what happened."

He didn't look over. "She told me the basics." Then, squeezing her hand in his lap, he added, "The rest I've figured out for myself, learning a little more about what makes you tick every time we've been together."

The way he said it made Noelle suspect he really did know her, very well. Maybe better than anyone else. Which made her even more anxious to know about him. Shifting sideways, facing him in the near darkness, she murmured, "So tell me why your family is so surprised to see you with a woman. You've got a nasty bump in your romantic track record too, don't you."

He nodded. "Yeah. I was engaged once, about five years ago, and it ended pretty badly." He didn't elaborate, leaving her to wonder if he, too, had been the victim of a faithless fiancée. How ironic if their stories were so similar.

"Hey, you asked my cousin about me," she said when he fell silent. "If you don't fill me in, I might just have to go to the family. Maybe Lottie."

Groaning, Mark turned his head to glare at her. "Don't even *think* about it." His tone sounded more horrified than angry, and Noelle couldn't help laughing. Obviously his sister was the person to approach if she ever needed the dirt on anything.

"You might as well just get it over with and tell me."

He again tried to refuse. "You don't want to know this."

She stroked his fingers gently. "Yes, I really do. You once loved someone enough to propose marriage and I'd like to know what she did to make you swear off relationships for five years."

With a deep sigh, he admitted, "She turned out to be a thief."

She sucked in a surprised breath.

"And she drew a line in the sand, saying if I truly loved her, I had to betray my principles and become someone I wasn't in order to cover for her."

Noelle was momentarily shocked into silence, almost regretting prodding him so hard. This had been a lot worse than a cheating tramp of an ex who'd broken his heart. She'd actually tried to break his *spirit,* to turn this proud, honest man into someone else, simply to suit her own purposes.

"I hate her."

He laughed softly. But before he could respond, they reached their destination, and Noelle realized the conversation was better dropped, anyway. She honestly didn't want to know any more about the bitch who'd had Mark's heart and had crushed it between her thieving hands.

Pulling into town, Noelle couldn't help smiling in delight, remembering, suddenly, what this place looked like at night as its namesake holiday drew ever nearer. Darkness having descended completely, the town had put on all her holiday finery. Christmas, Illinois, was lit up like the proverbial Christmas tree. Clean and bright, the whole place washed away the darkness of their previous conversation.

Each house outlined with lights, the streets were something out of a holiday movie. Santas and reindeer perched on roofs and nutcrackers stood guard on porches. There were toy workshops and elves, and a living nativity standing sentry outside a local church. They'd be there every night until the twenty-fourth, she had no doubt.

"Wow," Mark murmured, looking around wide-eyed as they drove through the heavy traffic clogging the streets. There were always a lot of out-of-town visitors coming through at this time of year.

"It is pretty, in a Clark Griswald kind of way," she said with a smile of rueful amusement.

"I need to get Tony and Gloria to bring my nephews out here," he murmured. "It's like a holiday fantasyland." He sounded admiring, not jaded. In his wide eyes, twinkling under the lights of the garland strung every ten feet across the main street through town, Noelle caught a glimpse of the little boy who'd once loved Christmas enough to take the blame for his sister's schoolyard fight.

"So," she said softly, "maybe there are one or two things you like about Christmas, after all?"

His gaze shifted over. "The holiday or the town?"

"Both," she said with a laugh.

"Yeah," he said, joining her in her laughter. "I guess there are."

WHEN THEY'D ARRIVED at the Candy Cane Inn, Mark had enjoyed the hour of conversation with Randy and Sue. For a pregnant woman, Noelle's cousin could put away a whole lot of pizza. It was a good thing they'd brought three pies, because she'd wanted to sample each kind. He just hoped the baby liked pepperoni, green pepper and mushrooms.

Yeah, it'd been a nice, quiet evening. At least, until Noelle's ex had shown up.

"I still can't believe you were engaged to that guy," he said as they sat in Sue's bedroom, a few minutes after Randy had left to escort his cousin Jeremy to the door.

Meeting the other man had been something of a shock, but not one that had given Mark a moment's concern. Because Noelle's ex was absolutely nothing to be threatened by.

Jeremy Taggert was probably considered good looking by female standards, with his sandy-colored hair and boyish face. But he was a skinny-ass loser as far as Mark was concerned.

"Me, either," Sue said, her mouth full of pizza. She swilled it down with a big sip of grapefruit juice. "That's what I call a lucky escape." Then she giggled. "Did you see his face? I wanted to jump out of this bed and kiss you when you put your arm around Noelle," she told Mark.

Noelle was quiet, still sitting on a chair beside Sue's bed, as she had throughout the brief visit of the man she'd been set to marry one year ago. Mark had kept a close eye on her for the excruciating five minutes of the visit. She'd done a good job of playing the cool, completely recovered ex-girl-friend. But when Mark had seen the way her hands were clenched tightly in her lap, he'd known she wasn't. So he'd moved closer, sitting on the arm of the chair and dropping his arm across her shoulders.

Her ex hadn't liked it. Which had made Mark drop a kiss on the top of Noelle's head and rub lazy, possessive circles on her upper arm.

At that point, he'd seriously thought the other guy's eyes were gonna bug clear out of his head.

"He looks like a teenager," Mark muttered. "Too young to even have hair on his balls."

Sue snorted, as did her husband, who'd just returned to the room. Noelle was the only one who remained silent.

"What'd you say he does again? Grocery store clerk?"

Randy explained, "He's actually in the family business, working for my uncle Ralph at his car dealership and helping to run the Santa school, which is open from September to December." The other man shrugged. "This year business wasn't so great at either place so Jeremy had to get a job part-time at the supermarket."

The Santa school. The very school he'd been looking into last weekend. The coincidence didn't escape him. "You said the school is a family business?"

Randy nodded. "Yeah, my grandfather started it as a gag but it really got popular."

"Randy worked there, too, until we got married and took over the inn together," said Sue.

Maybe it was just his dislike of Jeremy Taggert, but something made Mark anxious to learn more. The Santa crime spree investigation was going nowhere else fast and he was damned if he wanted any more kids robbed if there was anything he could do to prevent it. "Do you mind giving me your uncle's name and phone number?" he asked. "He might be able to help me with something I'm working on back in the city."

Randy nodded. "Of course! I have a bunch of brochures right downstairs that you can take with you, and Uncle Ralph's contact information is right on it." Then, looking curious he asked, "Are you hosting some kind of holiday event at your family restaurant? Looking for a reference for one of our students?"

He shook his head. "Not exactly." But he didn't elaborate. Randy might not be actively involved in the business now, but he had been. And it was still run by his family.

No, he didn't seriously think Randy could be involved in anything illegal coming out of that school. But he'd learned his lesson long ago about playing things close to his chest when it came to his job.

Looking down at Noelle, he realized he hadn't been following that advice when it came to his personal life. Because there was no doubt in his mind that he was falling for the woman. Falling hard.

The desire to follow Jeremy Taggert and unload on him for what he'd done to Noelle warred with his desire to see what was making her frown in thought like she was. "You okay?" he asked, his hand still on her shoulder. Though he couldn't imagine that Noelle would mourn the loss of the dork who'd just left, she did seem awfully quiet.

Not answering his question, she instead addressed one to her cousin. "You set that up, didn't you?"

Sue's face pinkened.

"You had him come over here to bump into me on purpose." Noelle's voice wasn't angry, merely quietly curious. Analytical.

"Well, he deserves to remember what he lost."

Sue sounded so self-righteous and unapologetic, obviously still furious about what Jeremy the jerk had done. Noelle didn't appear upset at all, just very deep in thought. As if Jeremy's arrival had set some wheels turning in her brain. He only wished he knew what kind of wild thoughts they were spinning.

During the drive back to Chicago later that night, he tried to think of a way to find out. They'd left Christmas at around ten. Traffic had been even heavier than it was two hours ago. Each car they passed was loaded with indulgent-looking parents and bouncing children, some probably already wearing their pajamas under their heavy coats, just like he and his siblings used to do. And just like them, these kids were filling their eyes and imaginations with all Christmas had to offer.

Eventually, after they made it past the very last set of lights to the highway and were cruising toward home, he quietly asked, "You okay?"

"Sure. Why wouldn't I be?"

That same distracted tone. It bugged him, mainly because he felt a distance between them, which had not been there on their drive earlier tonight. "Did seeing *him* upset you?"

"Not in the way you might think."

"Well, in what way then?"

She turned a tiny bit toward her own window, her body language telling him a lot more than he really wanted to know.

Like, maybe she still cared for the prick who'd dumped her. His whole body stiff, he muttered, "Don't tell me you still have feelings for him."

That seemed to surprise her. She immediately shook her head. "No. None. Absolutely zero. I can't believe I ever mistook that boyish face to mean he was someone with integrity and a good heart." Her tone completely unfaltering, she added, "He's a creep and a loser."

"Glad we got that settled. And for what it's worth, I agree. Creep, loser, asswipe, whatever you want to call him. The guy's shifty and not worth another minute or your time."

He'd meant to make her laugh, or at least smile. Instead, Noelle settled deeper into her seat, drawing her arms across her chest. Rubbing her hands up and down her arms as if to ward off the cold, she murmured, "I thoroughly agree. I must have been out of my mind to think I loved him."

Mark reached for the heater switch, though the car was comfortably warm in his opinion. He was thinking about her words, and the soft, mournful tone in which she'd said them, but before he could ask her about it, his cell phone ring, distracting him. His brother Tony was calling to ask him if he needed a key to the back door of the restaurant, so he could return the insulated pizza bags they'd used to make their long distance delivery. The restaurant closed at eleven, and it was likely to be dark and locked up by the time they arrived.

As he was finishing his call, Mark saw their exit. Pulling off the highway, he headed downtown, noting the decorated homes along the way. Definitely not up to Christmas standards, but in a city as big as Chicago, it was nice to see evidence of the same holiday spirit.

A short time later, when they were parked in the alley behind Santori's, next to Noelle's car—which he'd had her move earlier—he remembered her words. "So what'd you mean a little while ago, about being out of your mind to think you loved Jeremy the jackass?"

Noelle didn't answer. Instead, to his complete surprise, she shifted in her seat and leaned across the console. Cupping his cheek in her hand, she tangled her fingers in his hair and tugged him close, whispering, "Kiss me, Mark."

Their mouths met and opened, heat snapping in the wet mating of their tongues, just as it always did. He instantly hardened with want for her, want he'd been suppressing for five long days, since the party Saturday night.

"I need you," she muttered between choppy breaths when the kiss ended.

"I know the feeling." He was about to ask her whether she wanted him to follow her or just wanted to go home in his car when Noelle climbed across the seat onto his lap. "What…"

"Shh," she said, wrapping her arms around his neck to kiss him again. She tilted her head, thrusting her tongue into his mouth with almost desperate hunger. Mark shifted in his seat, making room for her, and Noelle responded by sliding one leg across his legs so she could straddle him.

Groaning in tormented pleasure when the heated V of her thighs came in contact with his rock-hard erection, he tangled his hands in her hair for another mind-numbing kiss. She was hot and wanton in his arms, and they quickly steamed up the car windows. Noelle twisted and writhed, rubbing against him, making desperate little sounds of hunger. Tugging his thick cotton shirt out of his waistband, she moved her hands over his stomach, trailing fire on his skin. Then she reached for his belt.

"Noelle, honey, wait," he whispered, drawing on some previously undiscovered well of control. "Let's get out of here and go someplace more private."

"No." She started unbuckling, not even looking at him. "I want it here. Now."

Now. In the alley behind his family-owned restaurant. If that wasn't bad enough, they were inside a car which was moderately comfortable for driving, but not at all sufficient for the kind of lovemaking he wanted to share with this woman.

He covered her hands with his. "My place is close." Pressing a soft kiss on her cheek, he breathed deeply, inhaling her hair. "We have all night."

"I don't want all night," she said, her voice thick and shaking. "I want now. Just this, right now. Do it to me, Mark. Take me."

The desperate tone in Noelle's voice suddenly pierced through the haze of lazy lust that had been clouding his mind. Because despite her frenzy and her words, she didn't sound aroused and hungry. She sounded almost…desperate. Her demands, which had thrilled him their first day at the inn, suddenly sounded less about passion and secret longings and more about anxiety.

"Noelle, I'm not going to have sex with you on a freezing-cold night in a car on a dark street. Let's go home and I'll love you all night long."

She stiffened, simply staring at him. Her mouth opened, then closed, as if she had something to say but couldn't make herself say it. Finally she squared her shoulders. "I don't want love all night long from you. I want sex. Remember? Hot, wicked and erotic, with no repercussions." She paused before adding, "No blame, no expectations. No morning after."

He stared at her in disbelief, wondering what the hell she was talking about. This wasn't the same woman he'd held hands with earlier this evening, the woman who'd socialized with his family and charmed them all. She couldn't be the Noelle who'd shared her memories of childhood heartbreak in this very car a few hours ago. This wasn't even, he suspected, the hungry woman who'd given herself over to all her erotic fantasies at the Candy Cane Inn.

No, this was a desperate, anxious woman who seemed determined to return their relationship to the place they'd started. He just had no idea why.

Wondering what was driving this sudden reversal, he opened his mouth to ask her, but suddenly a sliver of light cast a long thin line of illumination on the ground. The back door of the restaurant was opening. His father appeared there, carrying a bulging bag of trash. Noelle dove to the other side of the car, even as Mark shifted around, thanking God his hard-on was at least contained by his straining zipper. "I thought everybody was gone," he muttered tightly.

Spying them in the car, Pop waved. Mark reached for the door handle, to go help the old man, saying, "I'll be right back and we can finish our conversation."

But as he stepped into the cold night and took the heavy trash bags out of his father's hands, he saw the passenger door of his car open. Noelle got out. "Thanks for your help tonight," she said, focusing only on Mark's father. "My cousin adored your pizza."

"Your cousin, she has good taste!" the old man said with a big smile. "Like my son."

Noelle didn't respond to his father's broad hint. Finally, she turned her lovely face toward Mark. Their stares met and held for a long, silent moment. He remained very still, asking dozens of questions, receiving absolutely no answers. None that made any sense, anyway.

Then, without a word, Noelle walked over to her own car, got in it and drove away.

11

NOELLE WAS in very serious trouble. She'd made a huge, enormous mistake, probably the biggest one in her entire life. The kind that was going to haunt her for a long, long time, unless she corrected the situation immediately.

Unfortunately, she didn't believe there was a way to fix the situation. How could she fix the longing, the ache in her heart? Because she'd done the unthinkable. She'd fallen in love with Mark Santori.

Over the next couple of days while she'd focused on the shopping, planning, wrapping and baking for the Give A Kid A Christmas program, she also screamed at herself for being such a complete fool. After all the talks she'd given herself, all the justifications and warnings, she'd somehow let her heart slip away.

She'd realized it when Jeremy had shown up at the inn the other night. Until that time, she'd been able to fool herself that what she felt for Mark was simply intoxicating lust. But when she saw her ex, the man she'd been set to marry, standing there with her lover, she'd been forced to confront the truth.

While sitting there staring impassively at the face she'd once thought she loved, she'd been comparing her old feelings to the ones she had for Mark. It was like comparing a child's Etch-a-Sketch to the Mona Lisa. And suddenly she'd understood. Her feelings had washed over her in a sudden rush, literally making her shake where she sat. Because Jeremy had made her feel nothing compared to the *everything* she felt when she was with Mark.

And oh, God, if there had ever been a moment that had left her feeling completely out of her depth, vulnerable and utterly exposed, it was that one. When she'd looked at the worthless man who'd betrayed her and hurt her so badly—even when, looking back, she knew she hadn't truly loved him—she'd felt terror roll through her. Because the sadness she'd felt at losing Jeremy was *nothing* next to what would happen to her the day Mark realized she wasn't enough for him. Whether he came to that realization first, or simply admitted that he wasn't going to allow himself to even try to love her because of his painful past, she was the one who was going to be crushed.

Panic. Pure, undiluted terror had made her sit there silently in Sue's bedroom while the world continued on around her, oblivious to her epiphany.

The feeling had set in throughout the long ride back to the city, and with every passing mile, she'd grown more and more terrified of what she'd done. Falling in love was not supposed to happen. She'd just wanted a fling, not to open up her heart and let somebody throw rocks at it again.

Which was why she'd been so stupid, so *awful,* when they'd arrived back at the restaurant. She still wondered how she'd ever have the nerve to face him after the way she'd behaved in his car.

So far, she hadn't had to. She'd ignored his calls and when he'd come by the shelter Saturday, she'd had Alice tell him she wasn't around. Even though she was avoiding him, the man had still handed Alice an envelope bulging with donations from the restaurant, and from Rachel's bridal shop. Alice had had joyful tears in her eyes when she'd handed it over to Noelle.

What an incredible, wonderful, loveable, sexy man.

And she had to shove him away, to save herself from even more heartache in the future.

"Sometimes life really sucks," she whispered in the stillness of her bare, undecorated apartment Sunday night. She looked around, wondering why she suddenly had a longing for the smell of evergreen. She'd been so sure she wouldn't miss Christmas that she'd mentally removed it from her to do list. Yet here it was, one week away, and she was wishing she could find the comfort of some pretty lights or tinsel, if only to escape the ugly mess she'd made of her life.

"You're going to have to face him eventually," she whispered. She just needed to pull her thoughts together enough to prepare for it. Somehow, Noelle would have to explain her way out of this without letting Mark know she'd fallen so hard for him.

It wasn't that he'd intentionally hurt her. She knew that, just as she knew he'd do anything to protect the kids in her care, or to stop a criminal. It was his nature to be a caretaker.

But love was a different matter entirely. They were both too closed-off, too self-protective, to even *think* of letting emotion cloud their relationship. Mark had given her only brief details about the heartbreak that had left him cold to romance for the past five years, but given the length of time, it had to have been bad. *Really* bad.

So no, the two of them had absolutely no business letting this physical attraction they shared get all tangled up in emotion. And if he found out she'd already done it, he'd either feel obligated to try to care for her in return, or he'd run for the hills. Either way didn't bode well for Noelle.

All that was firmly settled in her mind as she changed into a pair of warm sweats and fuzzy socks, figuring she'd down her sorrows in popcorn and a Christmas movie. Tomorrow, she'd call him and ask him to meet her for lunch. She'd make light of what had happened in his car, thank him for the great time, and let him know she intended to move on.

Thank God she had a physical escape to look forward to in another week. To her great happiness, they had managed to replace all the money that had been stolen a few weeks ago, and then some. Meaning Noelle wouldn't have to lose out on the nonrefundable hotel deposit or hand over the money she had saved to pay for her expenses in St. Lucia.

Late on Christmas Day, she was flying south. Not to hook up with a sexy stranger, but to recover emotionally from the incredible man she'd so foolishly fallen for already.

Opening the popcorn package, she was startled by a knock on the door of her apartment. She glanced at the clock and saw it was after nine. A tiny frisson of tension shot through her, considering she didn't have any friends in the building and had no idea who'd be stopping by this late on a Sunday evening.

Going to the door, she looked through the peephole and was shocked to see Mark standing in the hall. "Oh, God," she whispered.

He knocked again. "Noelle, come on, I saw your car in the parking lot. Let me in, I need to give you something."

Hmm, she could think of something she'd like the man to give her. A very big something. *Forget it. That's over with!*

Swallowing hard, she unlocked the door and slowly swung it open. "Hi," she said, wishing her heart would stop cartwheeling in her chest over how damned sexy he was. He looked, as always, incredible. Wearing his soft leather jacket and some faded jeans, he was unshaven, his hair windblown. Warmth trickled through Noelle's body, settling between her legs, just at the sight of him.

"Can I come in?"

Stepping out of the way on somewhat wobbly legs, she ushered him into the apartment. He looked around while she shut the door behind them. "I like your place."

"Thanks." Clearing her throat, she added, "You have something for me?"

Mark lifted his hand, in which he held a tissue-wrapped package. "Yeah. Another thank you gift from your cousin Sue. She slipped it to me the other night and I forgot to give it to you on the way home."

Noelle felt heat rise in her face, remembering exactly what Sue had given her the last time. God, if Mark ever found out he was hand-delivering X-rated videos, Noelle was going to die.

She took the package and hugged it close to her chest.

"Aren't you going to open it?"

"Nuh-uh." Her cheeks were flaming—she just knew it.

Mark finally seemed to notice. Stepping closer, he tilted his head and stared at her. "What's wrong?"

Noelle took a tiny step back. "Nothing, nothing at all. Sue's just got a crazy sense of humor. I can only imagine what's in here."

His lips parted, as if he was about to press the matter, but he finally let it go. She almost wished he'd pressed her on it because his next question was even more uncomfortable. "So, why have you been avoiding me?"

Noelle walked past him into the living area of her apartment, stuffing the lumpy package into the oversized front pouch of her hooded sweatshirt. "Avoiding you?"

Following her, Mark caught her arm and made her turn around to face him. "Don't deny it. You've been avoiding me even though you know you and I have some unfinished business." Through half-lowered eyes, he raked a slow, thorough glance over her, from the top of her head to her fuzzy-covered feet. And suddenly even before her mind had caught up, her body figured out exactly what kind of business he meant.

Her heart stopped cartwheeling and began to do flips instead. "Mark..."

"You said you wanted me," he murmured, reaching up and stroking the fleshy pad of his thumb across her bottom lip. His voice was low, intense, throaty. "You begged me to do it to you, Noelle. No strings. No repercussions. I know you want me to take you places you've never been."

She was breathing in short, raspy gasps, stunned by his intensity, by the almost dangerous look on his face.

"Are you denying it?" he asked in a silky whisper, stepping closer.

Crowded by the sofa behind her, Noelle couldn't move away. They were only an inch apart, close enough to feel the heat and sense the electric passion surging up between them, just as it always did. "I'm not denying it."

He smiled lazily. A slow, wicked smile. Saying nothing, he unzipped his jacket and tossed it away, as if the decision had already been made. His words confirmed it. "Where's your bedroom?"

Gulping, she thought for one split second about the choice she had to make. Despite everything she'd told herself earlier about why she needed to stop seeing Mark, there was absolutely no way she could stop desiring him. And now he was offering her what she'd wanted: a night of erotic delight, without any expectations or promises.

It could only be one night. Her heart couldn't take the battering of drawing this out any longer. So she only had a few hours to build up some amazing memories that would last her whole life. She'd be absolutely crazy to refuse.

Mark moved closer, eliminating that tiny bit of space between them. When he slid a hand in her hair to tug her to him for a deep, wet kiss, she *knew* she wasn't going to refuse. The excitement sending her blood roaring through her veins wouldn't allow her to. Neither would her heart, which wanted him despite her certainty that they could never make it work. That either she would never be enough for him in the long-term, or else he'd never be able to completely let her past his self-protective wall that had kept him single for five long years.

But for now—right now—she wanted him heart, body and soul. So Noelle gave up all pretense of resistance, even in her own mind. Pressing hard against his body, she gave him her answer.

His slow, devouring kiss matched his mood…quiet, deliberate, oh-so-sensuous. Noelle met the slow, lazy thrusts of his sweet tongue, even as she rubbed her cheek against his rough hand. She wanted that roughness on other parts of her body. "Through there," she whispered against his lips, nodding toward her closed bedroom door.

He bent and picked her up, easily carrying her across the living room. It was the first time any man had ever picked her up like this. Somehow, whenever Noelle had fantasized about being swept off her feet by a man—*literally*—she'd imagined a lovely, romantic, old-fashioned gesture.

This was hot. Mind-blowingly sexy. Rhett carrying Scarlett up the stairs, not about to take no for an answer.

Which was when she fully appreciated what was happening here. Mark wasn't seducing her to her room, he was *taking* her, his every stride revealing his determination and his hunger.

Whatever moisture was left in her body descended with a rush between her legs. She was dying for him, on fire, ready to take and have and grasp and devour.

Dropping her onto her bed, he didn't follow her down immediately. Instead, he tugged his Chicago Bulls sweatshirt off and stood before her, his massive chest making her breath catch in her throat as always.

"I want to see you," he said. Reaching for her shirt, he began tugging it up, but it got twisted over the package Noelle had stuck into the front packet. Quickly reaching for it, Noelle yanked it out and prepared to toss it away. But Mark caught her wrist in his hand and wouldn't let her. "What is that?"

She swallowed hard. "I...I don't know."

He watched her closely, a cop's stare that said he knew she was lying. "What is it, Noelle?"

Nibbling on her bottom lip, she admitted, "I really am not sure. But, uh, last time, that other package you delivered?"

"Yes?"

Her voice dropping to a whisper she said, "It was a dirty movie."

Mark's eyes glowed as he stared directly at her, still holding her wrist. "Open it."

Again, he wasn't asking, he wasn't seducing. He was demanding. Every word he said, every move he made reinforced the delicious strength he usually kept masked. Mark was in an intoxicating, demanding, sexual mood and he wasn't going to be denied any little thing he wanted.

He let her go so she could open the package. Holding her breath, she sent up a silent prayer that Sue had given her a nice wallet or, maybe an ice cream scoop, since the thing felt as if it had a thick round handle.

Tearing off the paper, she stared at her gift. It was *not* an ice cream scoop.

Casting a quick glance at Mark, she saw him watching impassively, his only reaction a slight tightening in his jaw. "Does your cousin think you need that?" he asked, a smile of pure self-assurance widening his lips the tiniest bit, "when you're getting so much...more?"

Laughing nervously, Noelle clutched the flesh-colored sex toy in her lap, making a quick mental assessment that confirmed Mark's words. "Up until recently, I wasn't getting it at all."

He nodded.

"So I d-definitely don't need this tonight," she stammered, about to toss the dildo away. She wasn't throwing it in the trash, because after tonight, she might very well have use for it.

"Hold on to it."

Noelle gasped.

"And show me the movie she sent you."

Her jaw dropping open, she couldn't prevent a quick glance toward her bedside table. Mark noticed, of course. Opening the drawer, he dug around inside until he retrieved the video case. He barely spared a glance for the lurid photo on the cover, simply popping it open and dropping the tape into his hand. Then he walked over to her TV stand, where she had a small color TV/VCR combo.

"What are you…"

"You wanted it wild and daring, didn't you?" he asked, casting her a challenging look over her shoulder. "Tell me, have you ever done anything like this?"

Almost mesmerized, she shook her head.

"But you want to. Don't you, Noelle?"

After a split second of hesitation, she nodded, her mouth going dry and her whole body trembling. Because she *did*. She wanted everything and anything she'd ever dreamed about having, all in one night. With him.

Mark thrust the tape into the machine and punched the play button, then turned to face her. She didn't even glance at the TV screen, totally focused on the thick, hungry man walking toward her. His steps were slow. Deliberate. And they never faltered, not even when he reached for his belt, unfastened it, then unbuttoned his jeans, pushing them down to ride low on his hips. The darkened bedroom was suddenly illuminated by the flicker of light from the TV as the movie started, and a soundtrack with a heavy bass beat broke the silence. Reaching for the remote, Noelle turned it down until it became mere background noise. She wanted no distractions, no sounds of pleasure but the ones she and Mark made themselves.

She didn't, however, turn off the television.

Still never breaking their stare, Mark kicked off his shoes, then pushed his jeans all the way down and removed the rest of his clothes. Standing by the bed, just a foot away, he stared down at her, all big, masculine and fully erect, until Noelle wanted to cry at how beautiful he was.

She reached for him, wanting to touch his hot skin, but again, he caught her wrist. Sliding his fingers down her arms, he pulled her now-untangled sweatshirt off. She wore nothing underneath, and the cool air in the bedroom instantly brought goosebumps to her flesh. Before she could even react to them, Mark was warming her. She cried out as, in one move, he tossed her shirt away, then bent to cover her tight nipple with his mouth.

"Oh, yes," she cried, tangling her fingers in his hair.

He sucked one breast, then the other, as he pulled her sweatpants and panties down over her hips and bottom, taking her fuzzy socks with them. Noelle kicked the clothes away, wanting absolutely nothing separating their bodies.

Kissing and licking a path up her throat, he finally kissed her again, his tongue plunging deep. Then he shocked her, dropping his hand between her legs and thrusting two fingers into her drenched body, taking her completely by surprise.

"You're dripping," he growled, drawing his fingers out as he flicked her clit with his thumb.

"Yes."

Part of her expected Mark to climb right on top of her and dive in now, with no further buildup, and she was dying for him to. But he suddenly moved away, just out of reach, and sat down on the bed behind her. When she tried to turn around, he put his hand on her shoulder and held her still, kissing and nipping the nape of her neck. "Don't turn around."

She did as he ordered, remaining upright on the bed as he pushed her toward the end of it, following her. When her feet dangled off the edge and touched the floor, Mark parted his legs around hers and tucked in close behind her, their bodies pressed tight. She felt his huge erection rubbing the small of her back and was unable to resist pressing her bottom a little harder against his groin. This position was, indeed, one she'd fantasized about, though, in her fantasies, they hadn't been sitting up. They'd been, in fact, kneeling.

She wriggled again as more heat sluiced through her until she was certain she'd dampened her bedspread.

"Part your legs for me," he growled against her shoulder. When she hesitated for a second, he sucked a bit of her skin into his mouth and nibbled it, causing a tiny, delicious flash of dangerous sensation. She shifted her legs a few inches.

That didn't seem to satisfy him. Dropping one hand down the front of her body in a long, deliberate stroke that left her breathless, he brushed the side of his hand against her dark curls, but didn't touch her more intimately. "More. Open wide for me, Noelle." His tone told her he wouldn't proceed until she obeyed him.

Doing as he'd asked, she shifted her legs apart, completely exposing her sex for his exploration, wanting desperately to be explored. Dropping her head back onto his shoulder, she arched toward his hand, craving his touch. Wanting his fingers again.

He didn't give them to her. Instead, he murmured. "Now *look*."

At first she thought he meant to look at the movie. Unable to resist, she lifted her head and opened her eyes, almost too numb with erotic pleasure to grasp what she was seeing. It didn't take long to figure out. She hissed a little as she watched the flickering screen where two men were sharing a busty blonde who moaned in pleasure. "Oh," she whispered, shocked, surprised, knowing she should be turned off but instead feeling wickedly titillated.

A threesome *hadn't* been one of her fantasies, and it still wasn't. That was one part of the wild side Noelle had no intention of crossing over to. But there was something magnetic about *seeing* what was happening, and she couldn't tear her gaze away.

From behind her, Mark continued to stroke her belly and her thighs, watching over her shoulder as the woman in the movie—supposedly a southern belle comforting a couple of Confederate soldiers—was touched, licked and pleasured. And, eventually, driven into by both men at the same time.

"My God," she whispered, repelled but fascinated and completely unable to look away.

At least until Mark whispered, "Interesting. But that wasn't what I meant. Look in the *mirror*."

Turning her head a little, she glanced toward her closed closet door, and found herself staring into the full-length mirror. Mark was watching her, an expression of avarice and need on his handsome face. Her hungry, glazed-over eyes stared back at her, and below was her completely exposed body, legs spread, all her secrets exposed. *Very* exposed.

She tried to move.

Mark, however, wouldn't allow it. "Don't, Noelle. Stay very still." With his hands firmly on her thighs, holding them open so they could both see the gleam of moisture on her sex in the reflection, he continued. "Tonight is about letting go of everything. No inhibitions, no holding back. You wanted mindless eroticism, and you're going to get it."

MARK DIDN'T THINK he'd ever been more aroused in his life than he was as he gazed into the mirror and watched the last of Noelle's inhibitions fall away. After just a moment's hesitation, one last moment of sweet embarrassment, she nodded at him, then dropped her hand to cover his own on her thigh.

"Touch me," she pleaded.

And he would. He planned to. He was going to give her the kind of fantasy night neither one of them had ever thought they'd really have, even if it killed him.

It just might. Because, heaven help him, as much as he planned to savor every sensuous delight he'd ever dreamed of with Noelle tonight, there was a much more detached, intellectual part of him that watched everything and wondered if he was making a mistake.

It had seemed like such a simple plan on the drive over here. Noelle had gotten scared and backed off emotionally— he'd figured that much out. The only avenue she'd left open between them was the physical one. She'd said as much Thursday night.

So he was going to go down that erotic road and drag her down it with him. Then, perhaps, having what she'd said she most wanted, Noelle would realize she wanted more. Like repercussions. Strings. Mornings after. Feelings.

Him.

Just as he wanted her. Because if the past few days had proved anything at all, it was that he truly wanted her in his life, and not just in his bed. He greatly feared she'd already taken up residence in his heart, which he'd been sure would never open up to any woman again.

"I'm melting and burning up and shaking and shivering all at the same time," she whispered in a voice hoarse with need.

"Good. Whatever you do, don't close your eyes."

He certainly didn't intend to. Not when the most beautiful woman he'd ever seen was in his arms, silently begging him to do wicked things with her.

He knew just where to start. Remaining tucked up behind her, with his cock throbbing against the delectable cheeks of her ass, he reached to the side of the bed, where Noelle had dropped her *present*.

"Mark? What are you doing?" she asked, peering at his reflection, obviously unable to see in the shadowy light.

Not answering, he tore open the wrapping covering the sex toy, the crinkle of plastic competing with their heavy breathing and the sultry music oozing from the TV speakers.

When he looked at her reflection, he realized she'd heard the rustlings and correctly interpreted what he'd done. Her breaths were shallow, her mouth trembling with anticipation, and, perhaps, a bit of nervousness.

Moving his hand back to her leg, he flicked the switch on the side of the rubbery sex toy and let it begin to hum against her skin. Noelle flinched in surprise. "It vibrates."

"Mm-hmm."

He moved the thing a few inches down her leg, letting her grow accustomed to the sensation, and to the idea. Feeling some of the tension ease from her body as she settled back against him, Mark brought the phallus up to the tuft of dark curls between her thighs. Running it lightly over them, he heard her hiss and knew exactly when she'd felt the vibration on her pretty pink clit.

Mark knew she wanted more, that she was dying for more. Knowing, however, that the greatest release came after the slowest buildup, he moved the toy away, tracing a light, delicate line along the seam where her thigh met her pelvis.

Needing to touch her, he filled his other hand with her breast, tweaking her nipple, rolling it between his fingers until she squirmed. Kissing her neck, he breathed into her ear, then began moving the dildo again, this time right up the creamy crevice between her swollen lips.

"Oooh," she whispered, still watching every move he made in the mirror. Her senses were overwhelming her, he knew. The sounds from the television, the hum of the device, and their own raging pulses filled his head, too. The feel of him cupping her, stroking her, teasing her with the sex toy…it was all driving her wild. When he inhaled, he caught the scent of their passion. And all the while they watched. Everything. It only remained to taste, and before the night was out, they would be doing that, too, he had no doubt.

Noelle was shifting now, tilting her hips, so Mark turned up the intensity, setting the vibration a little faster. Giving her a lazy smile, he murmured, "I never imagined how much I'd want to see something other than me going into your sweet body."

With a wicked smile of her own, she covered his hand and guided the rubber toy lower, until its tip slid into her. He considered teasing her with it, but his own need was building. He didn't know how much more he was going to be able to take of this erotic playing. Seeing the thing disappear into her wet channel was going to make him want to plunge into her himself. But he couldn't resist doing it, sliding it slowly into her body, watching her reaction as it filled her. Her lips parted as she whimpered, and her hips tilted toward his hand until he could feel her moisture.

"Good?" he growled into her ear as he slowly moved the dildo in and out, watching the pleasure wash over her face.

She nodded, then admitted, "But not as good as you."

That was all he needed to hear. Mark tossed the thing to the bed, tugging her around to face him. He cupped her face in both hands, his fingers tangling in her hair, and covered her lips with his. Exploring the inner recesses of her mouth with his tongue, he began to slide back on the bed, bringing Noelle with him toward the headboard. Never breaking the connection of their lips, he rolled them both over until she was flat on her back beneath him.

She stared up at him, unblinking, unsmiling. "I want you, Mark," she whispered.

And he was absolutely dying for her.

He only wondered if Noelle was even aware of the sweet longing in her tone. There were no wild, raw demands. She didn't lose her inhibitions and beg for the utmost carnality. No, she simply whispered for him, which, without a doubt, inflamed him more than her wild demands or begging ever had.

Reaching for the condom he'd dropped on the bedside table, he sheathed himself, watching her watch him. When he moved over her, she closed her eyes and arched her head back into the pillow, her legs instinctively parting in warm, sultry welcome. Kissing her jaw and her cheek, he began to slide into her, slowly, losing himself in the pleasure of her body.

"You are so beautiful," he whispered, studying her face as she reacted to his possession. Her eyes remained closed, but her mouth parted on a tiny, helpless gasp. The pulse in her throat fluttered visibly and a warm pink glow washed up through her cheeks.

Sliding her arms up to encircle his neck, Noelle clenched him deep inside. Mark groaned, unable to remain still, needing to move, to empty her and fill her over and over again until she conceded—at least in her own mind—that this was no longer about sex. This was lovemaking.

Which is exactly what he did. With tender kisses, gentle touches, and gazes meant to silently tell her how much she meant to him, he possessed her for as long as his body could manage. Deep, slow thrusts followed by pauses to whisper and caress, to moan and to sigh, drew their interlude out long into the night. Until finally, when the unrelenting waves of pleasure caught him and carried him toward completion, he brought them both to shuddering climaxes, then fell asleep, still wrapped in her arms.

WHEN NOELLE WOKE UP the following morning, it was to an empty bed. She lay in the tangled sheets for a moment, just to make sure she hadn't dreamed the amazing night she'd shared with Mark. The indentation on her other pillow, and her naked body, told her she hadn't. So did the delicious soreness between her thighs.

Figuring Mark was in the bathroom, she curled beneath the covers to ward off the chilly morning and thought about everything that had happened in the last twelve hours. Though alone, she couldn't help blushing over some of the wild things they'd done together. But on deeper reflection, she realized she wasn't truly embarrassed.

Part of her wondered how she'd face him, knowing he had to be thinking of the incredible intimacy they'd shared. What prevented her from feeling that way was the memory of the sweet tenderness with which Mark had made love to her for the rest of the night. It had been incredibly passionate, but also deeply emotional and intimate. A contrast to the eroticism they'd experienced at first.

What an unusual man he was.

Wondering if he'd gotten in the shower, and considering joining him, she rolled over and glanced toward the bathroom door. It stood open, and the light was off.

"Breakfast," she mumbled, figuring he was in the kitchen. Then she spied the piece of paper on her bedside table, and knew she was wrong. Mark wasn't in the kitchen. He wasn't in the apartment at all.

She'd never been the recipient of a "morning-after" note and her heart thudded in her chest as she stared at it. Sitting up in the bed, she let the covers drop to her lap, her wild hair dropping over her naked breasts as she picked it up and read the words from her lover.

"Wild and erotic, no repercussions, no strings. Happy?"

That was all.

Noelle couldn't prevent hot moisture from rising in her eyes as she realized the truth. Mark had given her what she'd wanted—what she'd demanded. And then he'd left.

She couldn't even muster up any anger because she knew better than to think this was a brush off. His final word made that clear. Without ever confronting her, or accusing her of a single thing, he was forcing her to evaluate every decision she'd made since the day they'd met. To decide if her short-term affair idea was truly what she wanted, or if, in the glow of a night like the previous one, she'd realized it couldn't possibly be enough for them.

Which meant she had some serious thinking to do.

12

MARK WASN'T FOOLISH ENOUGH to think Noelle would read his note Monday morning, decide she couldn't live without him, follow him home and declare her undying love. No. He knew she was going to have to think things over, to figure out what she wanted and how she wanted to go after it. So he backed off, giving her some time and some space to do just that.

Only, he hadn't figured she'd need *this* much time. Days had passed and he hadn't heard from her at all. It was early Friday morning, the day before Christmas Eve, and he hadn't heard word one all week. If he hadn't been so focused on the unexpected developments in the Santa robberies investigation, he'd have been climbing the walls.

It was because of those developments that he'd refrained from going over to the shelter, or to Noelle's apartment, and confronting her once and for all. Either that, or giving her damn video and sex toy another serious workout. Because the case had taken a strange turn, and, frankly, he wasn't in a position to discuss it with Noelle yet.

Not when she had a personal connection to the primary suspect.

Stretching, he changed positions in his uncomfortable metal chair just thinking about Sunday night, as he had quite often in the past few days. Fortunately, Harriet didn't seem to notice. She was too busy watching their latest witness go through a pile of flyers—searching for a familiar face—to pay attention to her desperate partner.

"It was *him*," the witness said. The woman worked as a receptionist at a local temp agency. That same agency had hired out the costumed Santa who'd robbed the department store a few weeks ago.

They'd talked to this witness before, and she'd cooperated, going through books of mug shots. But it'd been a shot in the dark, just as it had initially been with the grocery store clerk. Now, however, they were no longer shooting blind.

The woman tapped her finger on a picture in the corner of a color brochure. "I definitely recognize this guy. He looked too cute and skinny to want to play Santa Claus and I told him that when he applied."

Mark glanced down. Though not surprised by what he saw, he couldn't prevent an internal grunt of disgust.

Five of the flyers spread on the table in the interrogation room of the precinct were decoys. He and Harriet had gathered advertisements for businesses, tour companies, training academies—anything with decent color shots of the people involved. All to one purpose: to see if the witnesses would pick out anyone on the *sixth* one. The only one that mattered.

And once again, it had worked. This woman had zoomed right in on the target. Just as the five other people they'd questioned over the past two days had done.

Harriet met his eye and Mark nodded, displaying no overt reaction. They had the bastards, there was no doubt in his mind. Every witness—every interview—put another nail in the coffin of the prick they believed was behind this whole thing.

He just still couldn't believe who that person was.

After escorting this latest witness out, Harriet returned to sit with him, and with the state police investigators who'd been assigned to work the case with them. Since the suspects resided outside Chicago, they'd brought in the state guys. Knowing just how small and close-knit the community under investigation was, they hadn't gone to the Christmas police yet, planning to wait until the day of the search to prevent any possible leaks.

"Is there any doubt at all now that we'll be able to get a warrant to tear that school apart?" Harriet asked.

Mark shook his head, as did the guys from state. With this many witness identifications, as well as the paper trail that linked one careless suspect who'd been dumb enough to use his real social security number back to the Santa college in Christmas, they had enough to go after the owners of that college.

Jeremy Taggert and his father.

He sighed heavily, wondering why he hadn't seen the truth when he'd met the asshole face to face last week. The man had, after all, perfectly matched the description given to them by the grocery store clerk, the one who'd been the target of some sleazy pickup line by the costumed Santa. *Sleazy. Definitely.*

The clerk had, in fact, been the one to break the case wide open Monday afternoon. She'd come into the station to try looking through more mug shots, though they all knew it was pretty useless. Sitting across from Mark and Harriet, the young woman had happened to notice the brochures for the Santa training school in Christmas lying on Mark's desk…the ones Randy had given him Thursday night. Her mouth had dropped open in shock as she'd pointed directly at Jeremy Taggert, pictured with his father and some of their "students" in front of the school building. "That's the guy. Definitely!" she'd said.

Thinking about it, he and Harriet had quickly realized that the "Jerry" the clerk had heard coming out of the Santa's bearded mouth had actually been "Jeremy."

From there, everything had fallen into place. With the flyers and a bunch of witnesses, they'd gotten IDs on four additional suspects, all of whom were pictured as students at the "Institute of Rotudifical Purveyors of Goodwill."

Yeah, they definitely had enough to obtain warrants on the school and pursue a serious investigation against its owners, and Mark was feeling damn good about it. There was just one problem...a big one. "I still don't see the need to question former owners of the company," he said, leaning across the table and staring at the lead guy from the state, and at Lieutenant Shaker, who'd entered the interrogation room. "Randy Halloran hasn't worked with his uncle at the college in a year and a half. He left long before these crimes started."

It wasn't the first time he'd made the argument. Beside him, he could see Harriet watching impassively, voicing no opinion, though she knew why Mark was making the case. He'd told her about Noelle's connection to everyone at the college, and she'd stayed quiet, letting him handle it his own way.

"He was an officer of the business."

"So was his mother and another uncle, but they've all sold out to Ralph Taggert over the past few years," Mark insisted. Then, knowing he needed to think clearly and speak calmly, he added, "Look, I've met Halloran. He's completely invested in the inn he runs with his wife." Thinking of Noelle's charming cousin, he continued. "As for the wife—she's on bed rest for a troubled pregnancy. I don't see how bursting into her home the day before Christmas Eve is going to generate much goodwill and cooperation in the town."

The investigator was silent for a minute and Mark almost held his breath, hoping he'd made an impact. When the other man spoke again, he realized he had…but not as great a one as he'd hoped. "Okay, we don't include the inn when we go to the judge this morning. But I do want to at least talk to Halloran."

Which, Mark realized, was as much of a concession as he was going to get. He only hoped it was enough to avoid any major difficulties for Noelle or her family.

And that she'd forgive him for not warning her of what was about to happen.

SUE HADN'T BEEN FEELING like herself for weeks, so she didn't realize she was feeling *worse* until early Saturday afternoon. She was so tired, that was the problem—much too fatigued for someone who hadn't been out of bed for two weeks.

Missing the excitement of the holidays, she had been lying in her room, listening to the chatter of their guests for the past several days. Randy and their few employees had done a great job taking care of the packed house, but this was the first year Sue was going to miss Christmas, and she wasn't very happy about it. That old holiday excitement should have had her bouncing in the bed in anticipation of tomorrow—as much as a woman with forty pounds packed onto the front of her body could bounce. Instead, she lay lethargically in her mound of pillows, wondering why she felt a vague sense of unease. And why she could barely keep her eyes open.

"Ready for a snack, sweetie?" Randy said as he entered the room.

"Tea?" she asked wearily, unable to muster up any enthusiasm for one more cup of decaffeinated tea when she was dying for her usual blast of the real stuff.

"Hot chocolate."

"Mmm," she mumbled, smiling weakly at him as he carried the tray over. The man was trying *so* hard to make her happy. Beside the steaming mug was a little plate with some mini marshmallows, and a few graham crackers. "Liquid s'mores?"

Nodding, he handed her the cocoa. But as she took it, Sue noticed that her hand was trembling. Some chocolaty liquid splashed out of the ceramic mug, splattering all over the saucer beneath it.

"Babe, are you hurt? Did you burn yourself?" Randy asked, instantly taking the drink away and reaching for her hand.

She shook her head, still staring at her fingers. They were fluttering, moving the tiniest bit. How funny. Because, as far as she could tell, she didn't *think* she was moving them at all.

"Sue?" he asked, raising his voice. "Honey, what's wrong? You look so pale."

"Do I?" That was her voice, coming out of her mouth, yet it sounded so far away, like the muffled tones of a stranger speaking in her dreams.

"I'm calling the doctor." He reached for the phone.

Sue said nothing, just watching him. Feeling so tired, so drained, she could barely lift her head to protest his bothering Dr. Franklin on Christmas Eve. Randy had to be calling the man at home, since his office would surely be closed today. But she couldn't form the words to ask her husband not to do it.

Randy spoke into the receiver for a moment, then, a little red-faced, he turned to her. "Honey, Dr. Franklin wants to know if you've had any more…spotting since that first incident."

Since she hadn't been able to get up to visit the bathroom on her own today, doubting her legs would hold her, Sue couldn't answer the question. With a helpless shrug, she tried to push at the heavy blankets and comforter which had been keeping her toasty warm.

"Hold on," Randy said. Setting the receiver down on the bedside table, he came to assist her, any embarrassment about helping her so intimately long since evaporated during her pregnancy. Once she was uncovered, she rolled carefully to her other side, shifting toward the edge of the bed. With her husband's help, she should be able to get up.

But as she slowly rose into a sitting position, she grew even more lightheaded—dizzy—as if she was floating. It was a strange, weightless sensation and for a moment she couldn't move at all. Not to stand up, not to lie back down. She could only sit there, as if a great, heavy blanket was pressing on her, holding her down. She remained completely still.

Until she saw the horror on her husband's face.

Looking down at the sheets and her own nightgown, Sue tried to understand the strange color. Red. All red. How funny. She'd thought the sheets were white.

She couldn't think about it for long because suddenly a loud, shrill noise filled her head, piercing and intrusive. Someone was screaming.

It wasn't until after she heard Randy shouting into the phone that Sue realized it was her.

EARLY SATURDAY AFTERNOON, Noelle continued with the nonstop activities that had been filling her every waking hour this week. The shelter was gaily decorated, filled with the smells of cookies and cinnamon, pine trees and poinsettias. Stacks of wrapped packages were hidden in the attic, and children were almost giddy with excitement.

She'd never have predicted this three weeks ago when they'd been targeted by a vicious thief.

The closer they'd gotten to the holiday, the more people had stepped up to help. They'd not only recouped all their losses from the robbery, they'd surpassed their original goal.

She and Alice had just returned from Super Dave's, where they'd bought the last of the toys they needed for the kids living here in the shelter. All the rest of the goodies had been purchased, wrapped, and delivered earlier this week to the grateful mothers making new lives for themselves elsewhere. Food, clothes, and gift certificates had accompanied each special delivery.

Nodding in satisfaction, Noelle couldn't help thinking it would be a merry Christmas for a lot of needy families, after all. The Christmas spirit seemed to have opened up many people's hearts. Maybe, she acknowledged, even hers.

When she hadn't been working herself into near exhaustion all week, she'd been thinking about Mark. About what they'd shared Sunday night, and the feelings she'd allowed herself to develop for him.

Love. She'd known it was love since last Thursday at the inn. But she hadn't realized until the last day or so that it was the kind of love *worth* risking a broken heart for. As the days had gone on without Mark in her world—without his voice on the phone or his visits to the shelter, or his smile—she'd realized there wasn't much she wouldn't do to make things work with him.

If only he felt the same way.

She couldn't help but think of him now, because at this very minute, the families in her care were sitting in the dining room, devouring the trayfuls of hot food Mark's mother and brother Tony had brought over here. Cartons of it.

Mrs. Santori had said she wasn't so good with turkeys, but she thought the children might enjoy a good Italian holiday meal for Christmas Eve. So a dozen children were now happily slurping long strands of spaghetti and picking the "white stuff" out of some fabulous lasagna.

They hadn't been the only Santoris to visit the shelter today. Out back was the big wooden jungle gym Joe and five of his workers had put together this morning while the kids were out ice skating. She, Alice, Casey and the mothers were being extra careful to make sure the kids didn't go out back for the rest of the day.

"So, what have you decided about your trip?" Casey asked as she popped into the office. Noelle waved at her to quickly shut the door. She was sitting on the floor, putting some finishing touches on the packages the children had wrapped for their moms yesterday. They'd all made hand-prints in cement, and the office currently had tons of little flecks of white plaster all over the floor. But she didn't care. It would be well worth it when the kids saw the happiness in their mothers' faces.

"I'm not sure," Noelle replied, looking up at Casey as the girl plopped on the edge of the desk. Casey's carrot red hair clashed with the red Santa hat on her head, but she looked so adorably happy, nobody really cared. "I'd decided last week that I really was going to go. Can't get a refund on the ticket and I have the money for the hotel since we didn't need it here. But then..."

Then she'd started thinking seriously about the man she'd be flying away from if she jetted off to the Caribbean.

"Then?"

"Then I wondered if I'd be making a mistake."

Peeling the plastic off a candy cane, Casey popped it into her mouth and sucked on one end. "You don't hate Christmas anymore, do you?" she asked with her mouth still wrapped around the peppermint stick.

"Nah. I really don't. I guess seeing the way complete strangers really came through for us when I thought they wouldn't made me realize there are still some people out there who value the spirit of the season."

"Or it could be that you had your own personal supersized elf to give you lots of presents," Casey said with a smirk.

Noelle knew what she meant and was about to roll her eyes when she realized Casey was no longer looking at her. She was staring at the door. Lifting her gaze and seeing Mark, she felt her heart thunk against her ribcage.

"Gotta scoot," Casey said as she hopped off the desk. "Have a good night, Noelle."

Dry-mouthed, she nodded, then looked at the handsome man watching her silently from a few feet away. Mark's big form ate up a lot of space in the office, and his presence even more of it. His hair was windblown, his face reddened from the cold outside air, and his green eyes glittered as he raked a thorough look over her, as if to catalog any changes. "I need to talk to you."

She taped the final bow on one package and slowly rose from the floor. "Yeah. I guess I need to talk to you, too."

No, she hadn't figured on having this conversation here. She hadn't been exactly sure *where* she wanted to be when she told Mark she'd fallen in love with him and wanted to give them a chance at a real relationship. But she knew she didn't want to wait any longer. Not with Christmas just a few hours away.

Not when she had finally found something fresh and new and wonderful to look forward to in the holiday.

"We've found the suspects involved in the Santa robberies."

Her mouth opened in surprise. She hadn't exactly been expecting declarations of undying love. Nor, however, had she been expecting Mark to go into cop mode right now, when they hadn't seen each other in five days. "I'm glad," she murmured. "I hope the bastards get a lot of jail time."

Striding toward the window to look outside, Mark thrust a hand through his hair, sending it tumbling even more wildly over his brow. "They will, I'm sure. But there's more."

Sensing by the clipped tone that she wasn't going to like what he had to say, Noelle slowly lowered herself onto the sofa. "Tell me."

He slowly turned around to watch her through hooded eyes. "We have a lot of witnesses who've connected the crimes to the Santa College in Christmas."

Now her mouth didn't just open, it dropped in complete shock.

"I was there yesterday afternoon," he added, not commenting on her reaction. "We served a warrant at the school and at Jeremy Taggert's house and found not only stolen merchandise, but a whole lot of cash."

Noelle's pulse roared in her veins, filling her ears as if she was being sucked into a giant vacuum. "That miserable son of a bitch," she mumbled.

"Yeah. He wasn't a very tough nut to crack. He admitted everything. Apparently his new wife has expensive tastes, and the school wasn't doing so well. He cooked up this whole thing with some of his former students and they've been raking it in pretty good."

Not quite knowing how she should feel, Noelle sat quietly, thinking it over. Should she be feeling stupid about having once been engaged to a thief? Lose faith in her own judgment again? Or just wonder how in heaven Jeremy's father was going to weather the controversy?

Deep down, she simply felt disgust. Jeremy had once

seemed like a nice guy but he was obviously very weak. He'd proved it in many ways—this was just one more. At least this final bit of evidence could help her admit what an enormous piece of good luck his cheating on her had been. Because if she'd actually married the creep a year ago, she might now be caught up in his crimes. "My God, how ironic. We were both once engaged to thieves."

He didn't respond, though he did nod slightly, appearing pensive.

"I'm so glad you caught him. Did you also find out who, exactly, robbed *us?* I know it wasn't Jeremy—I would have recognized his voice."

"No, it wasn't. It was one of his buddies, who also confessed once he found out he wasn't merely involved in some harmless pranks."

Pranks. Right. That would have been a great explanation to make to the kids if they hadn't managed to replace the stolen money.

"Turns out Jeremy's father was involved. He overheard your cousin talking to you on the phone about cashing out an account of Christmas donations one day a few weeks ago. He already had this guy in place at the party company you hired, and told him what to look for."

Noelle's head felt as if it was spinning on top of her shoulders. *She'd* been the one who'd leaked the information used by the thief!

"If it's any consolation, Jeremy didn't know you were a target until I told him myself. He appeared…unhappy."

Small consolation—not that she really cared about Jeremy's happiness. What really shocked her, though, was the revelation about blustery blowhard Ralph Taggert's involvement. "This is unbelievable. I can't even imagine how Randy's going to react to all this scandal about his family."

Mark looked away, suddenly clenching his fists and shoving them into the pockets of his leather jacket, which he still wore. "Yeah. I know."

Noelle was ready to change the subject, to forget about scummy Jeremy and his father and their crimes. It was time to talk about her and Mark. Maybe even time to ask him if he had any plans for tomorrow night...and if he'd maybe like to hop on a plane heading south with her.

"There's something else," he murmured, his voice low and his mouth grim. "Jeremy and his cronies weren't the only ones we questioned yesterday."

Noelle couldn't imagine what else there was to say that would be nearly as important, so she merely waited. But before Mark could elaborate, the phone rang. "Excuse me," she said, automatically grabbing for the receiver.

"Merry Christmas, this is Noelle Bradenton," she said, not having to wonder too hard about the unexpected Christmas spirit that made her voice sound so chipper. Now that the robbers had been caught and Mark was standing here in the room—so wonderful and desirable and amazing—she was anticipating a much better holiday than she'd ever have imagined a month ago.

"Noelle, we need you."

She almost didn't recognize the voice. Then she froze. "Randy?"

Her cousin-in-law's breaths were choppy and loud through the phone and a note of unfamiliar desperation tinged his words. "You gotta come. It's Sue. She's in the hospital." He sobbed, adding, "There was so much blood, Noelle."

Oh, God.

"Hemorrhage. Something abrupted, I don't know what the hell they're talking about. They're prepping her for surgery right now and she wants you here."

She didn't need to hear any more. "I'm on my way," she said, hanging up the phone.

Her whole body shaking in terror for her cousin, she grabbed her coat off the back of her chair and her purse from the bottom drawer. "It's Sue. Something's wrong."

Mark didn't ask stupid questions or even think twice. He merely said, "I'll drive."

And together they rushed out the door.

MARK DROVE AS FAST AS HE COULD from Chicago to Christmas, figuring it was better to talk his way out of a ticket than waste time obeying the speed limit. It still wasn't fast enough for Noelle. She sat forward in the passenger seat, her eyes wide with terror, her arms curled around her waist. She'd been mumbling a few words, and when he listened intently, he realized she was praying for her cousin and her cousin's baby.

He'd sent up a few of those prayers himself since Noelle had told him what was happening with Sue.

God, he felt so helpless. So inept. There was nothing he could say to comfort her, because he knew no more than she did. His sisters-in-law had had easy pregnancies and textbook deliveries, and he knew next to nothing about all the things that could go wrong when a child was born.

Absolutely the only thing he could do was torment himself with images of *why* Sue had started hemorrhaging. And if he'd had anything to do with it.

"Talk to me, tell me something, tell me it'll be all right," Noelle said, her voice shaking. She looked at him from the other side of the car.

"It will. She'll be *fine,* Noelle. Just keep sending up those prayers."

She didn't look convinced, continuing to chew a hole in her bottom lip. "What if she's not?"

"She will be." He allowed no doubt in his mind or in his voice. Realizing what day it was, he added, "Probably by the time we get there, there'll be a new Christmas baby to welcome into the world." His words suddenly made him remember something else, and he reached across the car to grab one of her cold hands in his. "Speaking of which, happy birthday. Today's yours, right? I can't believe I forgot." He laughed bitterly. "Some lover I am."

She stared at him, blinked a couple of times, as if weighing his words and deciding what to respond to—the forgetting her birthday part or the lover part. Not sure which he preferred, he waited until Noelle managed a small laugh. "Believe it or not, I forgot, too. I've been so busy with the shelter and everything."

"It looks fantastic. The kids have got to be bouncing off the walls with excitement," he said, glad she was allowing herself to be distracted. "Ginger and Mickey grabbed onto my legs as I walked in the door and asked me if I'd heard any bells outside because some of the older kids told them Santa's sleigh had already been spotted by the Air Force."

She managed a weary smile.

"You've done an incredible job," he added.

"With no small amount of help from your family," she replied.

Keeping himself so involved with the investigation in Christmas the previous day, he hadn't heard much about what his family had been up to. So he was mildly surprised when Noelle told him about the visit from Mama and Tony.

He was also glad to hear his brother Joe had followed through on the playground equipment, not that he'd ever doubted for a minute that he would. Joe was solid, reliable, and one of the most hard-working people he knew.

Thinking of the rest of the Santoris reminded him of the need to let them know he wouldn't be around tonight. Making a quick cell phone call to the restaurant, he filled Gloria in, then disconnected.

"Gloria said the whole family will pray for Sue and the baby tonight at midnight mass."

Noelle nodded, looking grateful.

Shaking his head and thinking of the typical Santori Christmas Eve, he added, "Thank God I have a good excuse for not being around this evening, because I know Rachel's gonna hate what I got her for Christmas."

Curiosity made her tilt her head to one side. "What was it?"

"Just a boring gift certificate," he said with a shrug. "Not very original, but my brother Joe swore she'd love this place. Someplace downtown called the Red Doors."

Noelle's tight mouth finally eased into a little smile and she nodded. "Yes, I've heard of it. And I think your brother's right. She'll definitely like it."

The smile relieved him. Noelle's ragged breathing had evened out, and she was no longer clenched and terrified-looking. He was just about to send up thanks that she'd been completely distracted from her terror when she remembered something he'd hoped she'd forgotten.

"You were about to tell me something else, right before Randy called," she said. "Something about the case."

Mark tensed, his hands curling tightly around the steering wheel. Tight enough to make his fingers turn white. "It's nothing."

She wasn't dissuaded. "It's not nothing, I can tell by the your expression. What happened? There's something else you're not telling me and I'd like to know what it is."

"Later, Noelle. We'll talk later after all this is over."

Maybe by then he'd have a way to explain that he'd been among a couple of cops who'd descended on the Candy Cane Inn yesterday and questioned her cousin's husband for two hours about his family's nefarious activities.

Christ, if the stress of that visit had caused Sue's health crisis, he was never going to forgive himself.

Noelle was watching him intently, giving him the assessing stare *he* often used on suspects he was trying to break. "I don't like being kept in the dark, especially when it was something you were ready to tell me an hour ago," she said, her tone stiff. "I'm involved in this, Mark, whether I like it or not. I was a victim of these crimes. And I actually have a connection to the primary suspect."

Mark couldn't prevent a sharp bark of humorless laughter. "Thank God you didn't marry that asshole."

She still wouldn't let it go, as tenacious as a kid going after a just-out-of-reach cookie jar. Only, when she got what she was after, she wasn't going to be happily enjoying some cookies. She could very well be hating him. Probably, though, not as much as he'd hate himself if he found out there was something he could have done to prevent Sue's emergency. Like, for instance, pushing harder to leave Randy out of the investigation.

"There's also the other family connection," she continued, ignoring him completely. "My cousin is a member of that family through marriage, remember."

Mark flinched, his head jerking up a little higher as he straightened even more in the seat. He didn't look over, wouldn't meet her eye, thinking he could keep cool, could hold things together until they got to the hospital and found out just what was wrong with Sue. Then, once they knew for sure what had happened—once he knew for sure he *hadn't* contributed to Sue's condition—he could tell Noelle everything.

He should have known his luck wasn't that good. "Oh, no, that's what's going on, isn't it?" Her eyes were wide, her mouth open. "That's what you were about to tell me about the 'someone else' you questioned. It was Randy, wasn't it? You accused Sue's husband of being part of Jeremy's crimes."

He wasn't going to lie to her, so he couldn't possibly deny it. He simply remained silent, too racked with guilt on his own to even try to defend himself.

"You're crazy if you think Randy was involved," she snapped. "Absolutely insane. Anybody in town will tell you he's the most honest man ever born." Becoming more indignant, she added, "My God, Randy turned himself in to the police when his car skidded in the rain and he accidentally hit a rabbit!"

She wasn't telling him anything he didn't already know. Having met Randy, he'd already suspected the guy would never be involved in anything illegal. The interview yesterday merely confirmed his opinion.

It hadn't, however, convinced the state investigators, who were still looking at Randy Halloran. Maybe not seriously, but at least still considering him.

"When did this happen?" Noelle asked, suddenly growing quiet. She sounded a lot more calm than he'd have expected this soon.

"We spoke to him late yesterday afternoon."

"Was he arrested?"

He shook his head. "Definitely not, and the inn wasn't part of the official search. We just sat down in his living room and talked to the man Noelle, I swear."

Staring straight ahead, appearing deep in thought, Noelle

fell silent. A long moment dragged into a few minutes of eerie quiet. Then, finally, when he had just about decided she was never going to speak to him again, not even while they drove the remaining ten minutes to the hospital, she whispered, "In his living room." She looked at him, her eyes suspiciously bright. "Do you think this had anything to do with Sue's emergency? Having the police accuse her husband of being a thief, right there in her own home, surrounded by their paying guests?"

Mark jerked as if he'd been struck. Her words were nothing he hadn't thought a dozen times in the past ninety minutes, since Randy's original call. But hearing her say it—seeing the horror on her face as she'd voiced the question—struck him to the core.

"I don't know," was all he could manage to mutter in his own defense.

He waited for her accusations, waited for her to scream at him that he'd put her cousin's baby's life at risk. Waited for *something*. Noelle simply curled her hands together on her lap and watched the bare trees passing by as they sped down the highway. Until finally she said, "Do you care about me, Mark?"

The question caught him completely off guard. "You know I do."

Turning in the seat, she said, "If you care about me, promise me right now that you won't let Randy be railroaded for something his cousin did."

That was completely without question. "I will do everything within my legal power to make sure that doesn't happen," he said, still surprised by her strange reaction. And wondering why she was suddenly bringing their emotions into the conversation, when she'd done a damn fine job of avoiding even mentioning them in the past month.

"That's not good enough," she replied, her jaw tight, belying the tears still glimmering on her lashes. "Everything in your *legal* power doesn't cut it. I'm not asking you as a cop, Mark, I'm asking you as a man, to do whatever it takes to make sure Randy gets out of this. Don't you dare let Sue lose her husband." Her voice breaking, she added, "Especially if there's a chance she might lose her baby."

Her tears, the way her voice shook, and her obvious terror for Sue were breaking his heart. But what she was asking him to do made his blood run cold in his veins. She hadn't said it specifically, hadn't asked him to choose between his oath as a cop and her. Somehow, though, deep in his head, he was hearing his ex-fiancée Renée's voice giving him that very choice. *Betray your principles for me.*

This is different. Completely different. Noelle wasn't asking him to do anything for her own selfish needs—she was merely trying to protect someone she loved. He knew that, knew it without question.

Yet some old, deeply rooted seed of anger or resentment for what had happened so many years ago wouldn't let him ignore the whispers in his mind. The whispers that said if Noelle loved him—the way he now knew he loved her—she wouldn't even think of asking him to become something he wasn't: a liar. A bad cop.

For someone else's good an internal voice reminded him.

God, it was too much. The guilt over Sue's condition, the concern about Randy's involvement, and now, this impossible promise Noelle had just asked him to make. He was out of his element, nearly out of his mind, and he had no idea what to say.

"Well?" she asked as he pulled the car into the hospital entrance.

Mark took a deep breath, reminding himself that this was Noelle, the sweet, funny, sexy, decent woman he loved. Not some phantom from his past.

"Go see your cousin, Noelle," he said through a tightly clenched jaw.

Without another word, he pulled up to the emergency doors of the hospital and turned his head away, not wanting to watch her get out. He couldn't stand to see her face dissolve into dismay and loathing when she finally came to the realization that not only had he possibly contributed to her cousin's condition, but he was not going to break the law to help Sue's husband if he was indeed guilty.

Not even for her.

His silence appeared to be answer enough. Because without another word, she opened the car door. He heard the slide of her hand across the leather seat as she slid out, noticed the loss of her warmth immediately as frigid winter air rushed in.

When the door slammed, leaving him alone, he suddenly realized the cold wasn't coming from the outside, but rather deep within himself.

13

For Noelle, the next hour was one of the most terrifying and heartbreaking of her life.

She'd found Randy and Aunt Leila in the obstetrics waiting room. Randy was pacing back and forth, mumbling, his hair wild and his eyes wilder. When she'd first walked in and seen the spots of blood on his clothes, she'd thought she was going to be sick. Even more than she'd already felt sick over the confrontation she'd just had with Mark. Somehow she'd managed to join the quiet vigil without losing her mind, though, as the minutes ticked by, she felt less and less in control.

"What's taking so long?" she muttered, talking more to herself than to the others. "I thought C-sections were routine."

"The doctor said the tricky part would be the…hemorrhaging, not the delivery," Randy said, his voice breaking.

Beside her, Aunt Leila's hands, which had been busy knitting something soft and yellow, stilled. A drop of moisture plopped onto her slender finger, obviously having fallen from her eye. Noelle reached over and slid her arm around the older woman's shoulders. "They'll be fine, I know it."

"I know, I know. Just the light in here hurts my eyes," the older woman said, stiffening her shoulders and getting back to work. "Better hurry—we're going to have a Christmas baby who's going to need a nice warm blanket."

God, how she wished she were certain of that. And how she wished Mark was here with her, holding her hand, and giving her the same reassurances.

She still couldn't quite believe he'd dropped her off and driven away. Now, when she needed him most, he'd left her on her own, appearing wounded and devastated, as if he were the injured party. All because she'd asked him to help a man she *knew* was innocent prove that innocence. Was it really too much to ask the man she deeply loved to help find the best lawyers and give Randy whatever help and advice he could?

"Are you sure you don't want to call Mark?" Randy asked, abruptly stopping his frantic pacing. "I can't believe he just dropped you off and left."

She stared up at her cousin's husband, surprised by the question. She hadn't even realized Randy had heard her when she'd mentioned who'd driven her down from Chicago. "Maybe he feels like you won't want him here," she said, wondering if it was true. "Because of…things."

Randy stared at her quizzically, then blew out an impatient breath. "You mean with that shit Jeremy pulled? Come on, Noelle, you can't really think I'm involved in that."

"I know," she said carefully, not sure how much Aunt Leila knew. The old woman barely seemed to pay attention anyway as her knitting needles clicked together furiously. "I mean, well, maybe he's afraid you'll blame him for what's happening now. With Sue."

Randy's eyes immediately moved to the door, which had remained ominously closed since the nurse had last checked in a half-hour ago to say they would be delivering the baby any minute. Then he shook his head hard and stared at her. "What could that have to do with anything?"

"Maybe the stress?"

"Oh, babe, you're kidding, right? Sue laughed her ass off last night when I told her, saying she was really having fun picturing Jeremy being some dude's girlfriend in a jail cell." Randy's eyes grew bright. "God, she's feisty."

Yes. She was. Noelle's eyes grew hot, too.

Sniffing a little, Randy continued. "This wasn't about stress or about her sneaking a cup of tea with caffeine last week, or about her not staying still enough in bed—all of which she accused herself of on the ride over here. It would have happened no matter what. There's nothing she could have done. Whatever this placenta abruption is, it doesn't usually happen on top of the previa thing she had, but it does happen once in a while. Nobody knows why, it just…does."

Feeling a bit relieved, Noelle nodded. She'd never seriously believed Mark was in any way to blame for Sue's condition, but it was nice to have it confirmed by Sue's husband.

Too bad Mark wasn't here to hear it for himself. Because something made her suspect he was heaping a whole lot of guilt onto his own head.

"I'm glad to hear this whole situation didn't upset her."

"Jeremy's actions angered her more than anything else, but she certainly wasn't seriously worried about anybody thinking I was involved, any more than I am."

"Good."

He ran a weary hand over his face. "One look at our pathetically low bank account balances should convince anybody that I don't have any stolen bucks lying around. They have absolutely nothing, Noelle. I sold my shares in the school to Uncle Ralph ages ago, which is how Sue and I were able to buy your mothers out. I haven't even set foot at S.C.U. in a year and a half."

That was exactly what she'd figured.

"Hell, if the cop leading the investigation doesn't even think I'm guilty, what do I have to be worried about?" Then he looked at the door again, his expression growing somber and his voice soft. "That's nothing, compared to the things that are really worth worrying about."

Noelle understood his sudden melancholy, but she also couldn't stop thinking of his words. The cop leading the investigation…did he mean Mark? Needing to know, she cleared her throat. "Mark thinks you're innocent?"

Randy nodded absently. "He and his partner both. They told me as they were leaving. Mark gave me the name of one of the best lawyers in Chicago, not that either of us really thinks I'll need it. Your boyfriend swore he'd get the truth out of Jeremy—that I had nothing to do with what was going on—even if he had to ask the D.A. to make a deal with him."

Noelle sagged back in her chair, stunned by Randy's words. Mark had *already* gone out of his way to help Sue's husband? He'd done exactly what she'd hoped he'd do… and yet he'd still reacted as if she'd asked him to commit a murder or something when they'd spoken in the car. She just didn't understand it.

But whether she understood him or not, there was one thing she did know. Mark was feeling guilty about Sue, she had no doubt of that. And he didn't deserve to carry that weight. So rising to her feet and grabbing her coat, she said, "I'm going to go outside and make a call. Come get me if you hear anything, okay?"

Randy and Leila nodded as Noelle walked to the door. Once outside, wrapping her coat tightly around her body against the cold, she grabbed her cell phone out of her pocket. She'd memorized Mark's cell number already and quickly dialed it. Watching the little puffs of air caused by her breaths, she counted the rings, and was more than a little disappointed when a recording answered after five of them. "Mark," she said, having to clear her throat, "it's me, Noelle. I just want you to know, there's no word on Sue yet. But in case you were worrying…in case you thought you and the police investigation had anything to do with this, well, you didn't. Sue was absolutely fine right up until this morning when it just…happened. No one was to blame, and *nobody* blames you. So please stop blaming yourself."

She was probably running out of time and there really wasn't anything more to say. He would come back, or he wouldn't. Call her, or not.

Love her or forget her?

Something inside her broke at the very thought. "I wish you were here. I wish I didn't need you so much. I wish…"

But before she could finish her wish—and even she didn't know what it was—a beep told her she'd run out of time. Slowly turning off the phone, she dropped it back into her pocket and walked back inside.

Mark was sitting in a crowded bakery on Frosty Lane, eating steaming hot gingerbread and drinking hot cider, when he realized someone had called him on his cell phone. He hadn't heard the ring over the din of noisy customers, all stopping in to pick up preordered cakes and pies for the holiday. He'd come here after driving around Christmas for a little while, unable to leave town without knowing how Sue was. Deep inside, he also knew he was sticking around to make sure Noelle would be okay.

Dialing for his voice mail, he listened to the message, his body tensing at the first sound of her voice. Noelle's words, however, sent a wave of relief washing through him. He leaned back in the booth, breathing deeply. So deeply, he almost missed the final words of Noelle's message.

She needed him.

And, oh, he needed her, too. He needed to look into her eyes and ask her what she wanted from him, because right now, he just didn't know. A cop? A lover? An ally? A stranger?

There was only one way he was going to find out, so, tossing his napkin to the plate, he got up and headed out the door. He was at the small hospital within ten minutes, and quickly found the obstetrical waiting room.

Glancing through the small window in the door, he assumed the room was empty, but pushed it open just to be sure.

He'd been wrong. The room wasn't entirely empty. A woman sat in a chair in the corner, her legs drawn up and her arms wrapped tightly around them. Her head was down, her forehead resting on her knees. A curtain of long, dark hair fell across her cheek, tumbling over her jean-covered legs.

"Noelle?" he asked, his voice no more than a whisper.

She slowly raised her head, her lovely face drawn and fatigued. Her eyes were suspiciously bright and the streaks below them told him she'd shed a lot of tears.

Oh, God.

Without a word, he strode across the room and bent down in front of her, tugging her forward and into his embrace. She wrapped her arms around his neck and hugged him tightly, almost crushing his throat. Winding her fingers in his hair, she kissed her way down his cheek to his lips, then pressed her mouth to his in a quietly tender kiss.

"Tell me," he urged, still holding her.

She hesitated for a second, then finally said, "It's a boy. His name's Nicholas. Can you believe they did that to him after all the times Sue has heard me gripe about having a holiday name?" She was laughing and crying at the same time, as if completely overwhelmed by her feelings.

But there was more, much more. So Mark waited, almost holding his breath. "And?"

"And," Noelle said, pulling away to stare directly at him, "he and his beautiful mommy are doing just *fine*."

IT WAS LATE THAT NIGHT—close to midnight—when Noelle finally agreed to let Mark take her back to the Candy Cane Inn. They'd spent the entire evening at the hospital, visiting Sue for a few minutes every hour and peeking at the baby—a real Christmas angel, everyone was calling him. Apparently things had been a lot more serious than anyone had ever realized, and even the staff had thought for a while that they were going to have a tragic holiday in the quiet little hospital. But once Sue and her baby were declared stable and out of danger, everyone had gotten a bit giddy with the news.

Mark had been absolutely wonderful, taking care of everything he could. He'd gone back to the inn to get fresh clothes for Randy, and to get Sue's bag, which they'd left behind in the frenzy. When he came back, he was carrying a number of presents provided by the inn's guests, who weren't the least bit disgruntled at having to fend without their host and hostess. Mark also brought a box of cigars, which he presented to the proud dad... Noelle had no idea where he could have found them on Christmas Eve night.

Randy and Leila were still at the hospital, each of them wanting a few more private minutes with their children. They'd come home later. But for now, as Noelle wearily opened the front door of the Candy Cane Inn and led him into the quiet foyer, they were completely alone. Well, except for the guests who were, she sincerely hoped, asleep for the night, with visions of sugarplums and all that jazz.

Walking across the wood floors on her toes, to avoid making any noise, Noelle entered the large living room, where guests often read or enjoyed an evening cocktail in front of a roaring fire. Tonight the fire wasn't roaring—it was low, merely flickering, a few glowing embers casting shadows onto the hearth. In the corner stood an enormous Christmas tree, laden down with ornaments both new and old. Noelle recognized dozens of classic ones from her childhood, but, in typical Sue fashion, there were also some funky golfing Santas, bubble lights, and an entire collection of characters from Rudolph the Red Nosed Reindeer. She stared at them, smiling as she imagined next year, when little Nicholas would be so completely entranced by the colors dancing across the floor in a rainbow of reds, greens and golds.

"It's almost midnight," Mark murmured as he joined her beside the tree.

Noelle looked up at him, noting the way the tree lights caught the deep green of his eyes and turned them into glittering emeralds. He was beautiful. He was thoughtful. He was strong and caring. And oh, she did not want to let him go, even if holding onto him meant she might someday be hurt.

But there was one thing she needed to straighten out. Because throughout the evening, as she'd watched Mark celebrate with her family and the hospital staff, she'd noticed the shadow in his eyes whenever the family "troubles" were mentioned. "I'd like to ask you something. Earlier, in the car, when I asked you to help Randy, you acted so shocked. Yet I found out later that you'd already done it. You'd referred him to a lawyer, told him you believed him innocent. So why were you so upset?"

Mark turned to look directly at her. Saying nothing for a moment, he lifted his hand and brushed a strand of hair back, his fingers tracing a tender line across the top of her cheek. "You *were* just asking for that, weren't you? I know it, I knew it then, I suppose. But somehow, Noelle, I just had this moment of terror, this déjà vu...."

She gasped, drawing a hand to her mouth. "Oh, no, you thought I was like *her*. Asking you to lie, to betray your oath as a police officer? To break the law because I'd asked you to?"

He answered her horrified question with one short nod. "You said you were speaking to me not as a cop, but as a man."

"I was. *My* man." Not even thinking about whether she was wise or a fool, she rushed on. "I was asking the man I love if he'd do whatever he could to help me in a crisis. Not asking a cop to forget everything he stands for."

Mark's big shoulders moved visibly as his breaths deepened. *"Love?"*

Stepping closer, she rested one hand on his chest, right above his heart. "You asked me a question a week ago, Mark Santori. And I can honestly tell you that the answer is *no*."

His brow furrowed; Mark obviously didn't understand what she was talking about. "What question?"

"One word. One simple little word. 'Happy?' And the answer Monday morning when you left that note for me was that I was utterly blissful, satisfied and overdosed on physical pleasure." Lifting her hand to his cheek and cupping it, she added, "But I was not happy. Not when I thought that having you fulfill all my fantasies would mean you would walk away from me."

He turned his face into her hand and kissed her palm. "I thought you wanted to let yourself go completely with someone you didn't have to face in the cold light of day."

Shivering a little as his lips and tongue moved to her fingers, she said, "You've proved to me that I can't have one without the other. You took the fantasy and made it perfect because of the beautiful emotion that came with it." She leaned up a little, bringing her mouth close to his. "I want you more than I can say. I love you more than I could ever have imagined."

He closed his eyes, still holding her hand to his mouth. Time seemed to stop as she waited for some reaction to her declaration. Would he echo it? Thank her politely, then stammer excuses? Ask her to run away with him?

Breathing deeply, as if memorizing the scent of her skin, he finally whispered, "I love you, Noelle."

The world started turning again.

"I want to spend my whole life showing you how much I love you, and I'll do that until the day I die."

She didn't doubt it. The honesty in his voice could not be denied.

"It nearly killed me to think you wanted me for nothing more than sex when I was already out of my mind over you." His eyes suddenly growing heated, he added, "I have to admit, I was trying to teach you a lesson last Sunday night."

She shifted lightly. "Consider it taught. Oh, my God, I almost died when I woke up and you were gone, but that, uh, *device* was still on the bed."

He dropped his arms to encircle her waist and tugged her close against him, sharing the heat of his body. "I think I started to fall in love with you the minute I crash-landed on you in that dressing room." He laughed throatily, the sound sliding over her, warming every exposed inch of her skin, like a protective blanket. "And I knew it for sure when you told my sister you liked your kids medium-rare."

He kissed her forehead, rubbing his cheek against her temple. Then, growing more serious, he said, "I hope you meant it, because I think our children are going to be *very* rare and special."

Thinking of all the children in her life—like sweet red-haired Ginger and shy little Mickey, and her new godson, Nicholas—she knew she liked children any way she could get them. Today, in particular. For the first time in a long time, she allowed herself to dream of tucking a child of her own into bed, whispering stories of fairies and nutcrackers, of magical snowmen and elves.

Mostly of his or her daddy, who loved them both so much, and showed them every single day of their lives.

She started to respond, but before she could do it, his lips were brushing across hers, then returning to deepen the kiss. She sighed, her mouth opening in welcome. Mark tasted warm and sweet, spicy—like the Christmas holiday itself— and she savored the flavors, as well as the scent of his skin and the firmness of his body pressed against hers from neck to knee.

Behind them, the holiday clock on the mantel began to play a quiet rendition of "Silent Night." A signal that they'd reached the midnight hour. Noelle would have smiled if she hadn't been fully occupied kissing the man she loved.

It was Christmas. And she'd just been given the most perfect gift of her life.

Keeping his arm around her shoulder, Mark led her to the couch near the fireplace and pulled her down with him, holding her close. Behind them was the front window. Glancing outside, Noelle was startled to see a few flakes of snow drifting toward the ground. For all the cold weather they'd experienced recently, they hadn't seen a lot of snow. She truly hadn't expected a white Christmas, on top of all the other miracles she'd experienced this year, yet here it was.

The greatest one was sitting behind her, letting her curl up in his lap. And suddenly, she couldn't help thinking of the last time they'd been in this position.

She took a deep, shaky breath as that same lazy curl of desire drifted through her. Mark seemed to know exactly what she was thinking, because he began to stroke her arms, then to run the tips of his fingers over her stomach. When he slid his hand under her sweater and caressed her midriff, she held her breath. It eased out of her in a low hiss when he cupped her breast and delicately toyed with her nipple. Warm lethargy turned to a more consuming heat and Noelle turned in his arms, tugging him down for a deep, intimate kiss. Wanting that intense closeness, she slid one leg over him and straddled his lap, almost crying when she felt the thick ridge of his erection between her legs.

"Let's go to bed," he murmured.

Noelle was more than ready to do as he asked, but she suddenly remembered something Randy had said back at the hospital. "There's a full house."

Mark was kissing her neck, rolling his hands over her distended nipples until she could barely think. But she somehow managed to add, "Every room is full, even my old one. We're going to have to stay here all night."

He looked into her eyes, his green ones dancing with humor, and began to laugh. "No room at the inn, huh?"

She instantly caught his reference. "Nuh-uh."

But the man she loved was an ingenious one. She should have known he would find a way to get what he wanted. So, gently sliding out from under her and depositing her on the sofa, he walked to the living-room entrance and pushed the door shut. Then he took an antique chair from the front of a writing table and slid it under the handle to make sure no one could enter.

Noelle watched approvingly, smiling at him as he returned. He stopped a few feet away, reaching his hand out to her. Taking it, she rose and let him lead her closer to the fireplace.

Moving together, they knelt on the thick rug and slowly began to undress one another. Every bit of skin that was revealed shimmered under the warm glow of the fire and the twinkle of the tree lights. And soon, they were naked, awash with color, alive with desire, coming together in a sweet mating that surpassed anything they'd shared before.

Because this time, they really did hold nothing back. While their movements were slow and unrushed, their emotions— their words—were about as daring as either one of them had ever imagined.

"I love you, Mark."

"I love you, too. Happy birthday, Noelle."

She squeezed him deep inside her, even as she wrapped her arms around his neck and pulled him close for another one of his kisses that made her feel capable of anything.

Just before their lips touched, Noelle murmured, "And Merry Christmas."

Epilogue

"I CAN'T BELIEVE MARK GETS TO fly off to some Caribbean island and I'm sitting here scraping forty pounds of potatoes on Christmas day," Lottie Santori said as she stood in her mother's kitchen, along with all the other women of the family. They were crowded into the home where she'd grown up, and while the kitchen might have seemed sizeable when her folks had bought the place some thirty-odd years ago, now that all six of the Santori kids were grown and reproducing, it felt like an oversized oven.

"He's in love," her sister-in-law Meg said with a genuine smile and a sappy sigh.

Meg, who'd given birth to the family's first granddaughter a few months ago, still had that new-mother Madonna glow about her. She was also skinny as a rail, having lost all of her pregnancy weight. All except for in the boobs—there, Meg had retained her prepregnancy curves...and then some. It'd make her sick if Lottie didn't love Joe's wife so much.

"I really like Noelle," Rachel said, joining in the conversation. "She's a sweetie-pie." Her soft southern voice was very much at odds with everybody else's strong Chicago accents.

"What is not to like? She is Italian, I can tell, even though she doesn't say it," Mama said, obviously overhearing them as she entered the kitchen to survey her worker bees.

The men were all in the other room watching sports on TV and playing a cutthroat game of Monopoly that had been going on since right after breakfast. It was totally not fair. In her next life, Lottie was coming back as a man.

Then she thought about it, considered all the hair and those nasty uncontrollable body functions and decided it was okay to be female. Even if she did have to peel a zillion potatoes.

"Ya know," Gloria said as she piped some whipped cream around the edge of a pumpkin pie, "I can't believe neither of the twins are here today. The house feels empty."

She and Mama exchanged a tearful look. Lottie could have kicked Glo for reminding them all of the harsh truth. Not only was Mark off on some fabulous Caribbean vacation with his new girlfriend, but Nick was still a world away, possibly getting his ass shot up in the middle of a war.

She didn't want to think about it. *Wouldn't* think about it. So she instead focused on her other missing brother. "How did Mark get the week off work so quickly to go away with Noelle?"

"He already put in for the time off, you didn't know?" Mama said, quickly distracted by thoughts of her son's romance with a woman she approved of. "Had that—what do you call it—lose or lose time."

"It's use or lose, Ma," Lottie said.

"Yes. That's it. So when Noelle asks him to come with her on his trip, there is no reason for him to say no. How very lucky that he was able to get a room at that same hotel."

Lottie almost choked, but a quick kick in the ankle from Meg made her clamp her lips shut.

"Thank goodness they came by on the way to the airport or Rachel wouldn't have gotten her present," Lottie said, still wondering if it was possible her mother really thought Mark and Noelle would be sleeping in separate rooms. Judging by the way her brother had looked at the woman, she doubted he'd be in a separate seat on the damn plane.

Rachel shrugged, still basting the turkey, which was roasting upside down with bacon strewn all over its back. Apparently it was a southern thing. But considering Mama's turkey always tasted like jerky, Lottie wasn't going to complain.

"I'm looking forward to checking out that Red Doors store." Rachel cast a quick look toward Meg. "You've shopped there, haven't you?"

Nodding, Meg grabbed her iced tea and gulped it, her face turning a little pink. But before Lottie could ask her about it, they were called into the other room, probably to see the latest cute-and-adorable trick her baby niece had managed. Maybe she'd spit up on her red velvet dress this time, instead of the green one.

Following the rest of them through the door to the overcrowded living room of the rowhouse, she watched as her father popped open a few bottles of champagne and demanded that everyone take a glass for a holiday toast. He gave the same speech he'd been giving every Christmas for as long as Lottie could remember, which made her smile.

As the chatter and the celebration continued, Lottie drifted to the corner of the room, standing to the side. Watching all the people she loved, eating, drinking, laughing and having a marvelous time, she felt a tear prick her eye, thinking that despite her complaints, she wouldn't trade her family for the world.

Maybe for a hot man.

But not for the world.

She lifted her glass to her lips, saying a silent holiday toast in honor of her big brother Mark. Somewhere, in a country far away from here, she knew he would be celebrating with the woman he'd chosen to spend his life with. They all knew it, just by the way Mark and Noelle had looked at one another today.

Taking a second sip, she tried to make another toast. This one wasn't so easy, and finally, with a tear slipping out of the corner of her eye, she turned it into a prayer. For Nick.

Someday they'd *all* be here for Christmas. She had no doubt about it. So lifting her glass toward the ceiling and blowing a silent kiss, she murmured, "Merry Christmas, guys."

We'll see you soon.

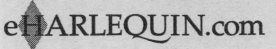